REVENGE AT RAVENSWICK

A FIONA FIGG MYSTERY

KELLY OLIVER

CHAPTER 1

I should have poisoned him. If only I'd had the chance. By the time he confessed to loving another woman and asked for a divorce, it was too late. When he left me, he took my desires with him, even my desire for death. If it weren't for an article in the Daily Times about a certain South African war correspondent living near Wickham Bishops, I might still be languishing in my bed, wishing I'd never been born.

I'd been such an idiot. Everyone knew Andrew was having an affair with his secretary—everyone except me. Clueless, I'd marveled at his tenderness when he brought me my headache powders last night—the night before I discovered the truth. That morning, he was off to work before I awoke.

. . .

THE SUN STREAMING through the window of our second-floor flat woke me, which was unusual because we rarely saw the sun in London, especially these days with the war dragging on. Bad news from the Front put a damper on even the brightest day. Today I was not going to think about the war. It was my day off, my headache was gone, and I was going to make the most of it.

I stretched out and enjoyed having the bed all to myself. "You're burning daylight." I heard my father's voice in my head. As always, he was right. I threw off the blankets, got up, fetched my robe, and trundled into the kitchen to make my first cup of tea for the day.

Andrew and I moved into this flat when we first got married. I'd just turned twenty and was happy to be out of my parents' house and setting up one of my own. Hard to believe it was 1916 and we'd been married for four years already.

I'd immediately fallen in love with the modest two bedroom with high ceilings and large windows facing Northwick Terrace, which was always bustling with life. The kitchen had the newest appliances—an enameled Smith & Philips gas stove, new paraffin lamps from Liberty's, and of course a telephone mounted on the wall. The glow of the double burner lamp reflecting off the black-and-white mosaic floor tiles gave it a cheerful feel, and, even then, I knew I'd be happy here.

Then the war started. And everything changed.

This morning, the war seemed far away as I sat at our small kitchen table, hands wrapped around my cup, enjoying its warmth. As I sipped the strong black tea with just a splash of milk, I recalled Andrew's cool hand on my throbbing forehead the night before. He'd been so sweet and caring, and I'd been such a wretch. I gulped down the rest of my tea and resolved to take the train into town and sweep him off to luncheon at the Criterion. It was my day off, so why not? I clasped my hands together. Wouldn't he be surprised?

I set about picking my wardrobe. I wanted to look casually appealing, not trying too hard, mind you, just naturally elegant and charming. I settled on a silky brown, low-waisted frock with black panels down one side. When I put on the matching hat, I looked like a nun in a floppy wimple. That wouldn't do.

I went back to the top shelf of my wardrobe where no less than a dozen hats reposed. I admit I have a weakness for hats. A hat added an air of mystery to even the plainest face. And mine was indeed one of the plainest faces in Northwick Terrace, if not all of London. Sometimes I wondered why Andrew married me when, with his fine features, silken hair, indigo eyes, and supple lips, he could have had any girl. Thank goodness for hats.

Given the constant threat of rain squalls, I reached for one of my all-purpose hats, a tan felt number that matched nearly any outfit. I went back to my dressing table, tried it on, and examined it in my hand mirror. I turned the brim up and then down. No, this was not the look I wanted. Too country house and not enough chic.

I went back to my wardrobe and replaced my country hat in its proper place. I picked up a round bandbox and removed my favorite hat, which was brown with gray feathers. It was a bit too fancy and formal for luncheon, but it brought out a certain feminine quality in my otherwise square-jawed countenance. I put it on. Yes, this was the one. It fit close to the head and was more durable than it looked. I reapplied my cherry lipstick, touched up my rouge, dabbed rose water on my wrists and neck, and smiled at my reflection. Andrew was in for a surprise... and, as it turned out, so was I.

· · ·

By the time I reached Andrew's office at Imperial and Foreign Corporation, I was perspiring. August in London is not for the faint of heart. I kept my arms glued to my sides for fear my dress had puddles forming under the arms. As I approached the heavy wooden door, I suddenly felt ridiculous. I considered bypassing the IFC and going next door to Liberty's to buy a new hat. I should have listened to that little voice urging me to go shopping instead of continuing to Andrew's office.

After two flights of stairs, I was panting and my hair was plastered to the sides of my face. I stood on the landing, rearranged my dress, blew the hat's feathers out of my face, then took a deep breath, forced a broad smile, and made a beeline for Andrew's office at the end of the hall. As I turned the doorknob, I heard laughter—really more like giggling. I stopped to listen, which was my first mistake.

"Don't worry, darling," said the familiar voice. "I'll take care of you."

He had said the very same thing to me the night before.

I flung the door open. There was Andrew, his arms around the little tart of a secretary, who was nibbling on his ear. He pulled away, but Nancy clung to him like a wet undershirt.

"How could you?" I cried.

Andrew came toward me, the curvaceous shadow trailing behind him. "I can explain—"

He'd only been home from the Front six months and already he'd taken up with his secretary?

"Sack her!" I shouted. "She goes or I will."

"Fio, don't get hysterical."

"Hysterical!" I stepped backward, my second mistake. I was backed into a corner. "Don't call me hysterical, you cheater."

Nancy giggled nervously and held onto the sleeve of his suit jacket. Her amber eyes flashed at me like a hungry cat's.

If I were a man, I'd have socked her in her pretty little nose.

How could he? How could Andrew do this to me? With that simpering imbecile no less. I didn't know which was worse, his infidelity or his insulting taste in women. "It's her or me," I shouted. "Take your pick." The ultimatum was my third mistake. As they say in America, three strikes and you're out.

"Fio, I've been meaning to tell you for weeks now." He glanced back at the little tart, and she smiled sweetly. "Nancy and I are in love. We want to get married."

My hand flew over my mouth. I pushed past him and ran out the door. How could he? How could I have been so clueless? What a nightmare!

Getting home was a blur. I remember I tripped running down the stairs and an army officer helped me to my feet. I don't know how I got myself to the railway station, on the right train, and back home to our flat. I couldn't see through my tears.

Andrew must have stayed at his club... or with her. Every evening, I waited for him to come home and apologize and beg me to take him back. But he never came. The next Tuesday when I got home from work, he'd cleared out. Two weeks later, I was served divorce papers. The barmy thing was, the papers said I had asked for the divorce for his infidelity with someone named Sarah Sample, not Nancy Nettles. At first, I was confused. It took me a while to work out he didn't want his darling Nancy's name dragged through the mud. Never mind me or my reputation—as a first-class dupe. I was devastated.

· · ·

FOR THE NEXT FOUR MONTHS, I got out of bed only when I had to go to work. I barely ate or slept. I lay on my four-poster bed memorizing the outlines of every leaf on the pale pink ceiling paper, wondering what I'd done wrong. I'd been a good wife, hadn't I? Was it because we couldn't have a baby? But that might have been his fault, not mine. What did she have that I didn't?

Alright, she was fleshier and a whole lot prettier. But she was a moron, whereas I was the head filing clerk at the War Office's top-secret Room 40, helping to decode military telegrams and win the bloody—I mean, blasted—war. Andrew claimed he'd always been attracted to smart women.

Maybe the war had affected his mind along with his body. Men were coming back from the Western Front unable to function, nearly catatonic, with what doctors called shell shock. Could shell shock make a man cheat on his wife of four years? Four blasted years! I rolled over and buried my head in the pillow. Andrew wasn't the only one suffering from shell shock. The war was taking its toll on us all.

Thoughts of war roused me from my bed. It was time to get to work. I suspected Andrew resented my taking a job at the War Office. But with so many men at the Front, women needed to keep things running back home. He should have been glad I didn't take a job at a factory or become a canary girl at a munitions plant. Anyway, his beloved Nancy was a working girl.

I glanced at the bedroom clock. I'd have to rush or I'd be late for work. I'd always prided myself on my punctuality. Since the divorce, I'd been slipping. I grabbed the matching gabardine skirt and blouse I'd worn the day before and slid them on. I removed my hairnet and tugged my felt hat over my mess of curls. I didn't have time to properly redo my hair. I'd have to remember not to remove my hat. No time for face paint either. When I looked in the mirror, for a moment I saw my Uncle Frank looking haggard and wearing a woman's hat. Ridiculous. I blinked and he was gone.

When I was young, I wanted to be an actor just like Uncle Frank. I'd dress up in my father's hats or my mother's heels and act out the characters from my detective novels. By the age of eighteen I'd grown taller and ganglier, but not a jot prettier. In my final year at North London Collegiate School for girls, Mrs. Benson, the drama teacher, said to me, "Sorry to be blunt, dear, but with that face, you'll never make it as an actress. You'd be better off putting on trousers and passing yourself off as a man."

Taking her advice, I gave up my dreams of acting. Although I admit, in my marriage, I'd employed my acting skills on many occasions, especially when entertaining Andrew's military colleagues and his school chums from Clifton College or the Royal Military Academy.

I gulped down a quick cup of tea, grabbed a biscuit, and headed to the railway station. I'd be lucky to make it to the War Office on time.

THE WAR OFFICE occupied several rooms in the Old Admiralty, a grand U-shaped brick building that housed government and military offices along with the top navy brass in well-appointed flats on the top floor. I arrived at Room 40 late—only by five minutes, but still late. Room 40 was a cavernous warehouse of a room with rows of drafting tables and desks. Men and women manned the desks, which sat one after the other, and were set up with Teletypes, typewriters, and desktop file cabinets. The room was so long and narrow that if you stood at one end, you could barely make out the other. Amid the clicking of typewriter keys and shuffling of papers, people talked in whispered voices.

A group of men huddled over a drafting table near my

desk. I whisked past them and busied myself at my filing cabinet. Absentmindedly, I filed a stack of papers. A photographic memory came in handy when filing while eavesdropping.

The excitement in the men's voices piqued my curiosity. Using the ruse of offering them coffee, I went to investigate. I darted into the kitchenette to prepare the coffee. Luckily, it was on the same end of the long room as my desk. You never knew what you'd find in the kitchen area. I steeled myself for bits of week-old sandwich and crusty teacups. Ruth must have cleaned up, because to my surprise it smelled of fresh pine instead of old cheese. I made a fresh pot of coffee, filled three cups, and put them on a tray.

"No thank you, Mrs. Cunningham," Mr. Montgomery said with a bow of his oblong head. "I just had a cup of tea." William Montgomery was the head of cryptography. Before the war, he had been a Presbyterian minister and an expert translator of German theological texts. Now he was one of Britain's premier codebreakers. He still looked more like a preacher than a spy.

"Thank you, I'll have a cup," Mr. Grey said. The men called him "the dormouse" because of his small stature and quiet demeanor. He gave me a sympathetic look. "Are you quite well, Mrs. Cunningham?"

"By all means, Mr. Grey." I forced a smile. "Don't worry about me."

The third man in the group was Dillwyn "Dilly" Knox, a former classics scholar and papyrologist at King's College, Cambridge. He was the most gregarious of the bunch and was said to have a notorious personal life that included both male and female lovers. He was the proverbial ladies' man, man's man, man about town. Not that I'm much for gossip, mind you. But with his full lips, sultry eyes, and thick hair, he didn't look like any professor I'd ever seen.

Mr. Knox nodded at me and took the cup from my hand. "The issue now is how to tell the Americans without them thinking we're spying on them, too," he said to the other men.

"This could be the turning point that brings the Americans into the war," Mr. Grey said, his small hand gripping the handle of his cup.

"And with the Americans on our side," Mr. Montgomery said, "we're sure to finally win this damn war. So many lives lost and for what?"

Ears pricked, I lingered around the table straightening some file folders. I had a reputation for sticking my nose where it didn't belong. The men wouldn't admit it, but I'd helped them crack code and plan espionage on several occasions.

"The devil is if the Americans find out we're intercepting their diplomatic communications, they might turn against us," Mr. Knox said. When he glanced my way, I busied myself shuffling some papers stacked on the end of the drafting table.

"It's a sticky wicket," Mr. Grey said. "On top of that, we have to prove to the Americans it's authentic. And to do that we have to give them cipher 13040, which risks the Germans discovering we've broken their code."

Picking up an empty coffee cup, I glanced down at the Western Union telegram they were decoding. It was issued from a Herr Zimmerman of the German Foreign Office to Ambassador Heinrich von Eckart, the German ambassador to Mexico. The entire telegraph was a laundry list of numbers. What did the Germans want with Mexico? Were they trying to bring Mexico into the bloody blasted war?

"We have to find a way to get word to the Americans without them knowing how we got it." Mr. Montgomery held out his empty cup as I passed by.

A light went on in my brain. "What about telling them you stole it in Mexico?" I blurted out. "Everyone knows corruption and bribery are rampant down there." Horsefeathers! What had I done? The impudence. I'd be sacked for sure. Not to mention, I really didn't know what went on "down there."

"Fiona, that's not a bad idea!" Mr. Knox said. "Hohler could pull it off."

My face grew hot. How did he know my first name? He was a forward chap.

"Yes, Mr. H could intercept the telegram in Mexico using whatever means necessary. And then we could tell the Americans we got it in Mexico." Mr. Montgomery beamed at me. "I say, it just might work."

"What about the Germans?" Mr. Grey asked. "Won't we still have to decipher it for the Americans? Then they'll know we've broken their code."

"What if your Mr. H stole the telegram already deciphered?" I asked. Glancing around at the men's rapt faces, I continued, "Surely someone has to decipher the code for the German ambassador to Mexico."

"Why, Mrs. Cunningham, that's genius." Mr. Grey gave me a full-faced smile.

"You do have a knack for espionage." Mr. Knox winked at me.

My cheeks burned. Still, I couldn't help but smile. It was the first time I'd felt useful since Andrew left.

A week later, when I arrived at Room 40, the men were celebrating.

"Mrs. Cunningham, congratulations," Mr. Grey exclaimed. He gestured me over to the planning table where they were gathered.

"What for?" I asked as I joined them.

"Your jolly clever scheme for the Zimmerman telegram

worked." Mr. Knox flashed a toothy smile, the kind that made nuns blush.

"It's only a matter of time until the Americans join the Allies and we finally end this bloody war." Mr. Grey tucked his pencil behind his mousy ear. "And it's all thanks to you, Mrs. Cunningham."

"We should make you an honorary consultant," Mr. Montgomery said, stroking his beard. "You've been cracking code and coming up with creative solutions with the best of them."

"Oh no. I couldn't—" I broke off. Why not? Why couldn't I? Because I'm a woman? Nonsense. I could match wits with any man. Anyway, it was true. I had been helping out a great deal, and it was nice to finally get recognition for my schemes instead of the men passing them off as their own.

"That's a jolly good idea," Mr. Knox said. He extended his hand to me.

I took it firmly and shook. He held my hand a bit too long for my liking. I gave him a stern look of reproach. Served him right. Cheeky devil.

"Welcome to Britain's premier intelligence-gathering agency." Mr. Montgomery extended his hand and gave me a polite handshake. "You can officially consider yourself an honorary consultant to the world's best codebreakers."

"Surely now the Americans know what the Germans are up to in their own back garden, they will have to join the war. And when they do, it will be curtains for the Huns," Mr. Knox said, and then disappeared into the kitchenette. He returned with a bottle of wine. "This calls for a celebration. I was saving this for the end of the war. But today marks the beginning of the end." With great fanfare, he popped the cork. "Fetch some glasses, will you, old girl," he said to me.

I scooted off to the kitchenette, which to my dismay was already a disaster area. Ruth and I were the only ones who even tried to keep it tidy. Cleaning up after men at war was a full-time job. I wiped out an odd assortment of glasses, put them on a tray, and brought them back into the planning room. "Here you are, Mr. Knox."

Mr. Knox poured wine into the glasses and the men each took one. "Where's yours?" He turned to me. "Silly girl, go get one for yourself." He pointed toward the kitchenette. "And stop calling me Mr. Knox. It's Dilly."

"Yes, sir."

I obeyed.

Mr. Grey raised his glass. "To the beginning of the end."

"To the Americans joining the Triple Entente!" Mr. Montgomery clinked his glass against each of the others'.

"To Fiona!" Mr. Knox downed his entire glass in one gulp.

I tightened my lips. The nerve! Using my first name without permission.

"Yes, to Mrs. Cunningham," Mr. Grey said and held out his glass to me.

I clinked and took a sip. The wine was sour, and I didn't particularly like it. I hadn't drunk wine since my last wedding anniversary. The memory stabbed me like a dagger through the heart.

"Are you sure you're quite well, Mrs. Cunningham?" Mr. Grey asked.

"Yes, yes."

"You know, you might have just changed the course of the war."

"Really?"

"Don't underestimate yourself, Mrs. Cunningham," Mr. Grey said. His soft eyes offered added encouragement. "You may have just helped us get the Americans into the war."

Mr. Knox refilled his glass and then raised it again. "To the new and improved espionage team."

"Mrs. Cunningham is an honorary consultant," Mr.

Montgomery said to Mr. Knox as if in warning. "Not officially part of the team."

Honorary or not, I raised my glass. Goodbye, Mrs. Andrew Cunningham. I made my own mental toast. To the new and improved Miss Fiona Figg.

CHAPTER 2

THE ASSIGNMENT

For the next month, every time I heard about Andrew's exploits at the Front, or ran into one of our old friends, I'd collapse back into my bed. Every place we'd been, everyone we knew, everything we'd done reminded me of him and his betrayal.

How could he have been so brutal? In the beginning, I'd found his brutality irresistible. Now the same qualities I'd so passionately loved I just as passionately despised. I hated him. I'd never hated anyone before, and the seed planted in my heart threatened to grow into a suffocating vine beyond my control. As much as I'd loved him, I loved being in control even more.

If only I could get out of London and everything that made me think of Andrew… or worse, Nancy. The first time I ran into her was a dreary Saturday in February. I was on my way to the hospital to tend to soldiers, when the sky opened and it started raining buckets. I'd forgotten my umbrella, so I ducked under the awning of Fortnum & Mason to wait out the downpour. Who did I run into coming out of the store? The little husband-stealing tart! I did an about-face and headed straight home to bed. The hospital would have to do without me.

On my days off from the War Office, I volunteered at Charing Cross Hospital, a teaching hospital with five wards commandeered by the War Office. All the local hospitals were overflowing with casualties, but given its location near the railway station, Charing Cross was an arrival point for thousands of injured servicemen. Caravans of canvas-covered lorries arrived daily. Many times, the hallways were full of cots where the wounded awaited treatment.

My greatest fear was one day I'd be looking into the terrified eyes of my former husband, crippled by the war. Or worse, find him in the morgue... not that it wouldn't serve him right. Andrew had been called back to the Royal Flying Corps shortly after he married her.

But it wasn't seeing Andrew lying on a stretcher that put me over the edge that day. It was seeing her. On another dreary Saturday a month or so later, I ran into her again. She had just started working at the hospital dispensary where I volunteered. She didn't seem to recognize me in my white uniform and cap. I gasped and my hands flew to my mouth. She was pregnant!

In my head, I counted the months since the divorce. Damn him! My heart sank. I turned on my heel and vowed to leave town at the first opportunity.

My opportunity came sooner than I expected.

THE ZIMMERMAN TELEGRAM may have been the beginning of the end of the war, but that end was slow in coming. The Americans still hadn't joined the Allied Powers. And the war continued. I settled into my role as honorary consultant to the team in Room 40. I kept improving my filing system, helped break code, fetched tea, and on occasion did field work. Given women could go some places men couldn't, from time to time they'd send me off to trail a new arrival from France or Belgium, a refugee they suspected might be doing more than taking refuge in Britain.

Following women of interest became my specialty. I could pass unnoticed in department stores, cafés, and schools. Following my female targets, I discovered how much more of the world belonged to men than to women. For there were many places where it was simply not proper for an unaccompanied woman to travel alone. And those were usually the more interesting places.

I'd just returned to the office from trailing a young woman mathematician who fled Brussels but had spent time in Berlin as a student. She ran me all over Mayfair before returning to her flat. Exhausted, I headed for the kitchenette to put on the kettle for tea. I was enjoying a strong cup with a dash of milk when I spotted the article that would change my life.

Sitting at my desk, sipping my tea, I passed my eyes over last week's Daily Times, looking at the pictures more than reading. A picture of a rugged young swashbuckler wearing a slouch hat, Duxbak jodhpurs, and pencil mustache caught my attention. A leather bandoleer filled with bullets crisscrossed his chest like a trophy adorned with tiger's teeth. I pulled the paper closer and began to read. The man was a wounded war hero and famous shooting instructor who had taken the American President, Theodore Roosevelt, big game hunting in Africa. A true renaissance man, he was also a war correspondent for an American newspaper. These days, he was recuperating from his war injuries at our very own Ravenswick Abbey. I studied the photograph, surprised that a grainy black-and-white photograph could stir such intense sensations in my torso.

"If this chap is a famous big game hunter and a war hero," Mr. Knox said over my shoulder.

"Don't sneak up on me like that," I gasped.

"Why is he living at the mercy of a wealthy English lady? The upper brass want to know what he's doing here." Mr. Knox peered down at the newspaper. "They've put a tail on him."

I should have known the mysterious hunter, hero-cum-war correspondent was already a person of interest to Room 40.

"Apparently, there isn't an animal he can't track," I said, glancing up at Mr. Knox.

He gave a little snort. "Great South African Huntsman, my eye."

I put my teacup down. "Listen to this." I read from the paper. "He wrote an article titled 'Fire Hunting with the Congo-Cannibals'." I immediately took an interest in the outrageous fellow and hoped to meet him one day.

"Why is this Tarzan gadding about, taking tea with ladies, and shopping for expensive mustache pomades?" Mr. Knox asked, arms akimbo. "He must be up to no good. He could be a German spy. He could even be the notorious Dionysus."

"Or a French spy," Mr. Montgomery said, joining Mr. Knox at my desk. "He has been living in Paris, and not so long ago, France was our mortal enemy—"

"He's South African," I interrupted. Although, according to the newspaper article, he was born in England, fluent in five languages and graduated from the Royal Military Academy in Brussels. On second thought, even the newspaper article didn't identify his origins. "Who's Dionysus?"

"A myth invented by the War Office. Something about a

super spy." Mr. Grey chuckled as he approached my desk, cup and saucer in hand. "Just a lot of rubbish and nonsense."

"I say he's working for the French." Mr. Montgomery lifted the newspaper from my desk.

"They're our allies," I said.

"Now they are, but we've been enemies for much longer than we've been friends." He dropped the paper back onto my desk.

It was true. A lot of people felt very uneasy about putting our lot in with France after all they'd done to us over the last century.

I studied the photo and its caption. "What an odd name—"

"French or not, he's a journalist and Kitchener has banned all reporters from the front lines," Mr. Montgomery said.

Mr. Grey's mousy nose twitched. "Complete censorship, that's what they want."

"National security, old boy," Mr. Knox said. "Churchill doesn't want us to read about our troops chewing barbed wire in Flanders. Too demoralizing."

"That's not right—" I started to say.

"It's a rum do about that chap who was to go to Essex and tail the newsman," Mr. Knox interrupted. "He's broken his leg, slipped getting on the train to go up there."

I wish these blasted men would quit interrupting me.

"I heard his cover was posing as a gynecologist on holiday for his nerves." Mr. Grey snickered. "I thought that sort of thing only happened in the theater."

You'll never make it as an actress. Mrs. Benson's words came back to me. You'd be better off putting on trousers and passing yourself off as a man. Was it such a daft idea?

"I'll do it!" I blurted out.

"What?" Mr. Montgomery's eyes widened.

"Do what?" Mr. Knox asked.

"Take the fellow's place…" I said, my voice trailing off.

"You want to impersonate a doctor and spy on the huntsman?" Mr. Grey dropped his spoon onto his saucer. "Are you mad? No one will believe a woman is a real doctor, not even a foreign one."

"I can do it," I said, dropping my deep voice another octave. "I've been told I make a passable man." I stood up, feet apart and hands on my hips.

Mouths open, the three men stared at me for several seconds.

"I say," Mr. Montgomery said.

Mr. Grey sat his cup and saucer down on my desk and fetched his hat from the rack. "Here," he said, handing it to me. "Say something doctorly."

I took the hat and placed it on top of my hair, which luckily, I always wore tightly pinned to my head. "The leg bone's connected to the ankle bone."

They laughed. But I was serious. Deadly serious. This was my chance to get out of London, to go on an adventure, and to meet the mysterious huntsman-cum-war correspondent.

I closed my eyes, inhaled, and slipped into character. Conjuring the words of Dr. Cornwall the last time he examined me, I said in a low voice, "Madame, you are suffering from an anxiety neurosis, most likely hysteria. I recommend bed rest, bland food, and seclusion. I will have some bromide powders prepared to help you sleep."

The men all quit laughing and gaped at me again.

"I say, it just might work!" Mr. Montgomery was the first to speak.

"Indeed, I've never seen anything like it," Mr. Grey said.

Mr. Knox gave me a wink. "You're a natural, old boy." When he clapped me on the back, I nearly fell over.

I had to bulk up if I was going to pull this off. "So, you'll recommend me for the job?"

"The head office is in a pickle." Mr. Montgomery scratched his head. "Oh, why not?" He chuckled.

"Thank you." I wanted to hug him.

"There's many a slip between the cup and the lip," he said. "Let's wait and see what they say in the head office."

After work, I walked directly to Foyles to buy some books on bodybuilding. The rain had finally stopped, and I was encouraged by a hint of sunshine warming the sky. Although as Mr. Montgomery had warned the gap between cup and lip could be a doozy, I was happier than I had been in a long time. The chance of tracking the Great South African Huntsman had cheered me considerably.

My new bodybuilding book in hand, I checked my timetable for the next train to Shaftesbury Avenue. Next stop, Angel's Fancy Dress, London's go-to shop for costumes. I'd been there many times as a child, begging my mother to take me there whenever we were in town.

As usual, the train was packed with people on their way home, most dressed in cream-colored trench coats holding black umbrellas like so many piano keys packed in a box. I was sandwiched between a bulky woman who smelled of garlic and an elderly gentleman wearing a top hat. I took a seat, opened my book, and admired the physiques of the muscular men who had competed in the Great Competition at the Royal Albert Hall sixteen years ago. My word! Sir Arthur Conan Doyle was one of the judges of the contest. As a child, I'd loved Sherlock Holmes. My mother had subscribed to the Strand Magazine, and after she'd abandoned them to be used as kindling, I'd sneaked the magazines to my room to devour Sherlock Holmes stories in private.

When I looked up from my book, the gentleman next to

me gave me a sly smile. I slapped the book shut, my cheeks burning. What must he think of me looking at pictures of scantily clad men? For the rest of the trip, I stared straight ahead, refusing to make eye contact with anyone.

I was so relieved when the train reached my stop that I jumped up and the blasted book slipped off my lap onto the floor. The gentleman bent to pick it up. I blushed as I snatched it away from him and scurried off the train. I didn't look back until I reached Angel's Fancy Dress shop.

With racks of brightly colored costumes and countertops covered in false mustaches, beards, and wigs, Angel's Fancy Dress shop was the perfect antidote to my awkwardness. I'd always felt more at home dressed as someone other than myself. You could be anyone you wanted at Angels. A shop girl could become a duchess, and an errand boy, a duke. A duchess could become a harem girl and her duke a sheik. From masquerade balls to motion pictures, Angels was the place for make-believe.

As I headed to the men's department, I passed a wall of eye masks, some with elegant colored feathers. Inhaling the musty smells that reminded me of my childhood, I tried on topcoats, hats, trousers, and bushy eyebrows, and I considered a set of false teeth. I settled on a great black beard and two reasonably priced outfits, one navy and one brown. I hoped I would grow into them with a steady course of weightlifting exercises prescribed by Eugen Sandow in the bodybuilding book.

Of course, I wasn't in possession of the dumbbells and pulleys recommended by Mr. Sandow. Although I didn't need it, I bought a sack of flour instead, which I could barely lift. I would have preferred a bag of sugar—which I did need —but with war rations, sugar was scarce. One advantage of the flour sack was if times got really tough, I could sew the fabric into a dress like they did in the wilds of North America. I hoped it wouldn't come to that as my flour sack was a ghastly shade of cement gray, sure to turn my complexion the color of stale porridge.

Another two weeks went by and no word came from the head office about the assignment. Seeing significant progress from my flour-sack exercises and eating an extra half tin of biscuits a day, I continued my bodybuilding even though I was sure they'd given the assignment to someone else. Probably to a man. On the other hand, men were almost as scarce as sugar—all of the able-bodied ones having been sent to the Western Front. Many didn't come back. And those who did come back were broken, bent, or barmy from witnessing the carnage of war.

The following Saturday, my day off, I took the train to Charing Cross to volunteer once again at the hospital. Five stories high and a couple of streets long, the hospital was an imposing structure. Its flat, unadorned façade made it look almost two-dimensional. I pushed my way through the crowded walkway, past the dark maw where the ambulances entered the inside court and slipped in through a side door. Two flights up, down an endless hallway, and I was at the dispensary, a quiet corner filled with bottles, tonics, and pills, tucked away from the masses of tangled flesh and missing limbs.

In addition to helping repair damaged men, these days I had another motive for going to the hospital. Still hoping I'd get the job spying on the huntsman, I was using my time in the dispensary to learn everything I could about tonics and poisons. The cover story already in place for the agent assigned to the case was a doctor specializing in toxicology and female maladies. Since I had some experience with the female maladies, I concentrated on the poisons.

Whenever there was a lull at the dispensary, I took the opportunity to study the medicines, which stood in neat rows in cabinets lining three of the four walls of the room. My tutor of sorts was a character named Daisy Nelson, a self-proclaimed "cunning woman" and practitioner of white magic, who ran the dispensary and was an expert on chemical tonics along with home remedies and medicinal plants both common and rare.

That afternoon, I was alone, standing next to one of the medicine cabinets, sniffing a bottle of mercury bichloride. I'd read it was colorless, odorless, and highly toxic. It was used to treat syphilis, more fallout of war judging by how many soldiers were suffering the consequences of visits to French maisons tolérées. Not quite odorless, the poison had a faint scent of daffodils. I recorked the bottle and carefully set it back on the shelf in the medicine cabinet.

"Planning to poison someone?" A woman's voice came from behind me. "Or do you suffer from the French disease?"

Blimey! I swung around and was face to face with the new Mrs. Andrew Cunningham. Her shiny black hair was perfectly coiffed in close curls, and her red lips formed a small heart in the center of her disgustingly symmetrical face. Her uniform accented her post-baby hourglass figure. I pulled my lab coat tight around my flat chest and wallowed in my deficiencies. I was half tempted to grab the mercury and gulp it down.

"I can think of a couple of people who deserve it," I spat out. I didn't specify whether I meant poisoning or syphilis. Either would do. I pushed past her and exited the dispensary. I didn't stop until I was out of sight of the hospital. Directionless and fractured, I stood on the curb shaking. Spitting rain mixed with my tears. I didn't want to go home. But I didn't know where else to go. Without thinking, I headed to the War Office.

. . .

ON THE OMNIBUS, people stared at my sopping wet clothes, but I didn't care. In a daze, I nearly missed the conductor calling out the Whitehall stop. I walked to Horse Guards Avenue and stood across from the imposing building, wondering what to do next. It was unlikely anyone would be in the office and probably the doors were locked. As I crossed the street, a motorcycle swerved to miss me, and in the process sprayed my skirt with mud. Could this day get any worse?

I picked up my pace to avoid getting run over. Taking shelter in the doorway, I considered my options. Since the door was locked and I didn't have a key, I couldn't get inside. Too bad I didn't bring the mercury bichloride with me, then I could just be done with it. I could go throw myself in the Thames. But frankly, after the trek from Charing Cross Hospital, I was exhausted. I leaned against the stone wall. I was even too tired to cry.

Looking down at the state of my attire, I decided I'd better go home before someone from the War Office saw me. My boots were wet and the leather was split; my skirt was covered in mud, and my coat was sticking to me. I was shivering from the damp. I took a deep breath and steeled myself for the trip home. I was not looking forward to encountering more ghosts of my dead marriage.

As I turned to go, the door opened and Mr. Montgomery stepped outside. At first, he didn't seem to recognize me. I stared down at my ruined boots, hoping he wouldn't. A sudden rain squall made him hesitate. I peeked up at him, and he glanced in my direction.

"I say, Miss Figg, is that you?"

"Mr. Montgomery—"

"Don't you look a sight." He took my elbow. "Come on, we'd better get you inside for a nice cuppa before you catch your death."

He removed a hefty key ring from his pocket and used one of his dozen keys to unlock the door. "Are you quite alright?"

"A cup of tea would be nice." I could barely force the words out, and they were nearly inaudible at that.

"Come on." He held the door open. "And if the tea doesn't fix you up, I've got some news that will."

I glanced back at him and he smiled.

The bitter black tea revived me a bit. Mr. Montgomery refilled my cup. I added a dash of milk and took a biscuit from the tin when Mr. Montgomery offered it. We were sitting at the little table in the kitchenette behind the planning room. It was a disgusting mess as usual, but I didn't have the energy to tidy up. Anyway, in my present state, I was in no position to criticize a blooming mess.

To my surprise, several men were working at their desks and a few women were manning the telephones. The hushed rhythm of their voices was comforting.

"Don't you take a day off?" I asked.

"The war doesn't take a day off, so neither do I." Mr. Montgomery ate a biscuit in two bites.

My biscuit still sat, untouched, on my saucer. I had no appetite for biscuits or anything else.

"You could have knocked me down with a feather when I got the news." Mr. Montgomery smiled. "The head office has approved my recommendation. You're to take that poor chappy's place at the abbey... you know, following the huntsman."

Stunned, I sat there blinking.

"The cover was already set, I'm afraid, a doctor named Vogel. Don't worry. You'll get intensive training for the next two weeks and then off you go."

I stared at Mr. Montgomery, unable to believe my ears.

"You're to report back to the War Office once a week. If

your position is compromised, then they'll find a way to extract you."

I gaped at him, unable to speak. Extract me. What exactly did he mean by that?

"That's what you wanted, isn't it?" He had a concerned look on his face.

I nodded. "Yes. Thank you, Mr. Montgomery. You've saved my life."

"You do have a flair for the dramatic, Miss Figg." Mr. Montgomery laughed.

I was deadly serious. The next encounter with my cheating ex or his fertile wife would have pushed me right over the edge.

CHAPTER 3

RAVENSWICK ABBEY

Two weeks later, after a crash course in espionage—and cutting off my most feminine feature, my beautiful auburn locks—I descended from the train at Wickham Bishops. Suspended above lush pastures and country paths, the platform was so small it could hardly be called a station. A lovely young woman was waiting on the platform. Her slim silhouette against the bright sunshine resembled a burning matchstick. She introduced herself as Mary Elliott.

"My mother-in-law sent me." She took the smaller of my two bags from my hand. "She would have come to welcome you herself, Dr. Vogel, but she's just recovered from a stomach malady, and she still has to prepare the house for a bazaar to benefit children orphaned in the munitions accident."

"Terrible tragedy, that." I remembered reading about the Silvertown accident in the newspaper. I was so shocked at the time that the story imprinted itself in my mind. Indeed, unfortunately, thanks to my photographic memory, I could see the headlines in my mind's eye now: *Tragedy struck the Silvertown munitions factory last night when a catastrophic explosion claimed seventy-three lives and left over 400 injured, devastating the surrounding East London neighborhood. Authorities suspect mishandling of TNT as the cause, but whispers of sabotage have already begun to circulate.* "Lord Elliott owns the concern, does he not?" I also remembered reading that Lord Bertram Elliott, Mary's father-in-law, owned Silvertown munitions, along with several other factories producing war machinery from ammunition to steam engines. The government may have commandeered his factories for the war effort, but from all accounts, the earl was still doing very well, profiting off other people's misery.

"He does. But it wasn't his fault." Lady Elliott narrowed her eyes and examined me. I looked away, vowing my countenance would not betray the fluttering of my heart. Had she found me out already?

The black beard itched and the bushy eyebrows threatened my lids. I lowered my voice to the limit of its depths. "Is something wrong, Lady Elliott?"

"Please, call me Mary. I know you're here on holiday." Her astonishing emerald eyes transmitted intelligence and warmth. "But I wonder if I might have a word with you about a delicate issue?" She blushed. "Not today, mind you. But whenever you have time. A personal matter."

"Of course." I nodded. "As I'm on holiday and have no schedule whatsoever, I'm at your beck and call." If she wanted me to treat her mother-in-law's sour stomach, I could think of no better cure than fresh ginger root tea. As for personal matters, my own life was such a disaster, I wouldn't have a clue what to prescribe.

She smiled and then piloted me out to the car.

"Thanks to my mother-in-law's charitable activities, and my work with the land girls, we get a limited supply of petrol." She pointed to a black automobile polished to a gleam like a shiny obsidian. "Our chauffeur was called up, so I'm afraid you've got me instead."

"I could drive if you like," I said, hoping she wouldn't take me up on it. Still, it seemed the manly thing to say.

"Oh no. Don't be silly." With a gloved hand, she waved me away. "Women are just as capable as men, you know."

"Yes, I know." Don't I just.

She took the wheel, and I climbed into the passenger's seat.

"You volunteer as a land girl?" I was surprised an aristocratic lady would drive her own car, let alone do manual labor.

"At the abbey, they call me Cinderella of the soil. I have an awfully green thumb. And everyone should do their part, don't you think, doctor?"

"Indeed, they should." I inhaled the scent of wildflowers. I was so used to the gray skies and smoky air of London that the brilliant blue sky and sweet country breeze took me by surprise. I'd forgotten what it was like to breathe fresh air. An energy so vibrant and alive emanated from the green pastures and flowered fields, it made me forget the death and destruction of the war.

"So, you were delayed?" She glanced over at me as she piloted the motor. "We expected you a month ago."

For a moment, I gaped at her like a cod out of water trying to remember my cover story—the poor lad who'd broke his leg, the fellow I replaced, the original good doctor who was really an undercover espionage agent hot on the trail of the notorious South African hunter, suspected German spy, and sometimes journalist, Fredrick Fredricks.

"Yes, well… I had a longtime patient take a turn for the worse, poor dear. I couldn't leave her, you see."

"And how is she now?" As she drove, Mary's fine chestnut hair blew in the breeze.

"I'm afraid she died. Poor Nancy Nettles." I sighed. "I did everything I could for her." Nancy Nettles was, of course, the name of my husband's mistress, now wife. The husband-stealing tart.

"Oh dear. That can't be good for business." Mary cranked the steering wheel and the motorcar jerked, barely missing a squirrel as it darted across the road.

"No, I suppose not." I grabbed at my hat to keep it from flying off my head.

After that conversation stopper, we both stared straight ahead for the rest of the journey.

We must have traveled about four miles before we reached the village of Wickham Bishops with its greengrocer, chemist shop, and, of course, public house. We passed a few ladies wearing hats and pleasant floral country frocks, holding parasols against the bright spring sun as they strolled along the side of the road. It was a nice change from the crowded streets of London and the hustle and bustle of the city. A trip to the country was just what the doctor ordered, if I did say so myself.

As we turned in at the manor house gates, Mary said, "I hope you don't mind. My mother-in-law has invited you to tea. Your cottage is just down the road." She pointed to a row of small stone houses. "It's very quiet down here, Dr. Vogel. I hope you find it restful."

Beyond the massive gates lay the estate grounds, and in the far distance, I saw a tiny dot of a house atop a hill that gleamed like the head of a pin.

"I'm sure I will," I said, knowing I was on the adventure of my life, hardly a restful holiday.

As the car rumbled over the gravel drive, my breath caught at the sight of Ravenswick Abbey, a sprawling estate that looked like it belonged in the pages of a romantic novel. The ivy-clad Gothic façade rose majestically against a backdrop of ancient oaks, its soaring turrets and arched windows glowing warmly in the golden hues of the afternoon sun. To my left, manicured lawns rolled into a shimmering lake where swans glided like ghostly sentinels, and to my right, a walled rose garden stood like a keeper of secrets behind its weathered gates. The whole place was stunning, yet there was an unmistakable stillness about it, as though the abbey itself was holding its breath, waiting for something—or someone—to stir its peace.

"I'll walk you to your cottage after tea. In the meantime, I'll have one of the staff take your cases down," she said as we drew up in front of a fine old house. "I hope you don't mind staying among the refugees, orphans, and other bits and bobs my mother-in-law collects."

"Bits and bobs?" As I scanned the grounds, I could barely keep my mouth from falling open in awe.

"She's practically running a guest house. She's taken in orphans, wounded soldiers, refugees, and one famous London doctor on holiday." She smiled.

Oh right. She meant me. The so-called famous doctor on holiday. I forced a chuckle and got out of the car.

"The abbey is a wonderful place to rest and recover." She led the way to the grand manor.

The three-story stone building had no less than six chimneys and a railing around the roof. I wondered if past lords of the manor facing financial ruin or scandalous affairs had thrown themselves off and the railing was installed to prevent the current occupants from doing the same. A circular drive was ringed by thick green grass, in the middle of which sat a sculpture of a giant vase. Perhaps before the war, the vase had held some magnificent plant or bush. The entrance to the manor house was crowned with four pillars that started above the ground floor. Judging by the garden, which was in bloom with roses and neatly trimmed shrubbery, the gardeners had not been called up.

A lady in a sailor blouse with a thick black belt and a scarf wrapped around her head was staring into a fishpond and then waved as we approached. Mary introduced her as her mother-in-law, the countess, Edith Elliott. You could have knocked me over with a feather. She looked every bit a gardener and not the least bit aristocratic.

"I heard you're here to rest. We don't get many famous doctors. Female maladies, is it?" The countess took my hand in her rubber glove. She was a fleshy woman in her sixties with squishy blue eyes in a moon face and an ample body balancing on tiny, booted feet. "All the fish have died. There's no one to clean the pond, you see. I don't suppose you—" Her shoulders slumped.

"Only too happy to help, Lady Edith." I bowed my head slightly in her direction and nonchalantly wiped the pond scum from my hand. The pond water had an oily sheen, and I sincerely hoped I wouldn't have to put my own hand into that muck.

"Are you coming to tea?" Mary asked her mother-in-law.

"I'll be there." She pulled off her rubber gloves. "Annabelle made a seed cake. Sadly, my appetite is still a bit off." With her abundant freckles and doughy face, the countess resembled a generous slice of seed cake.

I followed Mary around the house to the back garden. With sculpted shrubbery and rows of chrysanthemums giving off an earthy tobacco scent, the back garden was even more impressive than the front. And the back of the house, with its French windows and cheerful shrubs, was less intimidating and more charming.

Under an ancient beech, tea was spread out on a long table covered with a checkered tablecloth. Three men and a woman were seated at the table and another young lady lounged on the grass nearby. They were already tucking into the delicious-looking seed cake. One of the men rose from a wicker chair and wiped his hands on a napkin.

"May I present my husband, Viscount Elliott," Mary said. "Ernest, this is Dr. Vogel, who is visiting us from London."

Viscount Ernest Elliott was handsome in a country squire sort of way. He wore his affability on the sleeve of his well-pressed linen jacket. His handshake belied a man who hadn't done manual labor in his life. He gave me an appraising look as if sizing up an opponent in a game of cricket. I hoped it didn't come to that as I'm hopeless at sports.

"Do you shoot?" he asked.

"I'm afraid not," I said.

"But you ride?"

"No, not really."

"Do you play the ponies?"

I shook my head.

"The War Office has taken over Aintree, but you could come with me to the track at Gatwick if you like." He glanced over at his wife, who was now sitting on her hands, teeth clenched. I surmised she did not approve of her husband's visits to the racetrack.

"That's very kind, but I'm not much of a gambler." Of course, coming to Ravenswick dressed as a man, pretending to be a doctor, and chasing a possible German spy, was the gamble of my life.

"Oh well, Mary can entertain you then." He snorted and went back to the table, probably wondering what kind of man didn't shoot, ride, or gamble.

A well-dressed, white-haired woman with the air of a virtuoso, opened a French window and stepped out onto the terrace. Who is she? My espionage preparations in London, didn't inform me of another lady of the house.

Oh, my word. When she reached the table, I recognized her as a much-improved Lady Edith. No longer in the sailor blouse, her hair liberated from the scarf, and a generous helping of face powder had transformed her into what you might expect from a countess, a regal well-heeled woman wearing a lace collar over a lavender tea dress with a lovely cameo brooch.

I assumed the prune-faced man with his head bowed, shuffling along behind her must be her husband, the earl, Lord Bertram Elliott. The ashen color of his skin and the way he tottered to get to the table told me he was at least twenty years her senior. Mary jumped up to help him to the table. Good thing, too. He looked like he might keel over at any second.

Mary introduced me around the table. The countess's niece, a bright-eyed, rosy-cheeked, young woman named Lillian Mandrake tossed her cap to the ground and flung herself down on the grass next to the chair of a melancholy man who looked to be in his late thirties, and was introduced as the countess's younger son, Ian. I knew from my preparations that Lillian Mandrake was the orphaned child of the countess's younger sister, who like a fool had married their gardener's strapping son and then died in childbirth. The beefy gardener had been banished to the hinterlands of Wales, and Edith had taken in the unfortunate orphaned baby.

"Lillian, please take a seat at the table." The countess gestured for her niece to move away from Ian.

It was obvious the lady of the house did not approve of her son cavorting with an impoverished orphan, even if the orphan in question was her own niece. Perhaps especially so. After seeing the two young people in action, I surmised that the countess would not allow her youngest son, Ian, to make the same mistake and marry beneath his station. Although judging from the clandestine caresses passing between Ian and young Lillian as they sat on the grass, heads together, giggling, it was already too late.

"You don't want to neglect your guest, dear." Lady Edith gave a forced smile in the direction of another, older woman.

Lillian jumped up. "May I present Mrs. Millicent Garrett Fawcett." She beamed. "Millicent is a brilliant activist for women and children."

Mrs. Fawcett bowed her head slightly. "Thank you for having me to tea, Lady Edith."

Next to Mrs. Fawcett sat a clean-shaven man of about forty, with a receding hairline and long angular face, sitting legs crossed, wearing a wool suit—despite the heat—and fancy Italian lace-ups. He was introduced as Lieutenant Clifford Douglas, a wounded soldier just home from the Western Front, and a former schoolmate of Ernest Elliott.

I filed each person's name and biography into my mental filing cabinet. They made a pretty little party on an unseasonably hot spring day. Taking tea under the trees in the English countryside was not a bad way to spend an afternoon. My only regret was that the great South African Huntsman, Fredrick Fredricks, was not among the guests.

The lieutenant eyed me suspiciously. I instinctively touched my beard to make sure it was still attached. Something about the way he stared made me uneasy. I puffed up my chest and stood with my legs farther apart than necessary to compensate. I adjusted my eyeglasses and cleared my throat with a deep grunt.

The countess gestured for me to sit down. Feeling rather a spectacle standing before the rest of the party, I gladly complied. Unfortunately, the only open seat was next to the lieutenant.

"What will you do after the war ends, Lieutenant Douglas?" Mrs. Fawcett asked.

"I've always wanted to write." His teeth were too big to make his smile charming, but he tried.

"You mean for a newspaper?" Lillian asked.

"Promise me you won't laugh." He reached over and patted her hand. Did the good lieutenant flirt with all the ladies?

"I might," Mary said with a wink as she poured me a cup of tea.

"I'd like to try my hand at writing crime stories." The lieutenant's thin lips turned up into an embarrassed smile.

"Crime?" Mrs. Fawcett sucked her teeth. "Not to overstep, but isn't there enough crime in the world without making up stories? If you'd seen what I have," she said shaking her head. "Women beaten by their husbands. Children starving." She tutted. "War is one thing. We must defend ourselves. But what about poor defenseless women and children?"

Everyone stared down into their teacups. Lady Edith seemed especially agitated. The conversation ground to a halt. Of course, she had a point. Although, for my part, I loved a good detective story. "Sir Arthur Conan Doyle or Edgar Allan Poe?" I asked, trying to lighten the mood. I took a biscuit from the serving tray. I was about to take a sip of tea when the lieutenant gave me an odd look. I tucked my little finger into my palm and concentrated on manly slurping.

"You mean Sherlock Holmes or what's-his-name?" He'd stopped mid-bite and held a half-eaten biscuit in the air.

"Dupin." I sipped my tea. "Le Chevalier C. Auguste Dupin. Of course that was before the word detective had been coined." As a child, my secret pleasure was stealing off to my grandparents' haybarn with the latest issue of Strand Magazine to read the latest Sherlock Holmes story. The American, Edgar Allan Poe was another of my favorites.

"I say, aren't you clever?" The lieutenant popped the rest of his biscuit into his mouth. "But I want to write true crime."

"Right. Holmes and Dupin weren't real detectives." Mary stirred her tea with a tiny spoon. "Not like Scotland Yard."

"Damn Scotland Yard!" As if suddenly awakened from his stupor, old Lord Elliott straightened and pounded a feeble fist on the table. "They still don't have any idea what caused the explosion at the munitions factory." He sucked his teeth. "Blew up an entire neighborhood and they're too inept to find out why." Spittle flew from his mouth as he spoke and a bit of white foam gathered on his lips. "I suspect one of those daft cows working there lit a cigarette." He shook his head. "I knew we shouldn't have employed women to do men's work. And now my business must pay the price. No good deed goes unpunished, as they say."

"More men smoke cigarettes than women," I said, realizing too late that a reliable man may not be so quick to come to the defense of daft cows. I took another bite of biscuit to keep from saying more.

"Let's please not talk about that dreadful explosion." The countess troubled the edge of her napkin.

"Terrible tragedy," Mrs. Fawcett said sipping her tea. "My sister attended to some of the wounded." She fiddled with her napkin. "My father owns factories commandeered for the army and he worries something frightful might happen. We need to win this war and get our lives back—"

"That's the last time I let the government take over my operations." The old man's thin lips disappeared into his mouth. "I'm as patriotic as the next chap, but—"

"Please, Bertram." The countess held up her hand. "No more. My poor nerves can't take it. All those poor children orphaned."

"You and your orphans be damned." He pounded the table with his fist. "You've been crying about those poor unfortunates for months. It's time you faced facts and got on with it." He shook his head. "That's what I've had to do."

"Please, Bertram," she repeated, her voice quivering. "Let's not—"

"Well, you act as if you blew them to smithereens yourself, dammit."

She narrowed her gaze on her husband and a strange look passed between them. I wondered what it meant. "Not here, Bertram." She forced a weak smile. "Now where were we, before my husband so rudely interrupted? Lieutenant Douglas, you were saying?" Only a slight jerk of her head betraying her agitation. What a mercurial woman.

Lieutenant Douglas sputtered. "True crime," he finally got out. "Hunting down criminals."

"Have you tracked criminals before?" I asked, although I couldn't see the tidy man sitting next to me chasing down violent criminals—at least not in those shoes.

"Well, no." Lieutenant Douglas chuckled. "But I've had a lot of practice tracking animals. Tracking criminals can't be so different." He put down his fork. "You see, years ago, I met a great hunter in South Africa, and he taught me his technique. Only, I plan to apply it to stalking murderers instead of rhinoceroses. I've heard he's convalescing at Ravenswick and I'm hoping to renew our acquaintance."

Aha! Lieutenant Douglas knew the Great South African Huntsman. I'd have to stick close and see what I could find out. I wondered why the famed hunter was not part of the tea party. Perhaps his manners were too coarse for polite society.

"You think criminals can be tracked down like animals?" I sipped my tea in as manly a fashion as I could muster. "You must have a very low regard for human beings, either that or a high regard for animals. Or do you think all criminals are animals? Even petty pilfering to feed one's family?"

"Well, I suppose…" The lieutenant looked flustered. "Perhaps not all criminals."

"Technically, human beings are animals too," Lillian added.

"Jolly good." Lieutenant Douglas smiled. "And they leave tracks just like other animals."

"So, you plan to track criminals looking for their paw prints and scat?" I asked playfully.

"Scat." The lieutenant blushed. "Good lord." He gave me an odd look, examining my beard as if it were some rare mammal.

"Tell me more about this great hunter and his methods," I said, avoiding eye contact lest he suspect my interest in the Great South African Huntsman was untoward.

"I guess you could say he's a sort of Sherlock Holmes of the bush. It's a funny story how we met—" He dabbed at his mouth with a napkin. "I was hunting elephants in the Serengeti, you see."

I grimaced. Hunting elephants. Really, how barbaric. I almost voiced my abhorrence when I remembered I was a man and held my tongue.

"When Fredricks came out of the bush with his guide." He waved a fork in the air. "I nearly shot him. Although with that great hat of his, I don't know how I could ever have mistaken him for an elephant." He chuckled.

"Quite." I flashed an indulgent smile.

Old Lord Elliott started coughing, his face turning the color of a beet.

Lieutenant Douglas seemed to debate whether to continue his long-winded tale of bloodsport but thankfully thought better of it. Mary jumped up and patted the old fellow on the back. The countess gave him a sideways look and then tossed him her napkin, a look of exasperation on her face. Obviously, the transition from wife to nursemaid wasn't as easy as that from gardener to countess. Lillian ran to the house to fetch a shawl. She returned and placed it around the old man's shoulders. His face was red and blotchy and he sputtered a "Thank you, my dear" as he took her hand.

The party fell silent. The old man's malaise descended on the tea party like a thick fog. The countess took note of the damping effect of her husband and glowered at him. All the gayness of the afternoon evaporated as the earl slumped in the basket chair next to his wife.

After tea, Mary rose from the table and gestured for me to follow suit. "I'll show you to your cottage. I'm afraid it's very modest."

"I'm sure it will suit me fine." I wiped my mustache with my napkin, careful not to wipe it clean off, and then stood.

We bade farewell to the rest of the party, and Mary led me through the garden out toward the main gates. I admired the rose bushes, wishing I had a green thumb. Despite spending summers on my grandparents' farm, I was too much of a city girl now to grow anything except my hair, which was the only thing I missed about Miss Figg. Anyway, my days on the farm were wasted on reading, not something useful like milking daft cows. I inhaled the scent of sweet cherry blossoms with a hint of wild garlic. It was a beautiful day for a walk, and the fresh country air and brilliant sunshine chased away all the dreariness of my life in London.

We were still within earshot of the house when Lieutenant Douglas shouted, "Mary. Wait for me."

We turned to see him hurrying after us. "Mind if I join you?" He smiled and slapped his thigh. "Do my bum leg good to get some exercise." He looked at Mary as he spoke and acted as if I was invisible.

Mary, Lieutenant Douglas, and I continued on the path through the grounds toward the cottages. Scattered clouds dotted the sky and more gathered on the horizon. The few clouds were so low they cast great round shadows that rolled across the fields. After a few minutes, we came upon a group of charming stone cottages at the edge of the estate. They formed a neat line officially separating the estate from the village.

"Who lives here?" I asked, pointing.

"My mother-in-law is always hosting refugees and wounded soldiers on the estate." Mary gave her head a wistful tilt. "But since January, most of the cottages are full of orphans from the munitions accident." She shook her head. "Such a tragedy."

"Rum do all around." I sighed, doing my best imitation of Lieutenant Douglas. "Very generous of her." I wondered where she'd put the Great South African Huntsman. The lieutenant had confirmed Fredricks was staying at Ravenswick Abbey. But where? I was eager to lay eyes on him.

"Yes, she is very generous," Mary said in a rueful tone.

"You know they've had it damned difficult with the Germans using Belgium as a welcome mat for France," Lieutenant Douglas said. "And then that explosion on our own soil, probably the result of sabotage." He touched his leg. His limp was barely discernible. "I wish I could get back on the battlefield and show those Germans a thing or two—"

"Indeed." Sabotage. I wondered. Could Fredrick Fredricks have been involved? Is that why the War Office sent me to follow him? What if I have to trail the blackguard until the end of the war? I hadn't thought of that. Being a spy was jolly exciting but a bit nerve-racking, always having to keep my voice lowered and my mustache on straight.

As Mary opened the wooden door to my cottage, a strapping figure of a man exited the house next door. He tipped his wide-brimmed slouch hat when he saw us. When he did, thick sheepdog locks fell over his handsome forehead and he jerked his head to move them back into place. Speak of the devil and he shall appear.

"Is that one of the wounded soldiers?" I asked, although I recognized him instantly from the photograph in the newspaper, the famous huntsman with his broad chest, pencil mustache waxed to perfection, oversized tweed riding jacket, swagger stick, and knee-high black boots. With his strong nose in the air, the Great South African Huntsman brushed imaginary dust from his sleeve and replaced his slouch hat on top of his ample head of dark hair. I had to admit, he cut a striking figure. If he was a spy, he certainly wasn't trying to blend in.

I peered at the chunky gold ring on his pinky finger, wondering what the insignia meant. Was it a tiger? Some kind of big cat? With his great mane and white incisors, Fredricks himself looked something like a big cat.

"No, that's a wounded war hero, Fredrick Fredricks. He's a war correspondent now," Mary said. "A dashed brave one too."

"Why, I say!" Lieutenant Douglas rushed up to the resident war hero. "If it isn't my old hunting partner."

Fredricks blanched. "Do I know you?"

Lieutenant Douglas laughed. "Why Fredricks, it's me, Clifford Douglas."

"Of course." The swarthy man waved his hand in the air. "My old friend." He gave his friend's hand a hearty shake. "Quelle surprise!"

Had the War Office gotten it wrong? Was Fredricks actually French and not from the South African Republic? With his startling dark eyes, jet-black locks, and ruffled shirt collar, he rather looked like something out of a fairytale or a Gothic romance.

"I'd heard you were here," Lieutenant Douglas said, still pumping the huntsman's hand.

"Madame Elliott," the man said, bowing gallantly to Mary.

He turned to me. "Permit me to introduce myself."

"I know who you are," I said, mustering my courage. "You're Fredricks, the famous big game hunter and reporter for the New York Herald."

"Oui, Monsieur. That's me." He smiled broadly and both pointy edges of his mustache turned up. "I'm flattered that my reputation precedes me. My friends call me Apollo."

"I bet they do," I said under my breath, trying to avoid staring at the smooth tanned skin revealed by his open shirt collar.

He held out his substantial palm as if it were a cricket bat.

I didn't know whether to duck or shake it.

"Fredricks and I met hunting elephants in Africa," Lieutenant Douglas said.

Yes, he'd already regaled us with the story of his hunting prowess over tea. I must say, hearing the gory details had quite ruined my appetite.

"Fredricks is the greatest big game tracker in the world," the lieutenant continued. "Why, once, he—"

Fredricks interrupted him with a hearty slap on the shoulder. "I'm a reporter now. A lowly war correspondent, just continuing to do my part after my injury in the battle of the Somme." He cradled his wounded arm like a baby. "And I'm sure these good people don't want to hear about our exploits in the barren plains of Africa." He turned to Mary. "Our stories of heathen cannibals are not fit for the delicate ears of such a beautiful lady." He bowed again to Mary.

The way he eyed Mary turned my stomach.

He twisted toward me. "I've actually made a bit of a name for myself in America as an investigative journalist."

From what I'd heard at the War Office, American

neutrality had protected correspondents from the harsh censorship of the British and French press. Now that they had entered the war too, I expected that would change.

The grin on Fredricks's face as he took me in, as if drinking me up through a straw, made my blood run cold. I knew I'd better get away from his keen gaze as quickly as possible. I felt as if he could see right through me. I shook his hand again with the firmest grip I could manage, and then ducked into my cottage, resolving to watch him from a safe distance, lest the big cat should decide to pounce.

CHAPTER 4

FOUL PLAY

For the next few days, I settled in and took in the lay of the land. Trying not to arouse suspicions, I chatted up the village merchants about the presence of the orphans and soldiers and the countess's "other guests," hoping one of them would tell me something about the Great South African Huntsman.

Young Mr. Sage at the chemist shop was more than happy to tell me about the expensive mustache pomades the "over-sized Frog" asked him to special order, and the girl at the cash desk at the greengrocer told of the "Aussie's" fondness for sweets. Another shop girl practically swooned, insisting the handsome stranger was an American film star. There seemed to be sufficient confusion over Fredrick Fredrick's origins to make it difficult to glean much information from the townspeople.

The rest of the week passed pleasantly with Mary visiting me daily. She invited me to the manor house for dinner, and we enjoyed leisurely walks through wooded paths. As long as we avoided the heat of midday, we had lovely strolls through the vast estate, which included the beautiful gardens surrounding the manor house, hardwood forests outside the gardens, and then farmlands beyond the forests.

Given my cover as a doctor specializing in poisons and female maladies, Mary confided in me about her troubled marriage. She complained about her husband's interest in a certain recently widowed assistant foreman's wife, reportedly a robust beauty. Although she admitted marrying Ernest Elliott more to escape the confines of her father's suffocating household than for passion, she had grown to love him and didn't want to lose him. In my opinion, her husband's wandering eye seemed more in line with male maladies best cured by poison.

Of course, I kept my opinion to myself and comforted her with gentle soothing words and recommended a mild bromide sleeping powder available at any chemist. She showed her appreciation by grasping my arm and listening to my made-up stories about my early days as a doctor in North London.

Thanks to the attention of Mary, I was happier than I had been since before my divorce. In some ways, our time together reminded me of the halcyon days of Andrew's courtship and the first months of our married life. If I weren't binding my chest and wearing a great itchy beard, I imagined Mary and I could be fast friends.

EARLY ONE AFTERNOON, I met Mary on the forest path. She was in a state, her eyes puffy and face blotchy. I suspected she'd been crying.

"What's wrong?" I asked.

She broke down sobbing.

I put my arm around her shaking shoulders. "There, there. It can't be that bad."

Just then a buxom woman with long flowing hair wearing a dusty split skirt and a distinctively buttery complexion galloped past us on a beautiful chestnut horse. I withdrew my arm for fear we'd cause a scandal. I'd almost forgotten I was a man escorting another man's wife along a secluded footpath.

"That's her," Mary whimpered.

"Who?" I glanced back at the horsewoman.

"Mrs. Roland, the assistant foreman's widow. Ernest's mistress." Her whole body was shaking now. "Her husband was killed in the munitions accident." She sniffled. "So, now she's after Ernest."

"Her? Why? You're ten times more attractive." I took her by the shoulders. "She's coarse and smells of horse manure." Of course, I didn't know the woman from Adam and had no idea what she smelled like, but having had my own husband stolen away, I chose to imagine the worst. "I'm sure Ernest would never—"

"Really? Ten times—" When she looked up at me with those startling eyes, now flooded with tears, for a moment I thought she might kiss me. Releasing her shoulders, I swallowed hard and patted her hand.

"Really." Quite unsettled, I quickly started back down the path, nearly tripping over a sycamore root.

"What if I had proof he was having an affair?" Mary wiped her eyes with the backs of her hands.

"What kind of proof?" I couldn't imagine Mary peeping through keyholes or hiding behind bushes with a camera and popping out to catch her husband in a compromising pose.

"Yesterday, my mother-in-law received a letter." She bit her lip. "I'm sure it's about Ernest."

"How can you be—"

"I know it!" She cut me off. "Annabelle told me her mistress was quite out of sorts about it." She grasped my sleeve. "Later, I heard Edith quarrelling with Ernest." Her cheeks flushed and tears welled in her eyes. "I distinctly heard Edith say, your attachment to her is unseemly and I insist you give it up at once. And another one of the staff told me one day she found the horrible woman lurking upstairs in the family's private quarters."

"Oh dear." It did sound as if Lady Edith had found out something troubling. "What did Ernest say to that?"

"What did he say to Edith? You mean in their row?" She sucked her teeth. "His voice was muffled. But he called his mother a traitor and told her she'd best drop it or she would regret it."

Goodness. Ernest threatened his own dear Mutti.

"Then this morning, the horrible woman visited the house, again." Mary yanked up a wild forget-me-not and started plucking off its petals. "On the pretense of delivering a basket of fresh-picked chanterelle mushrooms. The nerve!" She stomped her little foot into the ground. "She's trying to ruin my marriage and get Ernest for herself." As she stared down at a clump of grass, a tear followed her gaze and landed like a plump dewdrop on a bright green blade. "I asked Edith to see the letter," she continued. "But Edith locked it in her briefcase and told me it has nothing to do with me." She moved closer and seized my elbow. "But it has everything to do with me. I must see that letter." She looked up at me with desperate eyes. "At the risk of seeming forward, might you help me retrieve it?" Her lip trembled.

"What?" My cheeks warmed. "You want me to help you steal a letter?"

"The uncertainty is making me crazy." She kicked at the grass. "I just want to know." Her eyes pleaded and I had to look away. "And you're the only one I can trust."

Me, the only one she can trust. In that case, I felt sorry for the poor dear woman. After all, my whole persona was a lie. "If the letter is addressed to the countess, then you have no right to read it without her permission." I realized that sounded like a fussy schoolmaster, but if Edith didn't want Mary to read it, then what could she do? Pinching it wasn't the answer. I patted her sleeve. Unfortunately, however, I understood exactly how she felt. The image of Andrew in the arms of his secretary stabbed at my memory and I winced.

"I have a right to know if my husband is unfaithful, don't I?" She pouted.

She had a point. Before my arrival at Ravenswick, for months I'd kicked myself every day because I hadn't even suspected my own husband's infidelity. I'd been such a dupe. Could I allow Mary to suffer the same fate? "Perhaps—"

"I'll make you a deal," Mary implored. "You help me get the letter and I'll tell you everything I know about that ruddy hunter you're always asking about."

Fredrick Fredricks. I'd almost forgotten I was here to gather information on the huntsman. Was I that obvious? I'd better be more circumspect in future. I nodded. "What's your plan?"

"Come to the house this evening after dinner." Her voice was animated. "I'll distract Edith so you can sneak into the study and take the letter from the briefcase." She clapped her hands together.

"And how shall I do that?" Good grief. She really did expect me to flinch the letter.

"I'll make sure the window is open." She smiled.

"You want me to crawl through a window?" My voice rose an octave before I caught myself. I cleared my throat loudly. Crawl through a window, was she barmy?

She shrugged, a forlorn shadow falling across her pale countenance. I thought she might start to cry again.

"Alright. I can't promise." I exhaled. "I'll see what I can do." Of all the crazy plans. I couldn't believe I was even considering it. What kind of spell had she cast on me?

LATER THAT EVENING, I strolled along the dirt path from my cottage to the big house. It was a lovely walk through a meadow with a stand of sycamore near the manor house gate. The sun setting behind it formed a halo of orange and the big house looked majestic. As I approached the circular drive, I glanced around and, seeing no one, I quickened my pace and made my way across the grass to the side of the house. I paced back and forth in front of the study window before darting into the bushes underneath it.

Breathless, I listened for voices. Nothing. Not a sound. I pulled myself up onto the window ledge. My weightlifting had paid off. I swung one leg over. I was just swinging my other leg over when I heard footfalls from inside nearing the study door. I lurched backward and toppled into the shrubbery, slid down, and landed face first in the flowerbed. Blast! Sitting up, I patted my beard and adjusted my clothing. I crawled on all fours through the bushes, glanced around, and then stood up, hoping no one saw my graceless descent, not to mention my illicit ascent.

Wiping mud from my suit, I walked quickly back toward the gates. Double blast! I only had one other suit.

I hadn't gone far when I was intercepted by the viscount.

"Why Doctor Vogel!" he said. "What happened to you?"

"I-I-I saw an unusual herb there." I pointed in the vague direction of the garden. "The bell-shaped flower put me in mind of belladonna. I was trying to reach it to examine it when I slipped in the mud." I thought of Daisy Nelson's lessons on poisonous plants and my own boning-up on toxicology for my role as Dr. Vogel. I even carried a sample case and a couple of test tubes in hopes of increasing the veracity of my disguise.

"You'd better come to the house and have a brandy." He strode ahead.

"They say nightshade is dangerous, and now I know why." A nervous laugh bubbled up as I followed him.

Ernest insisted I accompany him into the house. He led me into the drawing room, where the family had retired for tea.

"I must look a sight. I'm not fit for the drawing room," I said, wiping my forehead with the back of my hand.

"What happened, doctor?" Mary rushed to my side.

"I'm terribly sorry to impose," I said. "Lord—"

"I say, Vogel, you are a sight." Lieutenant Douglas strolled in from the hall. "Come in. Have some tea and dry off." He chuckled. "You know, once when I was hunting ducks in Scotland, I fell into a pond and—"

"Enough hunting stories for one day, old boy." Ernest slapped him on the back

Once we were settled in the drawing room, I repeated my story about the dangerous herb and everyone laughed— everyone except the lieutenant, who shot me a nasty look. He was probably jealous because he wasn't the one telling stories. "I'm afraid I'm a mess," I said, hoping my beard was holding up.

"Dr. Vogel." Mary's clear voice startled me. "You must know a lot about poison. Toxicology is your specialty, is it not?" She smiled. "That and female troubles, correct?"

The senior Lord Elliott coughed and sputtered.

She'd caught me completely off guard. I shifted in my chair. "Why yes, it is. Some poisons are very difficult to detect. And some are remarkably easy to procure. Some are common household chemicals." Why in the world was she asking about poison? Did they plan on doing the old boy in?

"You mean to say, anyone can commit murder?" Lieutenant Douglas asked. "Present company excepted," he said, turning to Mary and then nodding to Miss Mandrake.

"Why except the ladies? Poison, you know, is the weapon of choice for women," Lillian said. "Even I know about poisons from working in the dispensary. If I wanted to poison someone, it would be easy."

"Surely, not." The countess glanced over at her husband, as if giving it some consideration.

"Almost anything can be poisonous in the right dosage," I said.

"Everything in moderation, eh, old boy?" When Ernest laughed, he sounded like a goose taking flight. "Even arsenic?"

The countess let out a disgusted scoff. "I wish someone would poison those warring Huns."

"What about the Saxe-Coburgs, Mutti?" Ernest asked, playfully. "You and our king are descended from those warring Huns."

"I thought you were proud of your German ancestry, mother dearest," Ian said in a mocking tone.

"Your mother is a patriot," the elder Lord Elliott said, defending his wife. "And so am I." In a huff, he threw his napkin on the table. The effort sent him into another coughing fit.

"Enough talk of death," the countess said abruptly. "Lillian, dear, could you help me get Bertram back to his room? And pick up those newspapers and take them to the larder. You know we don't waste paper in this household. Not with the war on."

"Of course, Aunt Edith." When Lillian jumped up, her comportment made me think her position as a dependent was something the benevolent countess relished, despite her terms of endearment toward the girl. It was obvious the orphaned girl was beholden to her aunt.

"Oh, I almost forgot." The elder Lord Elliott shuffled past me and turned back to his son. "The fetching Mrs. Roland was around looking for you earlier." The spark in his old eyes was undeniable. "If only I were twenty years younger! Even now, I could give her a good what for." His laugh was full of naughty mirth. The old boy was livelier than I'd seen him since my arrival.

Poor Mary stared down at her shoes.

The viscount cleared his throat. "I wonder whatever for." He fumbled with his teacup.

"Lillian." Ignoring her husband's lewd remarks, the countess stood up.

The girl dashed to her side. "Yes, Aunt."

"Can you bring my handbag, dearest?" She nodded toward the sofa where her beaded bag lay. "I don't feel well. I'm going to bed." Holding her teacup, she headed for the hall. "Have Annabelle light my fireplace, will you? And fetch my briefcase from the study." She shot a parting look at her husband. "I'm freezing."

Briefcase. Lady Mary and I exchanged glances.

"Certainly, Aunt Edith." Lillian followed behind her. "I'll take you up and then I'll come back for uncle."

The old man grunted and grumbled but sat back down until Lillian came back for him.

Something was off with the countess. It was obvious she and the earl didn't have a happy marriage. And lighting a fire in this weather. It was beastly hot for early May. Perhaps she had the chills. Mary had mentioned her mother-in-law had been ill. I hoped I wouldn't be called upon for medical advice.

I was about to take my leave when Mary pulled me aside and whispered, "Please come back tonight. Meet me at the front just before dawn." She handed me a heavy envelope. "A key to her room."

I tried to protest, but I didn't want to make a scene. As I tucked the envelope into my waistcoat, I swore to myself that I would not use that key to get into the countess's bedroom.

"I can't bear it alone," she said, her lip trembling.

I nodded. Until now, I hadn't imagined myself a hopeless romantic. Perhaps it wasn't so much romance as an overidentification with a wronged woman wanting vengeance that made me agree to Mary's treacherous plan. "Until dawn," I said with a bow.

A LITTLE WHILE LATER, as I ducked into my cottage, I had the sensation of being watched. The huntsman's cottage was next door, and I had the distinct impression Fredricks was watching me like a hawk from his first-floor window, which looked down at my doorstep. I quickly went inside, shut the door, and exhaled a sigh of relief. Finally, I was alone and could go back to being plain old Fiona Figg instead of a fancy London doctor whose face was covered in spirit gum.

The charming stone cottages were scattered at odd angles as if someone had thrown them like dice. With just one room, mine was the smallest of the lot. Dark wooden beams and whitewashed stucco walls made a cozy retreat from the anxiety of playing my part. And given I took at least one meal a day at the big house, my tiny kitchen with its ancient gas stove was perfect for making a cup of tea. My only complaint was the heat. Unless I opened my front door, in the afternoons my room was stifling.

Relieved to be back inside what had become my own little sanctuary, I changed into clean clothes and then removed my beard. Every time I took the blasted thing off, a layer of skin went with it. Underneath, my face was so red with rash I looked like a radish. No matter how slowly I pulled it off, it hurt like the dickens. I carefully washed my irritated face and applied Pond's Extract Vanishing Cream. My experience with the muddy flowerbeds of Ravenswick Abbey almost made me wish I could vanish back into my own life in London.

Sleeping with one eye open, I lay on my bed with my head at an angle to see the clock on the mantel. I watched the arms slowly tick off the time and again wondered if the countess was quite well.

I must have fallen asleep because the sound of a dog barking woke me shortly after four. I dragged myself out of bed and reluctantly glued my beard back in place. I replaced my spectacles, which were nothing but clear glass. I placed my straw boater on top of my head and then set out for the manor house at a good clip. I wasn't used to wandering about before dawn. Luckily, there was a full moon. By the time I reached the gate, I was panting, whether from exertion or fright I couldn't say.

To my surprise, a car was leaving the manor house gate. I jumped back to avoid getting run over. The driver stopped, rolled down the window, and shouted, "Hurry. It's the earl. He's having some kind of fit. I'm off to get Dr. Derby."

I ran to the house as fast as I could. Although I wasn't a real doctor, maybe I could be of use. I had volunteered at Charing Cross Hospital after all. And the household would expect even their resident doctor on holiday to attend to a sick earl.

The front door was wide open. I dashed inside. Voices drifted down from an upper floor. I took the stairs two at a time and followed the voices to a bedroom at the end of the hall.

Clad in nightclothes and robes, the entire family—except for the countess and Lillian—was gathered around the earl's bed. I dashed to his bedside. The front of his nightshirt was covered in dark stains, as were his bedcovers, and his frail body bowed in convulsion. I stared down at him, helpless to do anything.

His eyes glued to me, he cried out, "Der… Der…"

"Der?" I asked. Was he calling for Dr. Derby or trying to tell me something?

"Der-spitzel," he gasped, fell back onto the bed. "My eyes. I can't see." He whimpered.

"Help me move him to the floor," I said to one of the servants. Again, I was glad for my bodybuilding. He was slight but not light. As I lifted him, a faint scent of bitter almonds emanated from his person.

"Bring me those pillows," I shouted at another servant.

I waved at the onlookers to give us some space. The earl's body went rigid for a second and then limp as an empty glove.

Using the Silvester method of artificial respiration I'd learned at Charing Cross, I elevated his shoulders and allowed his head to drop backward. As I knelt behind his head and grasped his wrists, I smelled the bitter scent of cucumber mixed with the acrid smell of vomit. Crossing his wrists over his lower chest, I rocked forward, pressing on his chest and then backward, stretching his arms outward and upward. I counted to myself, making sure to repeat the cycle twelve times per minute. After several minutes, I stopped. It was no use. The pulse in his wrists had weakened to nothing and his eyes glassed over and stared with the eerie look of the dead.

I glanced up at the terrified family and shook my head. Lillian appeared in the doorway.

Buried faces and muted sobs met my gaze.

"Help me get the earl back on the bed," I ordered the servants.

Just then, Dr. Derby, the earl's own doctor, rushed in and began fussing over the old man. A plainspoken and kind little man, I'd met the doctor several times while taking tea at the house. He obviously was very close to the earl. The blood drained from his face and his lip quivered as he stared down at the lifeless form.

"Oh dear. Oh dear. Oh dear." Dr. Derby was wringing his hands. "He had a weak heart. I told him to slow down, but he didn't take care of himself." He looked as though he would break down at any minute. "Poor old fellow's heart finally gave out."

"I don't think it was his heart," I whispered. I put my hand in front of my mouth so the others couldn't hear. "Or if it was, it was not an accident."

Dr. Derby blinked. The others huddled nearby, mouths agape.

"Perhaps someone should make tea." I turned to the viscount. "It's been a shock, especially for the ladies." As one of the ladies, I knew it had been a shock for me.

"Of course." Ernest stretched out his arm. "Come, ladies, Ian." The viscount led them all away, leaving me alone with Dr. Derby.

After they were out of earshot, I turned to Dr. Derby. "The earl has been poisoned," I said, glancing around the room. A teacup was overturned on the floor. "I suspect it may have been in his tea." I pointed at a brown stain on his shirt and the carpet. I had conducted a thorough study of all known poisons to prepare myself for my assignment as an expert in poison, and this case was clearly one of poisoning, given the violent nature of his fit. "Was he taking any medication?"

"His medical history is confidential." The doctor's voice was anxious. "As you must know, vomiting is also consistent with cardiac arrest." Dr. Derby was pacing in circles. "It must have been his heart. Poor dear man."

"He suffered a very particular kind of convulsion before he died, a seizure more in line with poisoning than a heart attack. And he said he couldn't see, which is another sign of poisoning." I knelt next to the stain on the carpet. "It will be difficult to get a sample of the tea. But we should perform a postmortem to confirm my hypothesis." By we, I meant him. I was ready to do what it took to maintain the integrity of my cover, and I had worked in the morgue at the hospital, but performing a postmortem was going a bit too far, even for me.

"Yes, under the circumstances, I suppose you're right," Dr. Derby said. "Poor fellow." He wiped at his eyes with his handkerchief.

I surveyed the room for any more clues as to how the earl had been poisoned. A saucepan sat on the chest of drawers near the fireplace. It was half-full. I sniffed the milky amber liquid. Milk and rum.

"I should get a sample of this milk." Obviously, the earl was not a teetotaler. In fact, if I were a betting man—or any kind of man—I'd say he liked a regular nip. In his tea. In his coffee. In his milk.

I slipped a small vial from my waistcoat pocket, dipped its dropper in the liquid, and depressed its black bulb to suck the milk into the dropper. Given my recent study of poisons, I always carried a spare vial or two in case I ran into an interesting plant specimen.

"What is it?" Dr. Derby asked.

"Nothing." I stood up. "We'll need to notify the police."

"The police!" Dr. Derby looked insulted. "Certainly, we can spare the family scandal on top of tragedy."

"Under the circumstances, I don't see how," I said. "The earl has been murdered."

"We don't know that," Dr. Derby murmured, wringing his hands. "It could have been his heart."

"Why don't you go down and console the family?" I surveyed the room. "I'll be right behind you." I needed some time alone to conduct a search of the room.

"Right." Dr. Derby stepped out in the hall. A few seconds later, he poked his head back inside. "Maybe I'll just wait for you, old man."

Blast. "I'll be right there," I said, restraining my frustration. "You go ahead."

I patrolled the rest of the bedroom as quickly as I could. The only other items of interest were a small blue medicine bottle and a box of Ryno's Hay Fever and Catarrh Remedy, both in the washstand drawer. Without touching anything, I bent to examine them. I sniffed the bottle, which had a slight bitter smell like daffodils. I could see through the blue glass of the medicine bottle that it was almost empty except for two fingers of a heavy viscous liquid settled at the bottom. I uncorked the bottle and put a finger to the mouth, tipped it up, and then withdrew my finger. Quicksilver. Also known as mercury bichloride. Had the old man had syphilis? Mercury bichloride was the usual treatment for the sores. In this case, if he'd swallowed it by accident or intent, the cure may have been worse than the disease. Although, having seen some of the soldiers who'd contracted the French disease, I wondered. I examined the Ryno's Remedy, but dared not sniff it since I knew from my days at the dispensary the stuff was almost pure cocaine snuff, a very powerful stimulant. Too much Ryno's could be fatal, too.

I was about to exit the death chamber when I saw it. The countess's briefcase. I knew it was hers because it was beaded with the letters E.E. In its rectangular clasp, it held a tiny silver key. What was it doing in the earl's room? I thought of the letter Mary had asked me to retrieve. Had she taken it already? She wouldn't have murdered her father-in-law to get it, would she? I slipped my handkerchief from my pocket and turned the tiny key in the lock. The only contents were a neatly folded letter and a burgundy-colored cordial bottle with an adorable tiny cork covered in red wax. I examined the ornate red bottle. It had a tiny tag attached to its throat that read "To Lady Edith, Yours truly, J." Who was J? I unfolded the stationery and stared down at it.

"Vogel, are you coming?" Dr. Derby called out from the hallway.

"Yes, I'll be right there." I didn't have time to read it with that pesky Derby breathing down my neck. I scanned the ink on the page. Crikey. It was in German. What in the world? Did my photographic memory work in another language? It was about to be tested. I tried my best to take a mental photograph. But the words meant nothing to me. Some of them were three inches long. Was this the letter Lady Mary was going on about? The one she wanted me to fetch. It had to be. But why was it in German? Was the widow Roland's mother tongue German? Or was some other tattletale, who had reported on the viscount's wandering eye, a German? Strange business.

I was about to tuck the letter back into the briefcase when I saw a word I did understand. Fredrick Fredricks. Oh, my sainted aunt. I should have known. Fredrick Fredricks, the Great South African Huntsman and suspected German spy was somehow involved. I returned the tiny key to the lock. I needed to get the letter to the War Office. I was about to tuck it into my waistcoat when Dr. Derby appeared on the threshold.

"What are you doing?" He approached.

I glanced around the room for a place to stash the letter. "Just taking one final look around, trying to find the substance that poisoned the old fellow."

"Come now." Dr. Derby huffed. "He wasn't poisoned." He pointed at the letter in my hand. "And if he was, you'd best put that letter back and leave things as they are for your dear friends the police." He stomped over to the washstand and yanked the drawer open. "I can prove it was his heart." While his back was turned, I took the opportunity to stash the letter. A caramel-colored fedora with a dark brown band resting on a hat stand caught my eye. I quickly folded the letter into a tight accordion and tucked it inside the hat's velvet band and tossed the hat on the dressing table, which was a much larger target than the hat stand. I withdrew the envelope from my waistcoat. The one Lady Mary had given me. I was about to put it in the briefcase, when Dr. Derby appeared at my side.

"Vogel." He was holding two small bottles. The blue one I'd already examined and another, a clear one with a rubber dropper. "If you must know, Lord Elliott was taking two medicines." He held up the clear bottle. "Digitalis drops for his heart." He pocketed the bottle. "And mercury bichloride for another condition." He cleared his throat. "Are you going to put that letter back where it belongs?"

"I understand." He did have the French disease, then. "Could he have taken an overdose of the digitalis?" I knew the medication was prescribed for slow hearts but in large doses it could be fatal. And blindness was a symptom of digitalis toxicity. I slid the heavy envelope into Lady Edith's briefcase and then turned the tiny key in the lock.

He held the bottle up to the light. "He was very careful about his medicine." He pocketed the second bottle. "The countess gave him two drops and no more every evening before bed." He shook his head. "I told them it would be better to take them in the morning, but the countess insisted the evenings were more convenient." He shrugged. "So, she doled out his two drops in his nightcap. Poor fellow."

Given how the countess spoke to her husband, perhaps tonight she'd decided to dole out a fatal dose. By nightcap, did he mean the milk and rum or something else? I had a sample of the milk. I glanced around for another vehicle for poison. Unfortunately, the spilled tea had already soaked into the carpet. "We'd best get downstairs," I said. To ensure the murder scene wasn't disturbed—or should I say, further disturbed—I locked both adjoining doors, placed the keys in my waistcoat pocket, and then shut the main door and locked it on my way out.

Hopefully, the letter would be safe there until I could find someone to translate it and learn what it meant. Was it, as Mary insisted, a letter revealing her husband's affair with the widow Roland? Or was it something far more sinister? Indeed, was it the reason the old boy was poisoned? I patted the keys in my pockets. It was odd that the countess's brief-case was in her husband's room. Had he purloined his wife's case? Perhaps to get his hands on the letter? Or had she been in his room and forgotten it? And more to the point, why wasn't she at the scene? The rest of the house had heard the commotion and come running to the earl's room. Why wasn't the countess there? It didn't add up. One thing was for sure. Mr. Fredrick Fredricks was somehow involved. And I intended to find out how.

THE FAMILY WAS SOLEMNLY ASSEMBLED downstairs in the drawing room, the very room where last evening we'd enjoyed a hearty laugh together. A cloud hung over the once cheery room as everyone sat slumped in the dark.

"Viscount Elliott," I said. "I recommend an autopsy."

"Why?" Ernest sucked in his breath and then grimaced as if he'd been pricked by a pin.

"Surely it's natural causes," Ian said. He was sitting in the window seat, fiddling with a tassel on the curtains. "Like Derby said, a heart attack."

"Probably not," I said.

"You can't think someone…" Ernest's voice trailed off.

"Under the circumstances, it would be best to do a post-mortem, so we could issue a proper death certificate," I said. Technically, of course, I couldn't issue a death certificate under any circumstances. I looked to Dr. Derby for moral support.

Ernest bent his head and gave a slight nod.

"Vogel here thinks we should call the police." Dr. Derby held his hat in both hands, gently caressing the band with his thumb.

"Why do we need the police?" Mary asked, her voice trembling. "Wasn't it his heart?"

"I fear the earl has been poisoned." I scowled at Dr. Derby. Either he was being coy or he truly believed it was the man's weak heart.

"Poisoned!" Mary gasped. "Oh no!" Tears pooled in her eyes and she put both hands over her mouth.

"Vogel's right," Dr. Derby said. "We should consider all possibilities."

"Rubbish," cried Ian. "You see poison everywhere, Vogel." He waved me away. "Derby had no idea of poison until you put it into his mind." He ran a hand through his thick hair. "Father had a heart attack, and that's the end of it."

I was surprised by Ian's reaction. Usually so quiet and unassuming, I'd never seen him so worked up. No doubt, like the rest of us, he was in shock. Poor lad.

"Dr. Derby's postmortem will tell us soon enough." I drew the bedroom keys from my pocket and handed them to Viscount Elliott. "I've locked the earl's rooms until the police inspect the premises."

"Police? Come on, old boy," Ernest said. "You can't really suspect one of us killed Papa?"

"Where is the countess?" I asked. "She's the only one who didn't rush to his bedside."

"Mutti?" Ernest glanced around as if the countess were hiding in some corner. "She must have slept through the commotion." He gave a weak smile. "Mutti has the constitution of a horse. Sleeps like a log."

His mixed metaphors weren't the only thing that betrayed his unease.

"Shouldn't someone wake her and give her the news?" I asked, wondering why one of them hadn't roused her already.

"She took sleeping powders," Mary said. "I tried to wake her before coming down, but she was dead to the world." She blushed. "Oh, sorry… I didn't mean…"

"Best to let her sleep." Ernest sighed. "She deserves a few more hours of peace before the world tilts on its axis."

"Not to be indelicate, and I hope you don't mind me asking, do you inherit the estate now that your father—" I ventured, thinking it might give us a clue as to the murderer.

Ian cut me off. "How can you talk of such things at a time like this!" He stormed out of the room, and Lillian ran after him.

"I suppose I'm to inherit everything." Ernest sighed. "Heavens, does that make me a suspect?"

"What about the countess?" It seemed old-fashioned to say the least that the son should inherit before the wife.

"Mutti will be my dependent, I suppose." Ernest leaned an elbow on the table and put his head in his hands. "I really hope we can keep the police out of this. Losing father is bad enough without those—"

"What about calling on the famous investigative journalist staying at your cottages?" I offered, hoping I'd get to see the great hunter in action. "Perhaps Mr. Fredricks could get to the bottom of this." Although if my suspicions were true, Mr. Fredricks was already at the bottom of this.

"You mean, call in a reporter?" Ernest looked incredulous. "Are you mad?"

"If you refuse the police, and don't want the investigator, I could give it a go." Why not? I was here to investigate Fredricks and if he was involved, then so was I. Afterall, I was an official—if undercover—agent of British Intelligence.

"You!" Ernest jolted upright. "I might as well ask my old pal Clifford Douglas." He scoffed. "He has ambitions to be a detective." A curtain fell over his countenance and he grew serious. He caressed his chin. "Why not? What harm could it do." He stood up and came over to me. "Vogel, old boy, you and Clifford have a go at it. Just don't get the police involved. At least not yet." He ran a hand through his hair. "At least not until we have a better idea of what happened." He held out his hand to me. "The last thing we need is a scandal. We'll keep it hush-hush for now."

I took his hand and shook it. "Of course. I'm the sole of discretion."

At that, I took my cue and bid them farewell.

CHAPTER 5

LADY EDITH

*L*ater that morning, I walked back to the great house. There were several unsettling details about the earl's death still playing on my mind. First and foremost, who could have poisoned him? Running a close second, why did he have his wife's case in his room? No self-respecting woman left her confidential papers in her husband's bedroom. A lady has her secrets, after all. And that was just what worried me. Countess Elliott's secrets. If the letter in German wasn't suspicious enough, she was the only person in the house not roused by her husband's fit. Indeed, I didn't see hide-nor-hair of her during or after the tragic affair. Perhaps she was out of the house. While her absence from the manor would explain why she wasn't at the earl's bedside, it posed more questions than it answered. Where was she? Why was she out in the middle of the night? Very peculiar behavior all around.

Stepping around muddy puddles, I walked briskly up the

path from the cottages, through the meadow, and up the gravel drive to Ravenswick Abbey. The morning air was heavy with dew and the slight breeze a refreshing change from the unseasonable heat of the past few days. But the sun burning through the mist promised another scorcher.

When I arrived at the abbey, I was greeted by Lillian Mandrake. She was on her way to work at the dispensary. Was it a coincidence she worked at a pharmacy? Time would tell. When I asked after her aunt, she told me she wasn't up yet. Indeed, most of the household was sleeping in after the horrid events. She let me into the house and told me to make myself at home, promising that Annabelle had baked some very nice breakfast buns if I went through to the kitchen.

I took Lillian's advice, and found Annabelle standing over the stove, moping her brow with a dishcloth. She told me she was preparing a tray to take up to her mistress, and I asked if I might deliver the tray for her. Although she did look frazzled, relieving her of her burden was, of course, only a pretext for my real concern, which was questioning Lady Edith. Surely by now, someone had told her of her husband's death. Perhaps that was why she was taking a tray in her room instead of coming down for breakfast.

Annabelle gladly handed me the tray, which she'd arranged very neatly with the soft-boiled egg in a cup in the center of a plate surrounded by toasted soldiers. A cup of steaming black coffee stood next to an adorable little milk and sugar set. Careful to balance the tray so as not to spill the coffee, I took off toward the door. At the threshold I realized I had no idea which room belonged to the countess—except that it must be on either side of the chamber belonging to the earl. "To the right or left?" I turned back to Annabelle. "The countess, is her bedroom to the right or left of the earl's?"

"Right," Annabelle replied, stirring spices into a doughy mixture she had started in a giant bowl.

I nodded and off I went, down the hall and up the great staircase. As I passed in front of the door to the earl's bedroom, a shudder ran up my spine. What did my grandmother used to say? "An eerie sensation like someone had walked across my empty grave." I knocked on the countess's door. No answer. I knocked again. Nothing. I put my ear to the door and listened. If the countess had called for a tray, why wasn't she answering? "Lady Edith," I called. "It's me, Dr. Vogel." I waited. "I have your breakfast tray." I waited a bit longer. "I came to check on you after... after the shock. And..." I knocked again. "Lady Edith?" Alarm bells sounded in my head. I hoped to heaven the killer hadn't decided what was good for the goose was good for the gander.

Balancing the tray between my arm and my hip, I tried the doorknob. It was unlocked. The door swung open and standing before me in her dressing gown stood Lady Edith. Coffee splashing every which way, I nearly dropped the tray. I managed to save the eggs and toast, but the coffee had escaped the cup and was soaking into the linen. "I brought your breakfast."

"Dr. Vogel." She put a hand to her heart. "You startled me."

I could say the same. "I did knock."

"Yes." She glanced around. "I was looking for my briefcase." She tutted. "Can't imagine where I left it."

I looked over her shoulder into her room. The smell of ash combined with her lilac perfume. I caught a glimpse of her fireplace and noticed glowing embers. She had mentioned having a chill, but really who made a fire when it was nearly eighty degrees? "Where would you like your tray?" I took a step forward, hoping she'd invite me into her room to get a better look. "Sorry about the coffee."

She gestured me inside. "Just set it on my dressing table. My stomach is still dodgy. But I'll take the coffee with some milk."

The milk was intact, but she would have to suck on the linen to get any coffee. "I'll have to fetch you another cup," I said crossing the room, which was stuffy and hot.

On my way to the dressing table, I passed her writing desk. When I did, Lady Edith dashed over and rolled the top down as if there was something on the desk she didn't want me to see, which, of course made me all the more determined to see it. As the lid rolled shut, I caught a glimpse of a letter she was writing addressed to—I stopped in my tracks—none other than Mr. Fredrick Fredricks. Now I was certain that whatever was going on at Ravenswick Abbey, the great hunter was at the center of it. I tried to concentrate on what I'd seen. The salutation to Fredricks. And the words "found out." Found out what?

"Deepest condolences for your monumental loss," I said, setting the tray on the table.

She gave me a quizzical look. "Oh, right." Realization crossed her face. "Bertram. Silly old goat." Almost as an after-thought, she pulled a handkerchief from the sleeve of her dressing gown and dabbed at her right eye. The shock of her husband's death, and by poison no less, didn't seem to unsettle her as much as it should have. "Couldn't leave well enough alone," she muttered under her breath.

"Was he involved in something that might have got him killed?" I tried to make the question sound quotidian, if not cheerful. I loosened my collar to combat the stuffiness of the room.

She dropped onto the edge of her bed, which was made military-style and didn't look as if she'd slept in it. "He hasn't been the same since the accident at the plant." She slumped. "All those people… the children." It was clear that the deaths of strangers affected her more than the death of her own husband. "He blamed himself."

Odd. At tea, he didn't act like he blamed himself. If

anything, he blamed Scotland Yard for not finding the cause of the explosion—some daft cow to be precise. He seemed to care more about the cost to his business than the cost in human life. His wife, on the other hand, became distraught every time anyone mentioned the accident... or children or orphans.

"Do they have any idea what caused the accident?" I asked, rearranging the plate and saucer on the tray, trying to move the soiled linen to one side.

The blood drained from her face. Her Adam's apple bobbed up and down and she opened her mouth, but she couldn't seem to speak. She shook her head. "Those poor children," she repeated, her gaze askew.

"Kind of you to take them in," I said, following her gaze to the fireplace where the last of the embers gave up their glow.

"It's the least I can do." She dabbed at her eyes again. "How can I live with myself?"

"Surely, it wasn't your fault." I put my hand on her shoulder.

She looked up at me with tears in her eyes and nodded.

"I'll go fetch a fresh cup of coffee." I gave her a sympathetic smile.

She nodded again and forced a weak smile of her own.

As I went back down the stairs to the kitchen, I began to wonder why she felt responsible for the accident. The look she gave her husband when he brought it up at tea. And now her remark about the "least she could do." Combined with her excessive grief and concern for the orphans and none for "the silly old goat." Didn't she care that her husband had been poisoned? Unless, of course, she'd done the poisoning. Lillian Mandrake was right when she'd said poisoning was the murder weapon of choice of respectable women. Lady Edith had the opportunity—her bedchamber connected to his. There was evidence she'd been in his room before he died—her briefcase. Did she have access to poison? And what was her motive? More germane to my own assignment, what was her connection to Mr. Fredrick Fredricks?

When I reached the kitchen, Annabelle, her apron covered in flour dust, nattered on about funeral parties and all the cakes she'd need to bake. After a long-winded story about the last time someone died at Ravenswick Abbey—the Elliott's young daughter—she finally poured out a fresh cup of coffee. Along with the coffee, I had a host of questions for the countess. Careful not to spill again, I held the saucer in both hands. "I'm back," I said as I crossed the threshold, so as not to startle her.

Sprawled across her bed, her chignon undone and her silver hair spilling over the side like a frozen waterfall, the countess lay staring up at the ceiling. Next to her was her briefcase, which she must have retrieved from her husband's room.

"Lady Edith?" I put down the coffee cup and rushed to her bedside. "Is everything alright?"

Judging by the unnatural angle of her body and the blueish tint to her lips, not to mention her unearthly stare, the answer was decidedly NO. Grimacing, I reached out and put two fingers to her neck. Everything was not alright. My heart sank into my stomach like a rock. Countess Edith Elliott was dead. And if I was right, like her husband before her, she'd been murdered. But how? The same poison that had done in her husband?

Of course, I wanted to report the countess's death to the family as soon as possible. But I also wanted to investigate without prying eyes watching my every move. This time, at least, I had the room to myself. At this point, even if Fredricks was not involved—and I was confident he was—I was the last person to see Lady Edith alive, which made me a person of interest, if not the prime suspect. A reason to conduct my own investigation if there ever was one.

First, I lifted the briefcase. It was just as I'd left it earlier when I found it in the earl's bedroom. The tiny key was in the lock. I opened it. The contents consisted of the envelope I'd put there and nothing more. As I relocked the case, an embroidered handkerchief fell to the bed. It must have been stuck to the back of the briefcase. Along with purple flowers, it had the letters L and M sewn into one corner. There was only one person in the household with those initials: Lillian Mandrake. I carefully tucked it back under the case and arranged things just as I'd found them. I suspected Lady Edith had called on her to fetch the briefcase, which raised the question of whether the countess knew the case was in her husband's room, or Lillian told her it was, having seen it there when the earl had his fit. I blinked. What if Lillian said she was going to the dispensary but in actuality doubled back to the house? If she were planning to kill her aunt, surely she wouldn't have told me. No. She would try to establish an alibi.

Next, I inspected the breakfast tray. Lady Edith hadn't touched it. So, whatever had happened was not caused by the unhappy looking boiled egg and soggy soldiers. Hands behind my back, wincing as I went, I bent closer and sniffed near Lady Edith's mouth to see if I could identify any unusual odors. She smelled unusually floral, like lilacs and daffodils. If she hadn't been staring off into space with cold dead eyes, and if her blue lips didn't form a deadly silent O, I would say she smelled like spring.

As I took a step back to get a better look at the corpse in situ, I kicked something with my boot. I bent to pick it up. The small burgundy cordial bottle. The one I'd found in her briefcase. The one with the tag reading "To Lady Edith, Yours truly, J." Only now, it was empty. Kneeling on the carpet, I felt around. There was a damp spot where the bottle had been. Whatever had been left in the bottle had spilled. I looked around for the tiny cork and found it on the night table, along with a ribbon of red wax. Lady Edith must have drunk it. I wrapped the bottle and cork in a handkerchief and tucked them into my breast pocket. The liquid in this bottle was no doubt what had done her in. Was it the same poison used to kill the count? I doubted it. Her symptoms were different. Did our murderer have an entire arsenal of poisons? He—or she—had knowledge of toxicology.

Once again, Lillian Mandrake came to mind. She worked at a dispensary. Then there was the second son, Ian. He was studying to be a doctor himself. They would know poisons. But would they kill Lord and Lady Elliott simply because the parents wouldn't give them their blessing? Murder had been committed for less, especially when an inheritance was at stake. And they both had the means and opportunity. Not to mention the incriminating hanky I'd just found.

I opened the drawer to her nightstand and peeked inside. What's this? Another cordial bottle like the first, only this one was emerald green. I uncorked it and sniffed. It had been washed and now contained oil. I put my finger to its mouth and tipped it upside down and back again. Rubbing my finger and thumb together, I confirmed it was indeed mineral oil. Lying in the drawer was the same tiny tag, which read "To E, Yours Truly, J." Obviously this J person had delivered several bottles of liquor in different colors, burgundy and emerald. One of the tenants perhaps. Someone unhappy with a raise in the lease payment? I slipped both bottles into my jacket pocket and continued my investigation.

I walked the circumference of the room, taking in the scene. The embers in the fireplace reminded me of the countess's chill last evening. I stooped down to examine the ashes, which were still warm. Was the countess ill? Was that why she needed a fire? To combat chills. Could it be she died of some malady or long-standing disease? Or perhaps the shock of her husband's death did her in. It was confounded peculiar to light a fire in this heat. I made a mental note to ask Dr. Derby about the countess's medical history. Although, if he was as tight-lipped about hers as he had been about the earl's, then he wouldn't be much help. Then again, syphilis wasn't a disease without stigma, so it was understandable why the good doctor didn't want to mention it.

A corner of torn paper caught my eye. I debated whether to remove it. With two deaths at the abbey, now certainly they would have to call the police. I bent closer to examine the bit of paper without touching it. I held my breath to avoid breathing in ash. The thick paper was torn into such small bits, most of them burned, that I could barely make out the word in bold letters on one scrap: TEST.

Curious. The countess had made a point of telling us not a scrap of paper was wasted. So why had she ripped up and burned a perfectly good piece of paper? What had she been so eager to destroy?

CHAPTER 6

THE GREAT SOUTH AFRICAN HUNTSMAN

The next day, Lieutenant Douglas and his great pal Fredrick Fredricks were constantly about the manor "investigating" the murders and interviewing the staff. I watched and listened at a safe distance for fear he'd find me out. It wasn't just his reputation that had me worried. I'd seen something in his eyes the day we met, a discerning flash of brilliance, which threatened to reveal me as a fraud. The last thing I wanted was for the astute reporter to interview me. If I thought I could get away with it, however, I would very much like to interview him.

After lunch, I got the lieutenant alone and pumped him for information. Nothing new on the case. Husband and wife both dead within twenty-four hours and no real clues. They were waiting on Dr. Derby's autopsy reports. Given the family's attitude toward the police, I was surprised they allowed the autopsies. In fact, if it hadn't been for my insistence as Dr. Vogel, I doubt it would have occurred to anyone that the deaths could be murders.

Lieutenant Douglas was only too happy to talk. And talk he did. He nearly talked my ear off. I heard all about the "splendid hunter and war hero" and their feats killing poor beasts in Africa. As much as I wanted intel on the suspicious huntsman, after an hour listening to stories of "the brilliant Fredrick Fredricks," I had to make excuses to escape.

What kind of name is Fredrick Fredricks, anyway?

I came away from my one-sided conversations with the lieutenant having learned more than I wanted to know about his trips to Africa and his exploits in the trenches, but very little about his famous friend—except that "Apollo" Fredricks had helped President Theodore Roosevelt bag a lion. Thoroughly disgusting, if you asked me. To top it off, I still had the feeling Lieutenant Douglas didn't like me. Surely, the two men had found more clues than he let on. I didn't need their help anyway. I was conducting my own investigation.

LATER THAT EVENING, I was back at my cottage writing up some notes in a lovely little leather-bound journal with a new indigo fountain pen I'd purchased before I'd left London. I loved the feel of the cool smooth leather in my hands. And the ink flowed onto the page like silk. My weekly report to Captain Hall—the head of British Intelligence at the War Office and boss to us all—was due in two days and I had gathered precious little information on the Great South African Huntsman, except he fancied himself a Greek god and wore a ridiculous hunting outfit everywhere he went. Pen in hand, I stared at the blank page. I had to get more information on Fredricks, or the War Office might take me off the case.

I began writing everything I'd learned. Starting with the

mention of Fredricks in two particularly suspicious places: the German letter I'd purloined from the countess's case and the letter I'd glimpsed in her writing desk addressed to the scoundrel. What was her connection to Fredricks? And how was he connected to the deaths of both Earl and Countess Elliott. Surely, it was not a coincidence that no sooner does Fredricks arrive on the scene than two English aristocrats drop dead. Here was what I'd seen so far of the famed huntsman:

Fredrick Fredricks seemed completely out of his element living among the wounded soldiers and orphans, most of whom were down on their luck and availed themselves of the charity of women like the countess. They'd arrived at the estate with only the clothes on their backs and whatever they could carry in a knapsack, some of them had lost everything in the munition's explosion, including their parents. Given the way he dressed, the newsman, on the other hand, must have had a duke's wardrobe full of expensive hunting outfits and evening wear. Even the most successful big game hunter and war correspondent couldn't afford Mr. Fredricks's wealthy lifestyle of imported chocolates, expensive mustache pomades, ivory-and-gold-handled swagger sticks. Some people in Wickham Bishops speculated he was South African or Australian royalty disguised as a newspaper reporter. Others, less generous, surmised he must be a German spy. Most agreed he was well mannered and exceedingly charming, especially with the ladies, if also annoyingly perceptive.

In the past two days, living among the wounded and orphans, I had a chance to interview several of them. To my surprise, all the women loved Fredricks, who spoke to them in their native languages, whether French or Flemish. He lent them money while they were waiting to get work at the nearby munitions plant. Some of them had worked at Lord Elliott's factory before the explosion. Now, they were waiting for new work in another of his concerns. With so many of our own men fighting at the Front, the war effort at home needed any and all willing laborers.

Somehow, the Great South African Huntsman remained above all the turmoil. With his indistinct accent, he was sometimes mistaken for a wealthy French or Italian gentleman, and at other times an American cowboy or Australian bush baron. The English women swooned over him. I had to admit, he was a handsome devil. And if the English gentlemen treated him with resentment, it was not for being a foreigner—if he was a foreigner—it was for being a bombastic braggart.

Dilly Knox was right. Great South African Huntsman, my eye. Indeed, the sobriquet alone set my teeth on edge. The pinky ring, the swagger stick, the jodhpurs. It was all a bit much. Speaking of Dillwyn—I had to get back into the earl's bedchamber and retrieve the suspicious letter from the hatband so Dilly could translate it from the German.

I was finishing up my notes when there was a knock on my door. Perhaps the Fredrick Fredricks had come to interview me after all. My heart was racing as I went to the door. I was about to open it when my hands flew to my chin. My beard! I'd almost forgotten I wasn't wearing it. I rushed to my dressing table, applied the glue and the beard, patted it into place, adjusted my spectacles, and took a deep breath.

CHAPTER 7

ANOTHER SUSPECT

To my relief, Mary stood on the doorstep. Her forlorn countenance warned me something was wrong. She asked if we might go for a walk, so I fetched my hat and off we went.

"Any news?" I asked. "Have Mr. Fredricks or Lieutenant Douglas come to any conclusions?" At least at my insistence, they'd finally called in the police. To my astonishment it seemed as if both Ernest and Ian thought their status as lords somehow put them above the law.

Mary shook her head.

"Have they identified the poison?" I picked up a small branch that looked like a perfect walking stick. Pleased with myself for appearing so manly, I swung the stick as I walked. "Or found any signs of poison on the premises?"

Every time I mentioned poison, she flushed and went silent. I wondered once again if she'd poisoned the old man to get the letter. I hadn't mentioned that I'd hid the letter in the earl's hatband. I wasn't about to tell Mary that I'd found the letter until I'd had it translated and determined Fredricks's part in the whole mess. Even if the letter was merely about her husband's cheating, it was better to wait to learn its contents before sharing it with her. At that point, she'd need a friend, which I knew better than anyone. And if it was the letter she'd been after, why poison the countess, too? I thought of the cordial bottles I'd pinched from the scene of the countess's death. I needed to have them analyzed as soon as possible. But who could I trust? Certainly not Lillian Mandrake or Ian Elliott. I could turn them over to the police. Indeed, I should turn them over to the police. But before I did, I needed to know how Fredricks was involved and make sure I could prove that I was not involved.

"Is something wrong, doctor?" Mary asked.

I shook my head.

Mary didn't want to talk about the murders, and so we walked in silence. I admired the countryside with its lush green meadows and wildflowers in bloom. In the distance, a wood pigeon cooed its lamentation, joining the symphony of buzzing, whistling, and twittering of its fellow rural inhabitants. Again, I was struck by the contrast with the city's blaring horns and clacking hooves.

Finally, I broke the silence. "Are you sure you can't think of anyone who might have wanted to harm the earl and countess?"

Overcome with emotion, she stopped and buried her face in her hands. "It's my fault," she said, her voice muffled and trembling.

"Why do you say that?" I sincerely hoped she wasn't confessing to the murder of her father-in-law, or worse yet, a double murder. I'd come to like her a great deal, and I'd hate to see her hanged.

"I made the tea, you see," she said.

"Yes, but that doesn't mean you poisoned it." I put my hand on her shoulder. "Did you?"

"Not intentionally," she whispered.

Did she accidentally poison her father-in-law? I raised my glued-on eyebrows.

"Go on," I said encouragingly.

"Well, I added sleeping powders to his tea so I could go through his room into hers and take the letter after she went to sleep." She started sobbing. "I killed him—"

"Now, now, don't cry. The tea didn't kill him." I gently shook her shoulder. "You didn't kill him." Of course, for all I knew, she did kill him. I thought again of the cordial bottles and longed to return to my cottage to examine them properly. If only I knew who to trust to test them for poisons. "I don't think the earl died from sleeping powders." Although it was possible for bromide powder to interact with one of his other medications and lead to a fatal outcome. I would have to do some research. Maybe Daisy Nelson would know. If only I could get to a telephone, I could give her a ring.

"It was horrible, doctor." Mary sniffled. "He was screaming and writhing in pain."

"There, there, it's not your fault." I surmised Mary had found the earl in the throes of the poison when she went to retrieve the letter just before dawn, which also meant she didn't wait for me as planned. I patted her arm. "Don't upset yourself."

She put a finger to her mouth as if deciding whether to tell me something. "There's a rumor Bertram made a new will..." Her voice broke off. "Just before he died." She continued in a whisper. "According to Annabelle, who heard it from the chauffeur, Bertram made an appointment with his lawyer for the very next morning." Her cheeks were flushed and her words were coming fast. "And that night, he had Annabelle bring his writing paper into his bedchamber." She stopped in the middle of the path. "Annabelle heard him arguing with Edith, too."

"Arguing about what?" Good heavens. Could husband and wife have done for each other? Or a murder suicide?

"Quite a row, according to Annabelle." Mary started walking again.

"What did they say?" I was dying to know.

"That's just it." She stopped again. "Annabelle said they were shouting in German." She shrugged. "So, she didn't understand a bit of it. Too bad."

"Isn't it though?" I gently nudged her elbow and we started up again. "Were they both from German descent?" I knew the countess was because Ernest had mentioned her relation to the Saxe-Coburg at tea. But was the senior Lord Elliott also from German stock?

"Oh, yes." She nodded. "Didn't you know?" She sighed. "I suppose not. They didn't exactly advertise the fact with this beastly war on." Mary broke the end of a twig off a tree. "Mr. Fredricks has been snooping all through the house, inter-viewing the staff and everyone." She ripped the skin off the twig and threw strips to the ground. "He even questioned me."

"And what has the famous reporter found out?" I perked up my ears. "They say he is a student of human nature whose method is to dissect the human heart the same way he would dissect the organs of any other animal."

"This morning, he stormed past me like a tornado. He's really a brash fellow."

I tried to imagine the Great South African Huntsman as a tornado, but a tepid squall was the best I could do. "What upset him?"

"From what I hear from Ernest, who gets most of his information from Lieutenant Douglas, originally Mr.

Fredricks found Edith's briefcase locked. Only now it turns out someone has forced the lock and it's empty."

I gaped at her. "What?"

"It wasn't me," she said. "I did go through his room to get the letter, but he started having that frightful fit and it scared me and I dashed out and after that, everything's a blur."

I had been careful to leave the briefcase locked. And when I'd found it on the countess's bed, it was locked. So, if Fredricks took the key, then someone else had picked the lock after the countess's death. Someone looking for something. Were they after the German letter or the burgundy cordial bottle? Instead, they got the envelope containing the key to the earl's bedroom. The one Mary had given me. Again, I was tempted to tell Mary about the letter hidden in the hatband but restrained myself. It wouldn't do to have her sneak back into the bedroom to retrieve it and then find herself in a faint. I was the one who had to recover the letter and get it to London so Dilly Knox could translate it for me.

We'd been so engrossed in our conversation I hadn't noticed how far we'd walked. We were passing by the Roland farm, the last place Mary needed to be. As I guided her back in the other direction, in the distance I noticed two figures standing beside the Roland's barn. One tall hourglass silhouette and one pyramid of manhood. There was no doubt. It was Mrs. Roland and Fredrick Fredricks.

What did he want with Mrs. Roland? What could she possibly know about the murders or the murderer? If Ernest was having an affair with the munitions widow, could that be a motive for killing his parents? Perhaps he wanted a divorce and needed money. He did play the ponies, after all. Presumably "Mutti" wouldn't give him an allowance to divorce Mary and marry another woman, especially not one of her tenants' widows. I quickened my pace, hoping Mary didn't notice her rival.

"Tell me about the munitions factory," I said, hoping to distract her.

She tutted. "Such a tragedy."

"Indeed." I thought of all those innocent people sleeping in their beds getting blown up by our own munitions. They might as well have been bombed by the Germans. "Are there any other plants nearby?"

"There's one right here in Wickham Bishops and another in Woolwich." She shrugged. "After the accident, Bertram's foreman from Silvertown moved to the Fawcett's plant up north. Why do you ask?"

"I'd like to visit one of them and perhaps speak to someone from the Silvertown plant." I stuffed my hands in my pants pockets like I'd seen Ernest do.

"You want to interview one of the Canary Girls?" She narrowed her brows. "Why?"

"Who are the Canary Girls?"

"The girls who work at the munitions plants." She smiled. "That's what we call them because the TNT turns them yellow."

"Yellow!" I sputtered. "You're joking."

"No." She chuckled. "Completely yellow. Skin, hair, everything. Like a canary."

"Blimey," I said under my breath. Poor women. Anything that turned your skin and hair the color of a canary couldn't be healthy. I thought of Mrs. Roland's buttery complexion. I wanted to ask if she worked at the munitions factory but thought better of it. "Tell me about this foreman. You say he works up north now?"

"At Leiston Works." She blew out a breath. "Left us after the accident and went to work for Garrett and Sons." She smiled. "You've heard of the Garrett girls. You met Millicent and Elizabeth is a doctor."

I nodded my head

"Millicent is a great suffragist." She stabbed the air with a finger. "Activist for women's rights. Bully for her."

"Yes." I smiled. "I remember."

"And her sister Elizabeth Anderson is the first woman doctor in England." Mary grinned from ear to ear as if this Elizabeth Anderson were her own daughter. "She owns a dispensary in Marylebone."

"And the foreman. What is he called? The one who moved to Leiston." I planned to visit the man and find out more about the Silvertown accident. I had a hunch the accident was at the core of Lady Edith's disagreements with her husband. Disagreements in German, no less.

"Mr. Newson Dunnell." Mary gave me a quizzical look. "Why do you ask about him?"

Rather than explain my hunch, I changed the subject. "What else has Mr. Fredricks found?"

Mary's face lit up. "Well, Ernest says he made quite a scene about a piece of paper in the fireplace."

"The earl's fireplace?"

"No, Edith's." Her eyes were bright.

I nodded, remembering I thought it odd she'd asked for a fire since it was so blooming hot.

"Mr. Fredricks seems to think the murderer destroyed Bertram's new will in her fireplace." Mary gave a nervous giggle. "Isn't that preposterous!"

When I last saw Lady Edith, there were indeed embers in her fireplace. And I had found signs that paper had been burned. If, however, they were burned by the murderer, then Lady Edith would have been there and witnessed the killer destroying a freshly made will. No, if anyone destroyed a will in her fireplace, it was her.

"A new will, you say?" That would explain the word TEST I saw on a torn corner. Last will and testament. "And what of the existing will? The last legal will and testament made by the earl?"

Mary dropped the remnants of the twig. "The original will favored Ernest, of course. He is the older brother." She kicked at a rock with her small, booted foot. "I guess, after learning of Ernest's infidelity…" She stumbled over the word. "He made a new will favoring Ian."

Mary didn't seem to realize that this information gave Ernest the greatest motive to commit patricide. If it was true that Bertram was making a new will that did not favor Ernest, and the viscount learned either his father or his mother were planning to cut him out of their will, then he may have done away with them before they could execute new wills.

Mary leaned closer and whispered in my ear, "Which is why I suspect Ian did it."

I blanched. "Ian!" It was true. He did have a motive—with his parents gone he was free to marry Lillian. And with the new will, he would inherit the estate. But then why would he destroy it? Unless he and Lillian destroyed the old will. Not the new one. There was the little matter of Lillian's hanky in the dead woman's room. "What else has Mr. Fredricks's found?" I held my breath in anticipation.

"He suspects some foul play with the tea, and Lieutenant Douglas suspects the milk. They seem to have some competition going to see who can solve the case. It's quite funny, really." She chuckled.

"We know the tea was tampered with, do we not?" I asked, giving her a knowing smile.

She blushed. "I suppose we do." She stopped and gazed out at the cool glades. Even the chirping of the birds was faint and subdued. "I have a confession," she said suddenly. "I also put sleeping powders into Lillian's tea, and in Edith's, too."

"It's a wonder we aren't all still asleep!" I made a mental note not to take tea with Mary.

She bit her lip. "Was I very bad?"

I couldn't believe my ears. This lovely lady was capable of much more than I'd given her credit for. So, she'd drugged the entire household, it seemed. No wonder she was acting guilty. I scratched at my beard. The hideous thing itched like the dickens.

"You should really just cut that thing off if it bothers you so much," Mary said with a wry smile. "You'd look nice clean shaven. You have a handsome face."

No one had ever told me I had a handsome face, or even a pretty one. Now here I was, dressed as a man, wearing a beard and bushy brows, with a married woman telling me I had a handsome face. I stared at my boots. What would a real man do in this situation? I dared not think... "Tell me about Ian and Lillian."

"Well, Edith didn't approve of Ian marrying Lillian." She tightened her lips. "In fact, she downright forbade it. Said she'd cut them both off without a penny."

"Did Ian know about the new will?" I stopped and turned to face her. If he did, that was a reason not to kill anybody. He had a motive to protect the makers of the new will, not destroy them or it.

Mary thought for a moment, then tilted her head to one side and said, "Lieutenant Douglas thinks you did it."

"What?" I dropped my walking stick and stared at her in disbelief. I knew that man had something against me.

CHAPTER 8

THE LAMB AND THREE KINGS

That Friday, I was called to testify at the inquest. I'd never been more agitated in my life. This was a true test of my acting prowess, on stage for the whole village —including the astute reporter—to see. I felt as though I were the one on trial.

It didn't help that my boss had made it painfully clear I wasn't to call attention to myself, particularly not by involving myself in this murder case. In our last communiqué, he'd given me strict orders to watch Fredricks and nothing more. "Stay out of local affairs," he'd said in his telegram.

The inquest was held at the Lamb and Three Kings in the village. The pub had a rough stone façade and sported a heavy wooden sign hanging from a post, featuring a friar in a black robe with a tonsure. The irony of naming a public house after biblical kings and Christ would have amused me if I had not been so nervous.

The air inside the pub was heavy with the lingering smell of stale cigarette smoke, intensified by the unseasonable heat and the presence of so many unwashed bodies. The villagers jostled to get front-row seats. A murder was unheard of in the tiny village of Wickham Bishops, and many establishments had closed for the day so their employees could take in the spectacle of wealthy landowners on trial. Low ceilings, dark timber beams, uneven door frames, sweating stone walls, and a slab floor illuminated by only two oil lamps gave the pub an eerie feel.

A couple of old farmers with few teeth and even less hair were jabbering loudly near the front of the room. And a group of women in rough dresses and caps on their huddled heads stood near the door gossiping.

The coroner pounded his gavel on the counter. It took several loud whacks before the crowd settled down. The coroner asked the proprietor to open the windows and then called Viscount Elliott to take the makeshift witness stand, which was really a wooden chair placed next to the counter.

Dressed in a tweed suit and crisp shirt, Viscount Elliott sat in the designated chair and proceeded to describe the events at Ravenswick Abbey the night his father died: Just before dawn, he heard a commotion coming from the earl's bedroom and went to investigate. By this time, the rest of the family had awoken. He called for Dr. Derby, but Dr. Vogel arrived first. Still, it was too late.

"Is it true you've accumulated rather impressive gambling debts?" The coroner pursed his lips.

The viscount shifted in his seat. His cheeks flush, he sputtered, "I do occasionally like to play the ponies." His eyes flashed. "But I don't see what that has to do with anything!"

Perhaps not wanting to incur the wrath of the new earl of Ravenswick, the coroner let him off the hook.

I was called next. I winced when the coroner referred to

me as "the famous London specialist." The crush of bodies with their pongy smells mixed with smoke from the lamps was suffocating. The dark room started to close in on me, causing acute claustrophobia. My head was spinning as I made my way to the counter. A hush fell in the room as I took my seat.

Sitting on the hard chair, facing the entire village, I broke out in a sweat. I pulled a handkerchief from my waistcoat pocket and dabbed at my forehead. Why did men have to wear the full kit even when it was so bloody hot? At least women could wear skirts or dresses. I scanned the audience for Mary's kind face, but instead my gaze landed on the inscrutable countenance of Fredrick Fredricks.

Trying not to swoon, I recounted how I ran into the house from the gate just before dawn to find the earl in the throes of a violent episode. I explained the distinctive signs of poisoning's violent spasms.

The coroner frowned. "And what sort of poison do you suspect?"

"It could be any number of things, including an overdose of his own heart medicine." I swallowed hard. After all, I was not really an expert on poison.

"The postmortem did indeed establish the earl had digitalis in his blood."

"Right." My face grew even hotter. I wished I could rip off my beard and run for the exit. "Higher than his regular dose?"

"If you please." The coroner blinked. "I'm asking the questions." He paced the length of the room. "And what of the countess?" He stopped. "You were the last one to see her alive, is that correct?"

I nodded.

"Do you also think she was poisoned?"

"I do." I was feeling more confident now that the nausea

had subsided. The intrigue of the case had overpowered my urge to faint.

"Do you suspect her after-dinner tea, then?" He grinned. "And it took fourteen hours to kill her?"

"I suppose not." I thought of the bottles hidden back in my room. I desperately needed to get those bottles analyzed and then back into the countess's bed chamber. But how? It was locked. And, anyway, it was probably too late now. It would be deuced suspicious if they suddenly turned up.

"Is it possible, doctor, upon learning of her dear husband's death that the countess died of a broken heart?" He put a hand to his hip.

"It's possible, I suppose—"

He cut me off before I could finish. Possible, but not probable.

"It's often the case when a husband and wife are as close as they were that they travel to heaven together." The coroner's self-satisfied tone turned my stomach.

Finally, the coroner dismissed me. Much relieved, I moved to the back of the room. As I passed Lieutenant Douglas and Mr. Fredricks, they both looked up at me. I nodded, then quickly continued down the aisle and took a seat next to Mary, who was sitting just two rows behind them. I was eager to watch the huntsman's reactions to the testimonies.

Dr. Derby was called next and corroborated my testimony. Sputtering with indignation, he repudiated utterly the suggestion that it could have been suicide. His patient suffered from a weak heart but otherwise enjoyed perfect health. Unless you counted syphilis of course. Which he failed to mention. As for the countess, she was in perfect health and devoted herself to good deeds, such as taking in orphans and refugees. He gestured toward Mr. Fredricks, who nodded in return.

Ian Elliott took the stand next. Fiddling with a pewter button on his waistcoat, he confirmed his brother's account of the night of their father's death. Just as he was about to step down, he paused, and then, with hesitation in his voice, said, "With all due respect, my father's death was from natural causes."

Dr. Derby was recalled to the witness stand and vehemently rejected the accusation that his prescription could have caused his patient's death. He was practically fuming. "As to an overdose, he would have had to have taken the entire bottle, which is nonsense." Dr. Derby seemed personally insulted by this line of questioning.

I wondered.

The testimony of the next witness, the countess's maid, refuted the possibility that the deceased could have taken the entire bottle of heart medicine. "The med'cine weren't just made. It were nearly gone. He were on the last dose the night he passed." The maid sniffled and wadded her soiled handkerchief into a ball. "And she were always so careful with it. The countess, that is. She gave it to him, see."

She testified to overhearing her mistress having a row with her eldest son, "master Ernest," on the day before she died. "She were mad 'bout some lady who come by earlier and somethin' 'bout betrayal."

The jurors' ears perked up at the mention of betrayal. Mine perked up at the mention of some lady. What lady?

"She shouted, 'Give it to me.'"

"Give what to me?" the coroner asked.

"Dunno, sir." The maid shook her head.

Apropos of betrayal, the next witness was Mary. Her demeanor didn't give her away, but I could sense she was nervous. Although she stared clear-eyed into the crowd, her cheeks had the slightest flush and her voice an almost imperceptible tremor.

"My alarm clock woke me at half past four as usual. You see, with the war, I do much of the work on the farm, milking cows and such." She was perfectly composed. It was uncanny. In my presence, she would cry at the drop of a hat, but under pressure she was cool and distant. "As I was dressing, I heard a crash. Then the maid came running down the hall, and we all rushed to my father-in-law's room."

The coroner interrupted her. "Yes, we know. Could you tell us about the quarrel you overheard?"

"Quarrel?" She raised her hand to her throat and adjusted her necklace.

I noticed Lieutenant Douglas shifting in his chair. He whispered something to Fredricks, who ignored him.

She hesitated. "I don't remember."

What was she playing at? I could tell she was lying. In fact, if this courtroom drama was any indication, the wealthy had no qualms about prevaricating. Was it only the middle-class children like me, daughters of greengrocers, whose mothers would wash their mouths out with soap if they were caught telling fibs?

"You don't remember?"

Her lip quivered as she answered, "I couldn't make out the words… because Ernest had a cold. His voice, you see…" She stared down at her hands. Suddenly, she looked up. "Maybe it wasn't Ernest I heard." A weight seemed to lift from her countenance. "Now, that I think about it. No. It was Bertram."

"Are you quite sure?"

"Yes." Her voice grew stronger. "It was Bertram. Not Ernest."

"But your maid, Annabelle, said it was your—"

She cut him off. "She's wrong."

Mary had told me the countess received a letter that proved Ernest was having an affair with Mrs. Roland. The maid had suggested the offending woman had visited the countess earlier that day. Mary was jealous to the point of obsession. And even so, she was protecting her unfaithful husband. The coroner pressed, but Mary wouldn't admit to anything more. Finally, he dismissed her. She rejoined me in the back of the pub. Her face was pale, but she forced a little smile as she sat down next to me.

Next, a shop girl testified she'd had a will form sent over the day the earl died. Then two gardeners swore under oath the earl had called them in to witness a document and sign it for him. So, the old boy had made a new will. But where was it? Was it destroyed the very same day?

"And who was the beneficiary of this new will?" the coroner asked.

"Can't rightly say, sir," the gardener answered, troubling the rim of his hat.

"Can't or won't?" The coroner tapped on the counter. "Remember, you're under oath and sworn to tell the truth, so help you God."

The gardener's round cheeks turned the color of two ripe tomatoes. "From what I saw—not that I looked mind—everything were going to Mr. Ernest, that is Lord Elliott, the younger."

The audience broke into excited chatter. If the new will favored Ernest, then what about the old will? And why had everyone said Ernest had been the beneficiary of the original will? It made no sense. The next witness, Lord Elliott's lawyer, cleared up the matter of the will. Yes, the earl had called him to make a new will. No, he didn't know its contents.

"And the original will?" the coroner asked.

"The estate and all his money went to his wife, Lady Edith Elliott." The lawyer wiped his palms down his jacket front scraping away any suspicions that Ernest had killed his father to prevent him making a new will.

Chatter from the onlookers disrupted the proceedings. The coroner pounded his gavel.

The countess's niece, Lillian Mandrake, was called to testify. She claimed she had gone to bed early and nearly slept through the commotion, which fit with Mary's admission to me that she had put sleeping powders in Lillian's tea. Young Lillian slept the sound sleep of a clear conscience—assisted by narcotics. She arrived at the bedchamber only after the earl was already dead. The next morning before going to work, she went to check on the countess to see if she could get her aunt anything. Could that explain the hanky on the bed? Or perhaps the countess lying dead an hour later?

My head was pounding, and the heat in the room was oppressive. I had to get some air. I whispered to Mary, "I'm going to step out for a bit." I picked my way through the crowd to the entrance and fled onto the lawn.

I loosened my tie and gulped in fresh air. It occurred to me that I'd hidden the two pieces of evidence crucial to solving the murders. The cordial bottles and the German letter. I was convinced they both had something to do with Fredrick Fredricks. But what? If only I knew, I could go to Captain Hall and maybe he could put a stop to the inquest.

With everyone in the pub, perhaps I could sneak back to the house and retrieve the letter and replace the cordial bottle back into the countess's briefcase. How odd it would look, a bottle turning up after everyone, including the astute huntsman-cum-reporter, had seen the case was empty. If the murderer had gone looking to retrieve the letter—or the bottle—what must he have thought when he found it missing?

The street was deserted and most of the shops were

closed. I quickened my pace lest some straggler noticed me. Even though it was only a five-minute walk, by the time I reached my cottage, I was drenched in perspiration. My mother always told me that ladies did not sweat, but she didn't know any who wore men's woolen suits in May. The Scottish were onto something with their kilts.

Once inside, I threw off my jacket, unbuttoned my shirtwaist, and unwrapped my chest. The gauze I'd used to conceal my femininity was soaking wet. I stripped down to my underclothes, retrieved the bottle from the pocket of my other waistcoat, which was hanging in the wardrobe, and then flopped onto my bed. I giggled, imagining what I must look like in women's underthings and a great black beard. Something from the circus no doubt.

Relaxing on my pillow, I held the burgundy bottle up to the light. It had beveled edges, curves in its neck, and lattice designs on its sides. The dregs of a dark liquid stained the inside of its corners. In fact, there were a few drops left clinging to the bottom. Around its neck was a small piece of thick paper attached with a tiny pink ribbon. I brought the bottle closer to reread the tag, which was penned in an extravagant cursive, suggesting a lady's hand. Again, I wondered, who was J? I uncorked the bottle and sniffed. The unmistakable sweet smell of sloe berries rode on the pungent current of liquor. Someone had made Lady Edith a homemade aperitif, possibly a deadly brew designed to be her last.

I smelled the cork. Along with the berries and liquor, I sensed something dark and earthy, mushrooms perhaps, and the faint bitter smell of daffodils. Did one of the tenants hold a grudge? Everyone gushed about how well the countess treated her tenants. Yet perhaps one of the wounded soldiers or refugees resented the countess's charity. Enough to kill her.

. . .

I JUMPED up from the bed and searched my room for one of my vials and paper or cloth in which to wrap both bottles. Carefully, I used an eyedropper to remove a couple drops of liquid from the one still containing the cordial and dropped it into a tiny vial, capped it, and set it aside. Then, I settled on a strip of gauze from my chest-wrap and wound it around the bottle. I had to get it analyzed as soon as possible. Given that everyone else seemed to think the old boy died of natural causes, it was up to me to determine otherwise, which is why I decided not to return the evidence. As far as I was concerned, I was securing the evidence.

Lillian Mandrake worked at a hospital. Maybe she could help. Then again, she was a suspect. And even if she wasn't, asking her would be problematic. "I stole this cordial bottle from the countess's briefcase; could you analyze its contents?" Would anyone believe I accidentally removed it from the murder scene? If only I'd made more friends while volunteering at the hospital. If I hadn't been moping around pining for Andrew, I might have. Andrew. By some miracle, I'd gone two days in a row without thinking of Andrew—and his new wife. She worked at the hospital. I could ask her. What an absurd idea. The husband-stealing tart.

Then there was my friend Daisy Nelson at Charing Cross Hospital. She was the true expert in poisons both common and rare. But could she keep a secret? I wrapped the gauzy bottles in butcher paper and tied the package up with string. I'd have to take my chances with Daisy. As a cunning woman, she was a practitioner of dark arts and white magic, and therefore no stranger to secrets.

Putting my damp clothes back on made my skin crawl. I glanced out the window before departing. My uncanny bearded reflection stared back at me, distorted further by the thick glass. I dashed out the door. Careful not to be seen, I stopped at the post office and mailed my parcel special delivery to Daisy Nelson at Charing Cross. Then I darted back to the Lamb and Three Kings for the end of the inquest.

When I arrived back at the pub, the whole of Wickham Bishops was milling about on the lawn. I was too late. The inquest was over. I spotted Mary in a small group near the entrance. I made a beeline through the throng and landed at her side.

"You missed it!" She grabbed my elbow in excitement.

I stared down at her small white hand, which was still touching my wool jacket. "Missed what?"

Our conversation was interrupted by the coroner calling us back into the public house. Once we were all seated, he concluded the inquest, announcing the verdict, "In the case of the earl: Accidental overdose of digitalis, a medication he was taking for his heart. In the case of her ladyship: a broken heart."

Broken heart, my fake mustache!

CHAPTER 9

THE CANARY GIRLS

The next day, I decided to pay a visit to Lord Elliott's former munitions foreman at Garrett and Sons in Leiston. Over breakfast at the abbey, when I mentioned my intentions, and asked if I might borrow a chauffeur and/or a motor, Lieutenant Douglas was only too happy to offer to drive me.

"I say." His blue eyes sparked. "All those munitions girls, covered head to toe in overalls." He chuckled. "Must be a sight."

"You mean the Canary Girls," Mary said, munching on a piece of toast. "An entire flock of them would be a sight indeed."

Considering the abbey had recently suffered the loss of the lord and lady of the house, everyone seemed a bit too jolly. The viscount tucked into his full English breakfast with the gusto of a man who'd just hiked up Scafell Pike. Despite having to work at the hospital, Ian added a healthy dose of brandy to his coffee. And young Lillian's cheeks glowed like pink roses covered in morning dew. In all, it was a pretty scene. The dining room was adorned with flowers, some of them sent with condolences from neighbors and tenants. And the sun had left off scorching us and resumed a normal warm and welcome springtime radiance.

"One more cup." Lieutenant Douglas refilled his coffee. "And then I'll fetch my motor and we'll be off." He smiled. "You know…" He let out a snort. "I haven't been up north to Leiston since a fishing trip. When was that now? Must be nearly five years. Anyway…" No doubt his coffee would be cold by the time he finished his story. If I didn't stop him, it might be lunchtime before we departed.

Lieutenant Douglas regaled me with hunting stories and humorous anecdotes all the way from Wickham Bishops to Leiston—almost two hours of nonstop nattering. I tried to tune him out, but his driving was worse than his chatter. I suspected if he concentrated on one rather than the other, then both would be improved. Meaning, we would be quietly driving straight and steady north along the coast and could enjoy the scenery instead of holding on for dear life listening to tales of bloodsport.

Leiston was bustling with activity. Groups of soldiers milled about downtown near the railway station. At high noon, the sky was so dark with soot from the factories, it seemed almost dusk.

Garrett and Sons was a long, low rectangular pink brick building surrounded by a high barbed-wire fence. Around the building sat dozens of machines like I'd never seen before. Lieutenant Douglas informed me that what looked like open-air miniature railway cars were called Ramblers. Similar engines used by farmers were called tractors.

Wouldn't my grandfather fall over to see such wonders? Turned out they made engines of all sorts: portable engines, traction engines, steam roller, steam tractors, steam wagons, and large six-wheeled wagons that tipped their loads to save men having to shovel. Much of the works had been commandeered by the army to make war vehicles and a section of the plant was reserved for munitions. That was where I'd find Mr. Newson Dunnell, the foreman who'd left Silvertown after it was blown to smithereens.

Much to his consternation, I left Lieutenant Douglas waiting with the car while an army private showed me the way to Mr. Dunnell's office.

Mr. Newson Dunnell, a tall, lean man with a strong upright posture wearing woolen tweeds met us at the door. His office was on the second floor, overlooking the assembly line below. A wall of windows gave him a clear view of everything on the floor, which was covered with a mat-like material. Dressed in blue overalls and matching caps, rows of munitionettes sorted and filled artillery shells and assembled fuses. It was true. Their faces were the color of pale butter. Peeking out from under their caps, even their hair had a yellowish tint. The loud clatter of machinery was punctuated occasionally by the shout from a supervisor. Even from behind the glass, the smells were oppressive, a mix of burnt rubber, acrid chemicals, rancid lubricants, human sweat, and the sulfurous stench of rotten eggs. I fought the impulse to hold my nose.

Mr. Dunnell was accompanied by two women, one I recognized as Millicent Fawcett and the other bore such a resemblance I assumed it to be her sister Elizabeth. They were introduced as the owner's daughters, the Garrett sisters, Elizabeth and Millicent.

"Yes, Miss Millicent and I have met." I tipped my hat.

She nodded. "Before the horrible tragic deaths." She shook her head. "Poor Lillian."

Poor Lillian indeed. With the parents out of the way, she could freely pursue their younger son. And perhaps her aunt had left her something in her will. Not to mention, poor Lillian would no longer have to take orders from the woman.

Elizabeth Garrett Anderson, as she was called, was taller and sturdier and looked to be the oldest. She wore her dark hair coiled atop her head, and a white lab coat over her dress. Compared to her sister, Millicent had a slight, graceful build. Her dark hair was pinned up in a simple bun, she wore a high-collared blouse, and woolen skirt. Unlike the other women in the compound, their skin was not yellow and they were not wearing overalls.

Just as Lady Mary had said, Elizabeth was a doctor, the first woman doctor in England. She was at the plant checking on the workers who suffered from every manner of lung ailment due to the horrible fetid air in the plant. Millicent made the rounds with her sister, helping out with medicines and hoping to recruit the women into her cause. They were both pleasant, soft-spoken, dignified women and if I hadn't been dressed as Dr. Vogel, I'm certain we may have become friendly. As it was, I had a difficult time convincing them that I didn't have time to attend to sickly munitionettes because I was busy investigating not one but two murders. They were such kindly women, they even offered to help with my investigation.

"Now that you mention it." I dug in the pocket of my waistcoat for the tiny vial. "Perhaps you can identify the substance in this sample." I held out the vial to the doctor— the real doctor.

"Where is it from?" Elizabeth took it and examined it.

"I found it in a cordial bottle." I stuffed my hands in my

pockets in a manly fashion. "Smells like a berry liquor of some sort."

She uncorked the vial and sniffed. "Yes. Berries." She sniffed again. "Fermented fruit and berries. Right, a liquor." She put her finger to the opening and inverted it.

"I wouldn't do that." I suspected she might be about to taste it.

She gave me a funny look.

"It could be poisoned." I grimaced.

"Poisoned?" Millicent said. "Isn't it bad enough we're at war?" She shook her head. "Do we need to go around poisoning each other, too?"

Elizabeth recorked the vial and wiped her finger on a small hand towel she had tucked into her belt. "Smells organic. Like unripe tomatoes. Slightly sweet unripe tomatoes. And berries, of course. I can't say more without bringing it back to my dispensary and taking a closer look, maybe run a few tests."

"If it isn't too much trouble." I smiled. "I have another one, if you could manage. From a milk with rum drink." I retrieved a second vial from my pocket and handed it to her.

"No trouble." She held up the vial. "Can you part with this for a day or two?"

I nodded. "I'm staying in the cottages on the grounds of Ravenswick Abbey in Wickham Bishops. Perhaps you could send word to me there? Or I could meet you at your dispensary."

"We regularly go back and forth between London and Leiston." She smiled. "Wickham Bishops is on the way."

"Excellent." I was happy to finally unburden myself of the poison sample. Perhaps now I could get some answers.

"Dr. Vogel, where do you stand on votes for women?" Millicent asked, her tone pointed if still polite. "I hope you're not one of those men who think reason and commonsense are your purview alone."

"Mrs. Fawcett, I believe reason and commonsense know no gender," I said with a smile. "Though I must admit, I've found women possess them in greater measure." I picked a tiny piece of lint off my hat. "Which is why I often think in addition to voting, they should be governing, too."

The gleam in her intelligent eyes told me she was pleasantly surprised. "You're a good man, Dr. Vogel."

"I'm at least one of those things," I said with a wink.

The ladies joined me in a laugh.

"I hate to interrupt the fun," Mr. Dunnell said. "But I believe you came to see me, Dr. Vogel." He was leaning against his desk. "And I really should get back to work. The army expects maximum production, so we're always running at breakneck speed."

"Of course, sorry for the delay." I turned back to the charming Garrett sisters. "I do hope our paths cross again in the near future." And I'm not wearing this hideous beard. "Now, I would like to talk to Mr. Dunnell for a few minutes in private, if I may."

After the ladies (myself excepted) took their leave, I sat down in a chair across from Mr. Dunnell's desk. "I was wondering if I might ask you a few questions about the Silvertown munitions accident." I fiddled with my hatband.

He frowned. "It was no accident."

My eyes went wide.

"It was sabotage." His countenance turned from sunny to stormy in a matter of seconds.

"Sabotage?" Good heavens. "What makes you say that?"

He crossed his arms, his jaw tight. "Lots of things don't add up." He held up one finger. "First, the week before the explosion, tools went missing and some barrels were mislabeled." Another finger went up. "Second, the girls reported an odd bloke hanging around the back fence at all hours." A third finger. "An odd smell appeared the day before the explosion, near the TNT stores, but not like any chemical we use." He balled up his fist. "Add it up and I'd say it wasn't an accident." He closed his eyes and let out a long breath. "Someone wanted to blow us up." When he opened his eyes again, they were dull and he looked weary. "We're just lucky it was a holiday and not many people were in the plant." He shook his head. "Those poor folks living within two streets of the factory weren't so lucky." He hung his head. "And my buddy Joe Roland. I was supposed to be working that day. But my daughter got sick, so Joe took my place." His voice trembled. "It should have been me…"

"It most certainly should not." I tugged at the hem of my waistcoat. "It shouldn't have been any of those poor souls." I tutted. "Who would do such a thing?"

He gave me a look like that was the stupidest question ever asked. "I hope that's a rhetorical question."

A terrible thought was taking shape in my mind. Now, now, Fiona. Not all Germans are saboteurs. It was a daft notion. Surely, Lord Bertram or Lady Edith wouldn't sabotage their own factory. But it did put a whole new spin on my murder investigation.

CHAPTER 10

THE MAID RECONNOITERS

The following day, when Mary came for our morning walk, she reported that immediately after breakfast Fredricks asked if the coachman could take him to Colchester, to the chemist where the earl had his tinctures made up.

"Coachman?" I asked. "Not the chauffeur?"

"Ian had dibs on the car. So, Mr. Fredricks had to settle for the horse-drawn coach."

"Even better!"

"Better? Why it will take four times as long." Mary gave me a quizzical look.

"Indeed." I took her elbow. Given Colchester was a good sixteen miles away, I figured Fredricks wouldn't be back for at least another four hours. "Mary, would you mind going on without me? I'm afraid my bad knee is acting up."

"Oh dear. But you're so young."

"Sports injury. From my college days, playing… ruggers."

"Rugby?" She narrowed her brows. "I don't believe you." She looked me up and down.

"I'm joking, of course." I laughed. "It was tennis." I turned toward the cottages and hobbled back along the path.

"Poor dear," Mary called after me. "I'll come round this evening and collect you for dinner."

As soon as Mary was out of sight, I dashed back to my cottage. I soaked a cloth, wrung it out, and applied it damp to my beard. After a minute, I pulled off the blasted thing, tore off my fake eyebrows, and applied cream to my poor inflamed face. I flung off my oversized boots, wriggled out of my trousers, jacket, waistcoat, shirtwaist, and then pulled off my socks. I unwrapped my bosom, such as it was, threw on my knickers, and stepped into my chemise.

I went to my suitcase and removed another costume I'd purchased for just this occasion. The black dress fell just above my ankles. Its little white collar was starched stiff. I sat on my bed and rolled on black stockings and then slipped on black T-strap shoes. I lifted a white apron from the case and wore it over my dress. Luckily the white maid's cap covered most of my shorn head.

At the dressing table, I applied just a touch of kohl, rouge, and lipstick. I powdered my chin to cover the rash caused by that blasted beard. My transformation was complete. I'd gone from wiry bearded doctor to a proper English chambermaid. I smiled at my reflection in the hand mirror. The woman looking back at me wasn't a beauty, but at least she didn't have a beard.

Exercising my vocal cords, I sang a few notes from The Maid of the Mountains, the last musical theater I'd seen before I left London. "Love will find a way..." I raised it up an octave and tried again. As the doctor, I'd been using such a low range, my voice was unaccustomed to the upper registers.

I peeked out the door of my cottage, looking both ways to make sure no one saw me. Horsefeathers! I didn't need to sneak around. I was now a chambermaid here to clean the cottages. Perfectly normal. No one noticed servants anyway. If I kept my head bowed and didn't make eye contact, I should be able to go about my business pretty much as if I were invisible. At least, that's what my brain said. My stomach was another matter altogether.

Carrying a couple of rags for effect, I walked across the dirt path to Leastways cottage, the one Fredrick Fredricks shared with the wounded and orphans. It was the largest of the cottages. Its thick brown-gray thatch looked like a saddle blanket draped over the pitched roof. Two dormer windows peeked out from under the thatch like sleepy eyes. Red roses climbed up the sides of the green front door, creating a festive contrast of color. I headed up the two stone steps and then knocked on the door. When one of the Belgians answered, I curtsied slightly, and he gestured me inside.

"I haven't seen you before," he said with a thick accent.

"I'm new, sir," I said with my best cockney inflection. "Sent from the manor house."

"It's nice to see English girls working hard," he said.

"Yes, sir." I narrowed my brows but didn't ask what he meant. "I'll just go 'bout my work then."

I glanced around the front sitting room where two other men were playing a game of backgammon. Concentrating on their game, they didn't look up. I wiped off the fireplace mantel and dusted the tables. There was a heaviness in the room that couldn't be accounted for by the dark furnishings, thick drapes, or the men's pipe smoke. A sense of loss hung in the air mixed with sweet cherry tobacco. Although they were speaking French, I gathered from their conversation they were biding their time until positions opened up at the munitions factory. My ears perked up when one of the backgammon players mentioned Fredricks. I couldn't make out all the words, but his sentiment was clear—resentment.

"Où trouve-t-il son argent?" one of the players asked.

Where does he get his money? Indeed.

"Excuse me, sirs," I said timidly. "Don't mean to eavesdrop, but Monsieur Fredricks has been up at the big house investigating the murders and I wonder if he's qualified. I mean they took him on without knowing his credentials." I hoped I'd read the room correctly and these men weren't fans of Mr. Fredricks. It seems only the women fancied him.

"What do you know about him?" I asked, still dusting.

"He puts on airs and looks down his nose at us," said the other backgammon player, a lanky middle-aged man with close-set eyes and slicked-back hair parted down the middle. "We have only the clothes on our backs. We don't know whether our families are safe. We are waiting for work so we can pay for our next meal. We have lost everything. And Monsieur Fredricks has everything."

"I'll pray for your families," I said, passing my cloth over the back of a chair. "Does Monsieur Fredricks ever talk about his family?"

A man with a bushy mustache looked up from the game. "Monsieur Fredricks treats us like children, always instructing us on how to behave in our new country. As an Englishman, this is his home, but we want to go home. We don't belong here." He puffed his pipe and blew out a cloud of smoke that hung in the air like a melancholy note.

But was Mr. Fredricks truly an Englishman?

"My woman and babies are in Folkestone working for rich lady cleaning house while I work here in weapons factory," said the one with the mustache.

"And Monsieur Fredricks? Does he have a wife and babies someplace?" I asked, wiping off a small corner table.

"Monsieur Fredricks is une folle," the lanky one said with a sly smile.

"Folle?" Didn't folle mean crazy woman? Maybe my French was rustier than I thought.

"Une countess, how do you call them in English?"

"A countess, I see," I said with a blush, and went about pretending to clean. He clearly didn't mean a countess in the way Lady Edith had been a countess, but another meaning altogether.

After a cursory dusting of the front rooms, I headed upstairs, wiping the wooden banister with a rag as I went.

I'd seen Fredricks open his bedroom window, so I knew his room was the second on the left.

I stopped on the landing when I heard voices coming from one of the rooms. I held my breath and listened. I couldn't make out the words, but they were definitely speaking German. Was this whole place full of German spies? Of course, speaking German did not necessarily make one a spy or sympathetic to our enemies.

I heard a doorknob turn and a voice getting louder, so I dashed past the door and slipped into the second room on the left.

Fredricks's chamber held a small bed and nightstand in one corner, a washstand and a writing desk near the window, and another small table and two chairs along the center of the interior wall. A tall armoire sat next to the table. Books organized from largest to smallest were neatly stacked at the back of the table against the wall, and a pen and a notebook lay in the center, all exactly parallel to one another. Similarly precise was his bed, made military style with every corner tucked in. I never understood how a fleshy three-dimensional person could slide into sheets so firmly fitted.

After surveying the room, I started my search at the nightstand. In its center was a small oil lamp and next to it, a chain of beads. When I bent down to get a closer look, I recognized the necklace as a rosary made of rosewood beads with a silver crucifix attached. So, Fredricks was Catholic. I wouldn't have figured a man of his great prowess to be religious, let alone Catholic. I wondered how many Hail Marys he had to say to atone for his sins.

My next stop was the washstand, where a cream-colored jug with blue floral designs stood inside a matching bowl. Alongside it sat a straight razor, tiny scissors, a tiny comb, a small tin of D. R. Harris wax, a silk snood, and an ornately handled silver rod with a lever and clip, which I can only assume was for straightening the ends of his pencil mustache. Each of these items was placed as precisely as if on a surgeon's tray.

Examining Fredrick's mustache paraphernalia, I recalled one of Kipling's women saying being kissed by a man who didn't wax his mustache was like eating an egg without salt. I didn't particularly like eggs, with or without salt.

I sat down at the table and read the spines of his books: a couple of fat books in German, by someone called Edmund Husserl; Matière et Mémoire by Henri Bergson; Die Traumdeutung by Sigmund Freud (I'd heard of him—an Austrian doctor who attributed all illness to sexual frustration); the autobiography of Teresa of Ávila; Field Guide to Poisonous Plants (Could Fredricks be the murderer?); and on the very top of the stack, a well-worn copy of The Handy Black Cat English-French Dictionary. There were certainly enough German books to confirm my suspicions that he was a German spy. I took a mental note of all the titles, planning to research them later. Sometimes a photographic memory came in handy.

I took my gloves from the pocket of my apron, slipped them on, and carefully opened Fredricks's notebook. Each page was dated, and in a tight cursive written straight across the page was line after line of French. I should have paid more attention in my French classes at North London Collegiate. I could make out some of the words, and given the dates, it seems he was making notes on the murders. Why is he writing in French? Could this somehow mean he is a French spy? The French were our allies. Was the French actually some kind of code?

I glanced up at the clock on the mantel. If he had set out for Colchester directly after breakfast—say about nine—then he had been gone for just over three hours. I figured he would need at least four hours to get there and back. Still, I had to dust the rest of the rooms and get out of the house before he returned. I didn't want to risk running into the eagle-eyed man. He might notice a certain freckle or mole that would give me away.

Still wearing my gloves, I opened the armoire. Golly. He had a lot of clothes for a man. Jackets, waistcoats, and trousers were segregated and arranged by color, with each hanger the same distance apart. Three-feet-tall leather boots stood at attention on the floor of the wardrobe, and three slouch hats were lined up on the top shelf. An assortment of bow ties hung from special hooks on the inside of the armoire door, again arranged by color and by length. You couldn't find a more colorful arrangement of vestments at Harrod's department store. A clothes brush hung from a hook on the inside of the door. A tidier wardrobe I'd never seen. I gently closed the door so as not to disturb anything and then checked to make sure I hadn't moved the books or notebook. I straightened the notebook so it was exactly aligned with the pen. Why was this man so obsessed with order? What would Dr. Freud have to say? His outward order was compensation for inward chaos, perhaps.

I stood in the center of the room and slowly turned, surveying every nook to see if I had missed anything of interest. I knelt and on hands and knees peeked under the bed. Aha! A small leather case sat atop a large suitcase. I carefully slid them out from under the bed. I sat cross-legged on the floor and opened the small case. It contained several corked lab tubes, a pair of tweezers, a magnifying glass, a pen, and a pad of paper. Given every item had its own slot or leather restraint, it looked as though the case had been specially made. I closed the latch on the tool case and set it to one side. His greatest tool was not in this case. On more than one occasion, I'd overheard him say he didn't need any special equipment to solve a case, only his animal instincts housed deep inside his lizard brain.

I listened to make sure no one was coming, and then I depressed the latches on either side of the large suitcase. To my surprise, it was unlocked. The case was empty except for a photo album and a small box. I picked up the box and suppressed a chuckle. The vain man used coal hair dye. I shook the box. Sure enough, there was a bottle inside containing the liquid dye. I replaced the box, removed the album, and opened its heavy embossed leather cover. Inside the album, photographs were skillfully glued to each black page. The first was of a beautiful woman holding two babies. Did the huntsman-cum-reporter have a wife and children waiting for him somewhere? Were they still in Africa or America? Or perhaps he had lost them in the war. That would explain a good deal.

The album was full of photographs of the same dark beauty and two boys who grew with each turn of the page. About four years in, a baby joined the family. A couple of pages later, she was a gorgeous curly-headed little girl of probably four years old. Then she disappeared from the rest of the pictures. By the end, the boys—who looked to be identical twins—must have been around nine years of age. They both had strong noses like their father and dark features like their mother, and both were wearing matching knickerbocker suits and captain's hats. I wondered where they were now and why Fredricks never spoke of them.

As I lifted the album from my lap to replace it in the case, something fell out. At first, I thought it was an insect. I jumped up and the wretched thing tumbled off my apron onto the floor. What in the world? It was a false mustache. Why would Fredricks have a false mustache? Wasn't his mustache real? It looked real enough. Then again, I'd been sporting a false beard and so far—touch wood—no one was the wiser. Could Fredricks be wearing a disguise? His fancy hunting kit did look more like a costume than anyone's regular attire.

I picked up the caterpillar mustache, returned it to the album, and put the book back in the suitcase. Closing the latches, I sat the smaller case on top and glided them back under the bed. Finally, I was getting somewhere. I wasn't the only one living a double life. The Great South African Huntsman, it seemed, had secrets of his own.

I brushed myself off and had just reached the chamber door when the handle turned. My hand flew to my mouth and desperately I glanced around the room for some place to hide. Too late. In strode Mr. Fredrick Fredricks himself. You could have knocked me down with a feather. I felt the blood drain from my face until I'm sure my complexion matched my apron.

"I was just cleaning your room, sir," I said, my voice cracking.

"Mademoiselle," he said, tipping his hat. "And now you're finished, n'est-ce pas?"

"Yes, sir." I curtsied.

"Too bad." He stood in the doorway and wouldn't let me pass. "Might I ask your name?"

Crikey! What was my name?

"Teresa, sir," I blurted out.

"Mademoiselle Teresa…" He held an arm across the entrance, blocking my way. "And your family name?"

I felt like a trapped animal. Had he recognized me and now he was toying with me like a cat with a mouse?

"Baldasarré." I lowered my eyes and focused on the buckles on my shoes. "Teresa Baldasarré."

"That's a familiar name," he said. "Where have I heard it before?" He lifted my chin with his index finger. "Let me look at you, ma chérie."

Cheeky devil! If I weren't in disguise and trying not to call attention to myself, I might have slapped his face.

"And your eyes…" he said, staring into my face.

As I closed my eyes tight, I had the strangest sensation in the region of my stomach.

"You're not the regular domestic." He brushed a stray hair from my forehead. "You're much prettier."

My eyes flashed open in indignation. I had to admit, with his jet-black hair and full lips, he really was quite handsome.

"Teresa Baldasarré." He patted his heart. "Such a beautiful name for such a beautiful girl." A wolfish grin spread across his face. He took a deep breath. "And you smell good enough to eat. Like fresh peaches and cream." He was practically smacking his lips.

My cheeks aflame, I had the strongest urge to bolt.

"Would you like some brandy, Mademoiselle Teresa?" With one finger, he lightly stroked my sleeve.

I stifled a gasp and shook my head.

He smiled and bowed his head. "Papa Fredricks won't bite, you know."

Aha! Papa Fredricks. He does have children then. Or, perhaps, he merely thought himself old enough to be my father, in which case the man was a rotter and a cad.

"Unless you prefer it that way." He flashed a devilish grin.

My hand flew to my mouth. "No thank you, sir." I ducked under his arm and resisted the urge to run. "I'd best get back to work."

I barely escaped a pat on the bottom on my way out. I hurried up the hall and down the stairs before he realized Teresa and Baldasarré were the two leads of The Maid of the Mountains.

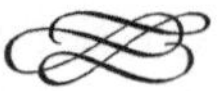

THE ENCOUNTER

The next morning was the countess's funeral, a glorious Monday with only a few puffy clouds. The entire village turned out to honor one of its prime benefactors. Even the Garrett sisters were in attendance. Arm-in-arm, they gave their condolences to the family. Many of the mourners were deeply indebted to the countess, including the Great South African Huntsman, and the refugees and orphans. With his slicked-back mane, the big game hunting reporter looked like a zebra in his black suit, white shirt, and dark glasses. He was accompanied by the irritating Lieutenant Douglas, also dressed in black. As usual, the lieutenant nattered on about killing something all the way to the church.

The quaint medieval church was round with a thatched roof upon which a turret was perched like a biretta atop the head of a bishop. We entered by a massive wooden door tucked into a stone archway. Inside, the church was built in stone blocks and contained a circular nave. Between the ambulatory and nave were eight massive Norman columns and round arches decorated with dogtooth ornamentation and carved human heads. Except for the light streaming through colorful stained-glass windows, the church was almost dark. An appropriate ambiance for a funeral.

Packed with mourners dressed in black, which contrasted with the light gray of the stone walls, the pews looked to be inundated by a flock of crows surging against a concrete sky. When Lord Ernest Elliott entered the sanctuary and took a place in the front pew, the crows clucked their tongues. His face remained impassive—if anything, he seemed to look down his nose at the other parishioners.

I positioned myself in the rear and off to one side of the chapel, which gave me an unobstructed view of Fredricks. So, Papa Zebra had foals. But why had he never mentioned them? And what of his wife, the dark beauty in the photo-graph? Why had he left her behind? And what about that fake mustache? I wished I could get a closer look at his mustache. To do so, however, would put him much too close to my own false facial hair. I stared at the altar without seeing, and the voice of the minister became background noise for my own nagging thoughts.

The heat in the church was stifling. I instinctively looked for something to fan myself with, and then remembered I was a man, and men don't fan themselves. Beads of sweat were forming under my beard. I patted it to make sure it was still in place. The last thing I needed was my beard sliding off during the countess's funeral.

As the minister droned on about the countess's good works and her importance to the community, I admired the arched ceiling and vibrant stained-glass windows, which depicted the last temptation of Christ—the morning sun was at the perfect angle to enliven the deathly scene with rich blood-soaked hues.

After the service, the mourners followed the pallbearers into the graveyard just outside the church. Centuries-old headstones sat at odd angles, giving the churchyard a whimsical feel. The countess's freshly carved headstone stood out straight and tall among its ancestors. Only her husband's new stone was taller.

During the burial, I hung back from the flock of mourners and planted myself under the shade of an oak tree to escape the beastly unseasonable heat. At least a skirt allowed for air circulation and some modest relief, though nothing a man had to endure in the way of clothing could compare to the dreaded corset. As a man, I could finally take a deep breath without feeling I was going to burst out of my stays.

A nightingale whistled a mournful lament overhead. I looked up and spotted the little caramel-colored creature bobbing up and down on a branch, its feathers soft with dappled sunshine filtering through the leaves. It seemed the whole world, even the birds, were mourning the dead. The earl's death was criminal, but he was an old man after all. The countess, on the other hand, had been cut down, if not quite in her prime, not in her dotage either.

At the hospital, I'd seen boys no more than fourteen for whom the loss of innocence meant the loss of limbs. Boys who would never whirl their sweetheart around a dance floor. Boys who would grow into men haunted for the rest of their lives by the atrocities of war. Men who would never truly find comfort in their lovers' arms, men who cowered whenever an airplane roared across the sky.

Instead of masquerading as a doctor, I should be helping in the hospital. Not for the war effort, but for all the boys and men who sacrificed everything to answer a call for help from our neighbors across the Channel.

My tawny feathered friend raised her voice in a final twittered song and then flew away. Goodbye, Florence Nightingale, the lady with the lamp. Guide our boys home safely.

"Excusez-moi."

My hand flew to my heart. "You startled me, Mr. Fredricks." In my surprise, I'd forgotten to properly lower my voice. I cleared my throat. "Catching a bit of a cold, I'm afraid."

He gave me an appraising look. "Might I ask you a few questions, s'il vous plaît?"

Why was he always speaking French? Was it because, like me, he was leading a double life? Or was it just to impress the ladies? I knew for a fact he was from South Africa.

"Of course," I said in the deepest tenor I could muster. "I'm at your service." Trying not to stare, I examined his mustache, looking for any signs of spirit glue.

"You were there when the earl died, n'est-ce pas?"

"Yes, but you don't think—"

"No, no, ma—monsieur." He gave me a reassuring smile. "And you were there when the countess died, n'est-ce pas? And you proposed poisoning for both?"

"I recognized the symptoms. With the earl. The tremors and violent spasms. At first, I suspected mercury bichloride. It's very easy to procure because... of the epidemic." For some reason, I couldn't bring myself to say syphilis, as if saying it risked infection. "But I was wrong, it seems. It was an over-dose of his own digitalis."

"An accident, then?" He stepped closer.

"Not necessarily." I didn't believe it was an accident. Not for a minute.

He moved even closer. Now I could feel his breath on my cheek. "And you are an expert on poisons, doctor?" He smelled of rosewood and peat.

I wiped my brow with my handkerchief. It had suddenly gotten much warmer. "Yes, poisons and female maladies are my specialties." I didn't mention that in my opinion most female maladies might be best cured by administering a lethal dose of poison to an unfaithful lover. I doubted the War Office made this connection when they came up with the cover story for the good Dr. Vogel.

"So, it was you who insisted on an autopsy, and rightly so." He leaned against the tree.

"Yes." My heart was racing. He was so close. The way he looked at me. Had he found me out? "Dr. Derby and the countess's son Ian thought it was his heart, but I knew otherwise." I tried to keep my voice strong and steady.

"Very correct, too." He fingered his mustache. "Did you notice anything strange in his boudoir?"

What could I say? You mean, dear Fredricks, did I notice anything strange other than the nearly empty tincture bottle, the Ryno's Remedy cocaine snuff, and a burgundy cordial bottle and incriminating letter in Lady Edith's case, which for some still unexplained reason was in her husband's bedroom? I troubled the edge of my hanky. "In the commotion, I didn't notice anything except the earl's distress." The nosy huntsman-cum-journalist German spy didn't need to know about Mary's mission to retrieve the letter implicating her husband, a letter still held hostage in a hatband in the earl's room, or the cordial bottles, which I had sent to Daisy Nelson at Charing Cross dispensary. Hopefully, Daisy could tell me more about the organic compounds Elizabeth Anderson had identified in the sample I'd collected. Innocent fruits and berries? Or poisonous toadstools and foxglove or oleander. There were plenty of deadly substances growing wild. Mother Nature didn't need man's help to kill.

"Perhaps you glanced at his medicine bottle or the little box of powders in his drawer?" When he smiled, his mustache turned up even more. "The ones Dr. Derby removed from the scene." He tutted. "So many things removed, n'est-ce pas?"

I stroked my beard. I wouldn't let this clever fellow unnerve me. "The medicine bottle was nearly empty. The powder was Ryno's Remedy, a snuff made of cocaine used to treat various ailments, including allergies."

He nodded encouragingly. "And is it safe to take the digitalis tincture along with cocaine powder?"

"They're both stimulants, so I suppose—"

"May I?" he asked and picked a speck off the shoulder of my jacket with his gloved fingers. He looked at the tiny ball on the end of his glove and then sniffed it. "Spirit gum, I think."

Blimey! He was on to me. "I really should be going." I stuffed my hanky into my breast pocket. "I have a... an appointment... a sick patient. Yes, I have to make a house call." I tugged on the rim of my hat.

"Do you smell that?" With both hands, he scooped the air into his nostrils.

"What?" All I smelled was my own fear.

"Peaches." A wide grin spread across his face. "Fresh peaches." He leaned closer and sniffed.

"I smell a rat," I said, taking off at a good clip.

He caught up to me. "May I walk with you?"

"I'm going in a different direction." I wasn't sure which direction he was going, but I was going to make sure it was different from mine.

He tipped his hat. "Very well." When he smiled, he had an

uncanny twinkle in his eyes. He started in the direction of the manor house and I went the opposite direction back toward the church.

Thank goodness. I was perspiring like a farmhand. I'd best contact the War Office and tell them the jig was up. I needed to find a telephone and tell them to extract me before Fredricks ripped off my beard and exposed me.

"Just one more question."

My hand flew to my heart. Fredricks's baritone voice caught me off guard. I swung around. What did he want now?

"Mein Freund." His disarming smile seemed rehearsed. "What were you doing out walking before dawn on the night of the murder? An odd time to be out for a stroll, n'est-ce pas?"

Was he speaking German and French? I'd read he was multilingual, but he really should make up his mind.

"You don't think I poisoned the earl, do you?"

"Did you?"

"Of course not."

"So why don't you answer my question?" he asked with that annoying, white-fanged grin of his.

"I couldn't sleep. Insomnia." I forced myself to make eye contact and speak with conviction. "I went out for a walk."

"Why don't you just take sleeping powders?" He might as well have added, like everyone else.

"I like to keep a clear head."

"You prescribe them, but you don't take them yourself?"

"They are better for the ladies."

"I see. And what doesn't let you sleep, doctor? You're troubled perhaps?"

"Nightmares. The blasted war has given everyone nightmares."

"Nightmares are for the guilty." He tapped his swagger stick on the ground for emphasis. "Which is why I have only sweet dreams."

I narrowed my fake bushy brows. "Then you, sir, are a lucky man."

"My clear conscience has nothing to do with luck, good doctor." That grin again. "Perhaps tonight, I will dream of the sweet chamber maid, Mademoiselle Teresa." He rubbed his hands together.

I blinked, ignoring his remark about the maid of the mountain. "Do you think I have a guilty conscience?"

"Do you?" he asked, giving me an unnerving stare.

"No more than any other man," I replied with more confidence than I felt.

"I suspect, good doctor, you aren't just any other man." The huntsman gave me a smug smile. "We should have a drink together very soon." He winked. "We could trade secrets on mustache wax." Chuckling, he turned on his heels.

I swallowed hard.

"I'll get to the bottom of it," he called over his shoulder as he strolled away. "And when I do, I'll leave no part untouched." His back as stiff as a windup toy, he swung his stick as he went.

Oh, my sainted aunt. He'd found me out. I leaned against the oak tree and removed my hat. That little interrogation had taken my breath away. I removed the handkerchief from my breast pocket, dabbed at my forehead again, and longed for a glass of cool lemonade. I hadn't seen a lemon in two years. The war had taken so much away from us, even the simplest of pleasures.

I closed my eyes and inhaled the scent of May in the countryside, damp grass and freesia so sweet it hinted at rotting fruit. I was going to have to leave the pleasures of the country and return to London without having fulfilled my assignment. Worse yet. I'd probably blown my cover. I certainly hadn't discovered the truth about Fredricks. I had no proof he was working for the Germans—or the French. After all, reading German philosophy didn't make him a spy.

The only certainty: he was deuced clever and a complete and utter rogue.

CHAPTER 12

THE WRONG MAN

Once I explained to Captain Hall my fears about Fredricks exposing me, he insisted on extracting me immediately. Even if I could figure out how to retrieve the damning letter, I couldn't ask the captain to give me more time. He was adamant about getting me out of Wickham Bishops as soon as possible. He didn't want me to compromise the mission. I tried not to be too contrite or admit failure just yet. After all, if my memory wasn't playing tricks on me, I could be instrumental in bringing a killer to justice. But how?

I couldn't tell the War Office I'd stolen a letter from the countess's briefcase and hidden it at the behest of a jealous wife who fancied me her savior. And until I could confirm the contents of the letter, I dared not make accusations that might turn out to be complete figments of my imagination. What was a bearded lady to do?

I was packing up my meager belongings: the maid's

outfit, the one suit I wasn't wearing, and my notebook, when there was a knock at the door. Luckily, I was still undercover as Doctor Vogel. I went to the cottage door and wasn't surprised to see Mary, as she was a regular visitor. I was going to miss our daily walks and sharing in her confidences.

"Mary, what a nice surprise!" For fear of rousing more gossip, I didn't invite her in.

"Doctor, you've got to help me!" She was quivering like a half-baked treacle pudding.

"Whatever is the matter?"

"They've arrested Ernest!"

"Ernest? Why?"

"They found a poison vial in his room. The police took him away to Scotland Yard."

I started. I thought the inquest ruled both deaths natural, which to my mind was of course a mistake.

"They've charged him with murder." She broke down and threw her head upon my shoulder. "They're keeping him in jail in London until the trial," she said in a muffled voice into my jacket.

I put my arm around her. "There, there. Don't worry. We'll sort it out. Aren't Mr. Fredricks and Lieutenant Douglas still on the case?"

A muffled "Yes" came from the vicinity of my armpit.

"I'm certain they can exonerate Ernest and catch the true killer." I wasn't certain at all. Especially if her husband's fate was in the hands of that absurd lieutenant. For all I knew, the great huntsman had planted the poison bottle in Ernest's room and the annoying Lieutenant Douglas was in on it. Then again, maybe Ernest was the true killer. If he had quarreled with his mother, and he was having an affair with Mrs. Roland, and the countess had threatened to tell Mary and cut him out of her will, especially considering his gambling debts, he had a motive. And he certainly had the means. But did he have the character?

Mr. Fredricks says anyone is capable of murder in the right circumstances. I disagree. Only a degenerate character is capable of murder under any circumstances. Although as far as I'm concerned, most men are degenerates. All the lives wasted and lost to wars, not to mention sons poisoning their mothers. If women ran the world, things would be decidedly different.

"Isn't there something you can do?" she pleaded.

"I'm a doctor, not a detective." I patted her shoulder. "Anyway, I'm afraid I must get back to London. I have a sick patient desperately in need of my care. She refuses to see any other doctor." I was pleased with myself for thinking that up on the spot.

"Oh, you can't leave me now!" she cried. "I'm desperately in need of your care." She stomped her foot. "I refuse to see any other doctor."

"I'm afraid I must." I went back to my packing, careful to cover my underthings and the maid's costume with more manly attire.

"Perhaps I could see you in London." She twisted a lock of her hair. "Ian has found us a house in Paddington where we can be near Ernest and await the trial."

"Good plan." I folded my socks and patted them into the corner of my case.

"They say it could be weeks, even months. Lieutenant Douglas is coming too. Why don't you join us? After you check on your patient, of course."

"Lieutenant Douglas?" I shuddered at the thought of sharing a house with that windbag.

"He's taken a job at the War Office." She went to my window. "Since he was wounded, he doesn't have to go back to the Front."

"At the War Office!" I couldn't help but blurt out.

"What's the matter with that?" She turned back to me. "He figures if he sticks it out, he may even be promoted to captain."

Captain Douglas. Horsefeathers! I doubted he could make the grade.

"Won't you join us at the house in Paddington?" She came to my side. "We've got plenty of room." She put her small hand on my sleeve. "I need you now more than ever. My nerves are ruined. Please, doctor."

I couldn't bear to look at her. I took a deep breath. "I'm afraid that's impossible. But I will promise to visit you when I can."

"I imagine you'll be called on to testify again at Ernest's trial." She sounded almost hopeful.

Oh, bother! I hadn't considered I would be called as a witness in London. I'd planned on discarding Doctor Vogel as soon as I reached a safe distance from Wickham Bishops. I'd better keep the two suits and the beard and brow set just in case. "Could be." I didn't relish the idea of reprising my role as Dr. Vogel on the London stage, even if that stage was a courtroom.

Mary's face fell. "What can we do, doctor? We can't let Ernest—" She didn't finish the sentence.

"No, we can't," I agreed. I needed to get that letter back. But how? If only I could remember what I'd seen. Fine time for my photographic memory to fail me, which was only because the blasted letter was in German.

The War Office expected me back in London tonight. I was to leave immediately. Furthermore, the diligent maid was keeping the room under lock and key on strict instructions from Mr. Fredricks. I doubted even Mary could get into the bedroom. Given Mary's role in the whole affair, she was not in the best position to find such a letter in any case.

Luckily, Ernest's trial was weeks off, so I had time to devise a plan to retrieve the letter. Most likely, I was imagining its damning contents. Maybe Mary was right, and it was about a marital betrayal and Ernest's affair with Mrs. Roland.

"What can we do to save Ernest?" Mary seemed to shrink in stature. "Poor Ernest, spending the next few weeks in prison."

"Don't worry. We have time. We'll think of something." I hoped I was right. I didn't feel as certain as I sounded.

"Thank you, doctor." Mary gave me a sad smile. "Until we meet in London." She held out her hand.

I took it, bent toward it and kissed the air in its general direction like I'd seen other gentlemen doing.

Once Mary left, I rushed about to finish packing my one suitcase and tidy up the cottage. I double-checked the night-stand and the chest of drawers. I didn't want to leave behind some telltale sign of my disguise. For a second time, I passed a rag over the counter of the kitchenette. I'd say it was even cleaner than when I arrived. I gathered my toiletries and spirit gum and tucked them into a corner of my suitcase, closed it, and sat on the small wooden chair, at the ready. A driver from the War Office would be fetching me in less than ten minutes, and I didn't want to keep him waiting.

A brusque knock on the door signaled his arrival. Although I would miss Mary and the sweet country air, I was eager to get back to my flat in London and take off my disguise. Suitcase in hand, I opened the door, ready to depart this place for good.

To my surprise, it was a boy delivering a telegram. I dropped my suitcase and fished in my pocket for a coin. I wasn't used to having pockets. But they were jolly handy. The second I closed the door, I ripped open the telegram. It was from Elizabeth Garrett Anderson. Stunned, I stood blinking down, rereading the two-word telegram. Arsenic.

Digitalis. I wished she'd specified if they were in the cordial or the milk. The earl didn't drink the cordial. But his wife did. The milk, on the other hand, could have been the vehicle for whatever did for the earl. And if he did get an overdose of digitalis, it very well could have caused cardiac arrest.

Bang. Bang. Bang. Another knock at the door startled me. When I opened the door, a uniformed officer was standing on my doorstep. I had expected someone undercover or at least wearing plain clothes, someone who wouldn't call attention to my departure. Instead, there was a police car with another uniformed officer waiting in the driver's seat—hardly a discreet send-off. The whole village would be talking. Probably thinking I had been arrested for the murders.

"Dr. Vogel?" the officer asked. Wearing the standard issue navy-blue overcoat and custodian helmet fastened under the chin, the poor fellow was sweating like a cold beverage on a hot day. "The expert on poisons?"

"Yes." I was distracted by thoughts of arsenic. What did it mean? Dr. Anderson must have found arsenic in the burgundy cordial bottle from Lady Edith's briefcase that I'd found on the floor near her body. Someone had poisoned the sloe-berry liquor with arsenic, which confirmed Lady Edith's death was indeed murder. Did her husband die from arsenic poisoning too? My head was spinning with questions.

"Come with me." The constable put his hand on my arm. "You're under arrest."

What nonsense? Had that blasted Lieutenant Douglas actually persuaded the police I killed the countess? "There must be some mistake."

"Come along." The officer took my suitcase from me and dropped it on the doorstep.

"Why? What's going on?"

"You'll find out soon 'nuff." He slapped metal ratcheted

bracelets around my wrists, picked up my case, and then gestured toward the car.

I had no choice but to comply. With its front fenders suspended above large white tires, its long shiny snout, two round lamps for eyes, and license plate mustache, the car looked like a menacing cartoon dog. The levered front window only added to the effect.

The constable opened the passenger door and roughly deposited me, along with my luggage, on the backseat. I'd never been in a police car before. In fact, having grown up in London, except for family holidays to the seaside, I'd only been in an automobile a few times in my life, the most memorable had been my wedding day when Andrew hired a car to take us to Torquay where we spent our honeymoon at The Grand Hotel. Andrew had tried to carry me over the threshold but tripped, and we both went crashing to the floor, his elbow jamming into my eye socket on the way down. I had a great shiner for the rest of the week. Those had been the happiest days of my life.

Strangely enough, even after his infidelity and the divorce, I didn't regret having given my whole heart to Andrew. Yet, I already regretted coming to Wickham Bishops, which could prove to be my last regret, if I ended up hanging for a crime I didn't commit.

The backseat of the Arrol-Johnston—as a tiny plaque on the bonnet announced—was cramped and claustrophobic, especially with my case on my lap. At least the top was up, hiding my shame. I'd hate to have to ride through the village with the top down, everyone gawking at me. They already thought I was carrying on an intrigue with a married woman.

As we drove past, several orphans from the cottages were standing on their doorsteps, smoking and watching the scene. A couple of others peered down from their first-floor windows. My arrest was the most exciting thing to happen in the village for months, next to Bertram's death (which the authorities still considered was the result of natural causes), the countess's murder, and the arrest of Viscount Ernest Elliott, of course. I was glad when the police car had left the village behind and we were driving along deserted country roads.

I hadn't realized Wickham Bishops was so close to the coast until I saw a giant concrete "ear" in the far distance across a green field, a large dot against a gray-blue horizon. I recognized the large dome as one of the new sound mirrors the War Office had installed along the coast to amplify the sounds of approaching enemy aircraft. The car continued along the coast, passing more fields of various grasses and an occasional stand of black poplars or other hardwood trees.

I was happy to see the green spire of Chelmsford Cathedral. I recognized it from when I was a child, and my mother and I would take the train from London to Chelmsford to visit my aunt. The police station couldn't be far away, and finally I could get out of this deuced uncomfortable automobile. Give me a train over a car any day.

Wait! What? We passed right by the Essex Constabulary. "Where are we going?" I asked. We'd already been driving on this bumpy horse path long enough for my back to hurt. Where were they taking me? Now I was getting nervous.

"London," the driver said. "Keep your shirt on."

They would be in for a surprise if I took it off!

"Might you at least tell me the charge against me?" I asked as politely as I could manage under the circumstances. Had they released Viscount Elliott and I was now to take his place in a London prison? My mind was racing.

"All in good time," the arresting officer said. "All in good time."

It was not a good time. Not by a long shot. But one didn't argue with bobbies armed with billy clubs.

Surely the War Office would help me sort this out once we got to the London police station. As my father used to say, "The day's not over till the cows come home." I just hope I'm not said cow heading for the slaughter.

On the outskirts of town, we passed an abandoned farm. The once bucolic landscape of rural England was haunted by what it lacked—able-bodied men.

I must have nodded off for quite a while because I awoke when the car stopped in front of the Essex Regiment Depot at Warley, or so the sign said. The depot was a big square brick building surrounded by scrubby lawns and dirt. Across the road, by the looks of it, the chapel had become the regiment's home church, and a group of men in uniform stood huddled in the churchyard, no doubt at another funeral for a fallen friend. Lorries carrying wounded soldiers pulled up in front of a makeshift hospital. And a group of men—some in wheelchairs and others on crutches, stood smoking near the entrance.

When the acrid smell of cigarette smoke reached my nostrils, it transformed into the familiar penetrating spirits smell of ether and brought the war back in all its vivid gore. I could practically feel the soldier's cold flesh under my palpating fingertips.

"Out you go," the driver said. "A break to use the lav."

"Don't let him out of your sight," his partner said.

I desperately needed to use the facilities, but I couldn't bloody well do so within his sight. Although, if I revealed my true identity perhaps the case against me would be dropped. Then again, I might appear even more suspicious for wearing a costume and posing as a doctor. In fact, they might think the whole ruse was devised in order to murder the countess.

I'd never traveled from Warley to London by car, but it

must be at least another two hours. I didn't know if my bladder could hold out against these blasted bumpy roads. Under the circumstances, I had no choice but to risk it.

"I'm fine," I lied.

"Alrighty then." The driver reached over the backseat and unlocked my hands.

Were they dumping me off in Warley? Or worse, enlisting me in the army? I was passing myself off as an able-bodied man, and a doctor no less. And the Warley Depot included a hospital central to the war effort. I'd seen the effects of war, and I could stomach the sight of bloody and severed limbs, but I definitely couldn't amputate one.

"Cuff him to the car," the driver said to his mate. He stretched out my right arm and handcuffed my wrist to the car's metal frame, while his partner took my left hand and cuffed my left wrist to the opposite side of the car frame. I was stretched out like Christ on the cross. What in blazes did they have planned for me? Was I to be horsewhipped while chained to this vehicle?

"Now see here," I said.

"Let's get us a pint," the driver said heading for the depot with his partner in tow.

"You can't just leave me!" I called after them.

The driver called back, "We'll see about that, ya dodgy berk." Then they both laughed.

I didn't know what a berk was, but it didn't sound good.

An hour later, the pair returned in good spirits, smelling of beer. I, on the other hand, was more than a bit miffed and planned to report them to the War Office as soon as I got the chance. My arms were aching and the cuffs bit into my wrists.

"Enjoy the view?" the driver asked as he uncuffed my right hand and then reached across to my left. He pocketed the extra cuffs and locked my wrists together again with the remaining set.

I scowled at him but said nothing. I didn't want to be conked on the head with a truncheon, or worse.

After thirty minutes on the road, the sky turned as dark as my mood. A crow sitting atop a dead tree alongside the road gave me an eerie feeling. Dotted with drooping thatched roofs and an occasional dilapidated farmhouse, the landscape spoke to me in a shadow language full of foreboding. By the time we reached the outskirts of London, I was convinced there was an apocalypse amid the hedgerows.

"Where we supposed to drop this dirty Hun spy?" the driver asked his partner.

"Spy!" I exclaimed. Truth be told, I was a spy, but not for the Germans.

"That's right," his partner said. "And you'll hang for it. Unless you gets the firing squad."

The driver snorted. "Hangin' or shootin's too good for the likes of him. He oughta be drawn and quartered or burned alive."

Burned alive! I shuddered.

"We should string him up by his ugly black beard," his partner chimed in.

As much as I'd been looking forward to losing the beard, that's not exactly how I'd imagined doing it.

CHAPTER 13

$\mathcal{I}$ was greatly relieved when we turned onto Whitehall Street and then pulled up in front of the Old Admiralty Building. If I could just talk to Captain Hall or Mr. Montgomery or one of the other men from Room 40, I could get this mess straightened out.

One of the constables grabbed my suitcase, dropped it on the curb, and then grabbed me. I stumbled as he pulled me out of the car. After five hours folded into the back of that car, I could barely walk… and my need for the facilities was dire.

"Might I talk to someone in Room 40?" I asked, with as much deference as I could muster. "Please, I know people there. They can vouch for me."

The driver pulled a piece of crumpled paper from his pocket and read it. "Says we're to take him to some bloke called Captain Hall." His colleague removed my handcuffs.

Thank goodness. I rubbed my wrists where the cuffs had cut into them.

Captain Reginald Hall—or "Blinker" as the lads called him—would save me. Surely, he wouldn't let me hang. Everyone in Room 40—Mr. Montgomery, Mr. Grey, Mr. Knox, and me—all worked under the command of Captain Hall.

The bobbies deposited me in the reception area outside Captain Hall's office. His secretary gave me an appraising look and reluctantly offered me a seat. When I made for an overstuffed upholstered chair near a low coffee table, she shook her head and pointed to a high-backed wooden chair in the corner. She pushed a button on a little box, announced me to a man on the other end, and then escorted me inside to the interior office.

Captain Hall's office was spacious and contained only the bare essentials—a desk and chair, which gave it a forsaken appearance. Unlike Room 40, his office had big windows facing Whitehall Street. The sound of cars and carriages created ambient background noise for our meeting. The captain was sitting at his desk. He was a slight man with a band of white hair encircling a bald head, sharp eyes, and a pleasant if tight-lipped smile. He was wearing a dark uniform decorated with the multicolored stripes of an officer, a stiff white collar, and a neat black necktie. He greeted me with a smile, stood up from his desk, and held out his hand.

I dropped my suitcase and reached out to take it, but he'd already withdrawn it with a chuckle.

"Brilliant disguise, Miss Figg," he said. "I nearly fell for it myself."

"Thank you, sir," I said with relief.

"But, if you don't mind me saying, you look a bit worse for wear." His eyes twitched and flashed like a Navy signal lamp. No wonder they called him Blinker.

"It was a long ride from Wickham Bishops, and those officers were convinced I'm a German spy. Needless to say, they weren't happy with me."

"Sorry about that, old boy—Miss Figg. We had to maintain your cover throughout the extraction. Standard procedure. Apologies if it was uncomfortable, but it's safer that way." He gestured to another high-backed wooden chair, the only other piece of furniture in the room besides his desk and chair.

"Perhaps I could freshen up before our interview?" My bladder was full to bursting.

"Of course. The gents'—ladies'," he corrected himself, "is just downstairs. I'm afraid there's not a ladies' on every floor." He cleared his throat. "Although I'm not sure you should visit the ladies dressed like that."

"Good point." A man in the powder room, and one in my disheveled state, would surely cause a panic. "Is there a place where I can change?" I pointed to my suitcase.

"My secretary will take care of you. After you've freshened up, tell her to bring us a couple of coffees, will you? Unless of course you prefer tea? I'm a coffee man myself." He chuckled. "You really are very convincing, Miss Figg. It's uncanny." He shook his head, and his eyes flashed their Morse code.

"Thank you, sir," I said, wondering if it was flattering that I could so easily pass as a man.

It took a while to persuade his secretary I didn't want to change my clothes in the men's lavatory. What would the Navy men think if I went in as a man and emerged as a maid? The secretary buzzed the captain again and asked if she could escort me to his private lavatory. She gave me a scornful look as she did so.

Besides my second suit, the maid's kit was my only option. I pulled off my trousers, jacket, waistcoat, and shirtwaist, and slipped into the black dress. I decided to do without the apron. I was on my way out the door when I caught my reflection in the glass. Good heavens! I'd forgotten to remove my beard and bushy brows. When I ripped off the beard, at least one layer of skin went with it. I peeled the brows off more slowly and then adjusted my maid's cap to cover my shorn hair. First thing tomorrow, I'd have to shop for a new hat to wear until my hair was long enough for a finger wave. Nothing like buying a new hat to lift the spirits.

I returned to Captain Hall's office. He looked up from his desk and stared at me with astonishment. "Uncanny." He gestured to the wooden chair. "Take a seat, Miss Figg."

I smoothed the skirt of my dress and sat down. I felt self-conscious about my legs. In my haste, I'd forgotten to put on my stockings. I tugged the dress down over my knees. A few minutes ago, I'd sat in the same chair with all the confidence of a man, and now here I was as fidgety as a schoolgirl called before the headmistress. It was amazing the difference wearing trousers made to one's confidence. If women wore trousers, we'd rule the world.

"I'd like a full report on this supposed American newspaperman and hunter, Mr. Fredrick Fredricks." He blinked. "Can you type it up and have it to me by next week? Handy you're a secretary too." When he chuckled, his eyelids fluttered. "You can do your own typing."

"Just so," I said with a forced smile.

"In a nutshell, what did you find out about the blighter? Is he spying for the Germans?" The blinking stopped and his gaze was unrelenting.

I didn't want to admit what I'd found out could actually fit inside a nutshell. "He's very secretive. Based on my investigation, I suspect he has a family somewhere, a family he never mentions."

"Did you find evidence of espionage?"

"He had several books in German."

"Books? What kind of books?" Captain Hall's mustache framed his scowl.

"From what I could tell, German psychology and philosophy."

"No coded messages or secret telegrams?"

I shook my head.

"Well, type up everything. Even the smallest detail could be relevant."

The captain sounded just like Fredricks. Anything, even the smallest detail, could be a clue. I hesitated for a moment, wondering whether I should bring it up, as I was expressly told in no uncertain terms to stay out of local intrigues unless they were directly connected to the suspicious huntsman-cum-reporter. "Remember I mentioned the murder investigation at Ravenswick Abbey?"

"Yes, and I told you to stay out of it." He tapped a pencil on his desk.

"I think Fredrick Fredricks is involved." I steeled my courage. "I found evidence."

The captain blinked a few times and furrowed his brows. "Involved? How?"

I cleared my throat. "He had a Field Guide to Poisonous Plants in his room." I tugged on the hem of my maid's uniform. "I found a couple of suspicious little cordial bottles—"

"Stay out of it, Miss Figg, and let Scotland Yard do their job. They don't interfere with our business, and we don't interfere with theirs. Is that clear?"

"But, sir—"

"The War Office can't get involved in local criminal cases. You're assigned to get information on our potential spy. Keep after Fred... Fred..." He stuttered over Fredrick Fredricks and gave up. "The suspicious newspaperman. Unless you can prove the country murders are connected to espionage, and Fredricks is the murderer, leave it alone. Stick to your mission." He shuffled some papers on his desk.

"But, sir, I saw—"

"Dismissed, Miss Figg," he said without looking up from his papers. "And stay out of it, that's an order!"

"Yes, sir." I nodded and took my leave. Tomorrow, I would follow up with Daisy Nelson and swear her to secrecy. In the meantime, I was eager to get home to a warm bath and a hot cup of tea.

CHAPTER 14

A BAD PENNY RETURNS

*I*t was good to be back in my flat after so many weeks away. Motes billowed into great clouds as I pulled open the drapes in the drawing room. Despite the fetid premature summer smells wafting up from the sweltering street below, I opened the windows to air out the place. London was malodorous and my flat was stuffy, but it was home. And I thought the cottage was oppressive. I'd have to start the ice delivery service again as soon as possible. If only I could get my hands on some lemons. I was dying for a glass of cold lemonade. With the war, icemen were replaced by ice girls, who delivered only once a week, and my beverage choices were limited to water or beer.

I'd say one thing for Dr. Vogel, he'd taught me how to hold my liquor. Before my assignment, I'd been a teetotaler. Now I enjoyed the occasional pint as much as the next bloke.

I surveyed the drawing room. Except for a layer of dust, it looked just as I had left it, and yet it felt different. Something had changed. The furniture was the same—four ornate chairs in crimson velvet inherited from my grandmother, a Charles II oak court cupboard, and a pink-and-blue Donegal carpet. The silver candelabra on the round oak table and my grandfather's cuckoo clock on the fireplace mantel were exactly where I'd left them. So, what is different? Is something missing? I walked around the room, touching my favorite pieces, the smooth wood of the cupboard, the soft plush of the velvet. Then it dawned on me. Incredible! I swirled around taking in the entire room. That's it! The overwhelming absence of Andrew; it had vanished.

I flew about the flat like a bird just released from its cage. I threw open the drapes. I sorted my mail. I put on the kettle. It was reassuring to sit at my own kitchen table and listen to the crescendo of the kettle reaching a boil. I poured the boiling water into my favorite teapot and waited for the reviving beverage to steep. I never imagined cobalt-blue and-white porcelain could bring such joy.

After my cuppa, I took a long hot bath, which made me sleepy. Sleep won out over food, and I went to bed without supper, which was just as well since my icebox was empty. When I lay in bed, looking up at the familiar wallpaper, a hint of the absence of Andrew was barely perceptible in the curve of a particular paisley or that faded patch near the chandelier. I closed my eyes to blot it out, but the presence of his absence spread from the wallpaper to my walled-in heart.

I thought of the evening at the Royal Caledonian Ball when my second cousin, who'd been at Eton with Andrew, dared him to dance with me. Apparently, I had a reputation for being prickly, and at the ripe old age of twenty was already considered a hopeless spinster. Andrew was a beautiful dancer, so graceful I felt like I was flying. Unlike other boys, he laughed at my zingers and quips instead of running away. To the chagrin of my mother, I scratched out the rest of my dance card and he abandoned his other partners. We danced together for the rest of the night. We were married three weeks later, on Christmas Eve.

Where is he now? I could almost feel his arms around me. Brushing tears from my cheeks, I closed my eyes and said a prayer for him. Then, completely knackered, I fell into a deathlike sleep.

The next morning, I awoke, disturbed by nightmares about Andrew and a terrible sense of foreboding. I was tempted to track down Nancy, the husband-stealing tart, and ask if he was alright. But first, I had to do something about my hair. Even if I wore a hat, I couldn't completely cover the black bristles sticking out of my head like a valet's brush. And I wasn't about to let her see me looking like a love-sick porcupine.

Famished, I searched my kitchen cupboards for something to eat. I had to settle for a couple of stale biscuits and a tin of beans. I made a cup of tea, dunked the biscuits, and resolved to restock my pantry as soon as possible.

After breakfast, such as it was, I picked out a flowered spring frock, my nicest silk stockings, a pair of low-heeled but stylish strappy pumps, and laid them out on the bed. Then I went to find a hat. Before the war—and the divorce— deciding on a hat to wear was the most difficult decision of my day. Now, I might find myself decoding a German telegram that could change the course of history or trailing a suspicious refugee.

I grabbed my fancy pink garden hat off the shelf. It was loaded with silk flowers and lace and looked like a great blooming meringue. I hurried to my dressing table and placed it atop my shorn head. Drat! I didn't have enough hair to pin it into and it kept sliding off. Mourning my auburn locks, I went back to my wardrobe to fetch my old stand-by, a beige bucket-shaped felt number. It wasn't as pretty, but at least it stayed on. I would have to leave the flat early enough to stop at Raoul's Wig Shop and find a suitable wig. I couldn't wear this ugly hat for the next six months waiting for my hair to grow back.

I may have overdone the lipstick and rouge just a tad. But it was so nice to be able to paint my face again. The reflection in the mirror didn't seem to belong to me, but to some long-lost twin, who looked like me but lived a parallel life more exciting than my own. I held the bottle of Atkinsons Lavender at arm's length, spritzed the air in front of my face, and walked through the fragrant mist. Ah, to smell like a woman again instead of a sweaty farm hand.

It was a rare fogless morning, and early enough that the early summer sun was still pleasant, so I decided to walk the mile to Raoul's. Excited to be back in the hubbub of the city, I enjoyed the bustle of women on their way to work. Before the war, the walkways would have been thick with the hard browns, grays, and whites of men's suits, but now they'd been replaced by the soft yellows, pinks, baby blues of tunics and skirts—and of course uniforms. It was easy to distinguish the shop girls from the munitions workers, and not just because of the yellow skin. The munitions workers wore overalls and boots. The shop girls donned aprons and Mary-Janes.

Since Raoul's wouldn't open for another twenty minutes, I decided I might as well continue on to the Italian Gardens, one of my favorite spots. Every Sunday before the war, Andrew and I would walk arm in arm through Hyde Park and stop in the Italian Gardens for tea. I hadn't visited the gardens since before the divorce. My life, it seems, had been divided into BD and AD, before-divorce and after-divorce.

Sadly, the fountains in the Italian Gardens were off, and the water lilies, flag iris, flowering rush, and purple loosestrife were dead—just like my life with Andrew. I plunked down on a bench and wondered what it would be like to have an everlasting love like Prince Albert and Queen Victoria. Albert made these gardens for her, his one-true love, as a token of his undying devotion. Look at them now. The war may have destroyed the earthly tokens of undying love, but I had faith it couldn't destroy what they represented. Even now, after everything, as hard as I tried, I couldn't squelch my love for Andrew.

With my spirits as brittle as the dried rush stalks, I headed back toward Raoul's.

The clerk seemed put out when she unlocked the door for me. Luckily, I didn't need her to direct me to the wigs. I knew the shop by heart since my mother was an avid wearer of wigs. I glanced around before taking off my hat. Anyone who saw my shorn head would think I suffered from some nasty tropical disease or contagious fungus. I selected a wig closest to my natural auburn hair color. It wasn't in the finger-curl style I preferred, but it would have to do. I tugged my felt bucket back over my brush of dyed hair, paid for the wig, and hurried to catch the train to Whitehall.

Parcel under my arm, I disembarked at Westminster Station. I'd have to run to make it to work on time.

Oh no, not him! The station was crowded, but I would recognize that gray fedora, long neck, and languid posture anywhere. Flustered, I faced the other direction so he wouldn't see me. What was Lieutenant Clifford Douglas doing getting off the train at my stop? And why was he heading up Whitehall Street? I ducked under the awning of the teashop next door to the Old Admiralty and watched him enter the building. Blimey! That's right. Mary had told me he was working here now. Hopefully, he's being recommissioned to the Front. Although I wouldn't wish the Front on my worst enemy, I would be pleased never to see the narky chap again.

I gave him a couple of minutes head start and then headed into the building myself. I arrived at Room 40 a good five minutes late thanks to blasted Lieutenant Douglas.

I hurried to my desk, which was exactly as I had left it, neat and tidy.

"Miss Figg." Mr. Grey greeted me with a big smile. "Or should I say Dr. Vogel?" He turned to the table where the rest of the team was working. "Look who's here!"

"The prodigal daughter returns." Mr. Montgomery waved me over. "Tell us all about your adventure at Ravenswick Abbey. Did you catch the little Frenchie in the act?"

I was so used to people confusing the Great South African Huntsman for a Frenchman I didn't bother correcting him.

"I'm afraid I wasn't much of a success," I said. "In fact, I think I rather messed it up."

"No." Mr. Knox held out his hand. "You could never do that, my dear."

When I didn't extend my hand in return, he grasped my bare arm. The cad. Some things never changed.

"Why don't you make us some tea and tell us all about it," Mr. Montgomery said.

Yes, some things never changed. I'd been commissioned by the War Office as a spy and was still expected to make the tea.

The fellows seemed so genuinely glad to see me, I was happy to make tea as long as I didn't have to do it wearing a beard. If only they could have seen me in my disguise. Amused by the thought of serving them tea in a beard, I turned the corner into the kitchenette.

"I say!" a familiar voice said. "You should be more careful."

I'd run smack into Lieutenant Clifford Douglas.

"Excuse me," I said, my face hot. I stared at the floor as I passed him.

"Have we met before?" he asked, following me to the sink.

"I'm sure we haven't." I averted my gaze.

"You look awfully familiar." He stared at me.

"I have one of those faces, I guess." I noticed the strap on my shoe needed mending.

"I'm sure I've seen you before. Didn't I meet you at a supper party…" He pulled a pipe from his breast pocket. "At Lord Gorman's house party, then?" He tilted his head. "Lady Hansberry's birthday do?" He lit the pipe.

I shook my head and busied myself with the kettle, but he wouldn't go away. He just stood there puffing on his pipe and watching me. I could feel his eyes on the back of my head. He had recognized me. I knew it. Now I was in the soup.

When I turned around, I caught him staring at my ankles. He certainly hadn't seen my ankles before!

"I say," he repeated. "Would you like to have lunch with me this afternoon? I know a nice tea shop next door."

"I'm afraid I'm busy during lunch." I rinsed out four cups, which of course were filthy. "Anyway, I don't know you." Given the state of the kitchenette, I should tell Mr. Montgomery to bomb the place and start over.

"Oh, so sorry." He tipped his hat. "Captain Douglas."

Captain! Had he been promoted or was he promoting himself?

"But why don't you call me Clifford?" He smiled. He had very good teeth, especially for a forty-something Englishman.

"Glad to meet you, Captain." I sat the four cups on a tray, poured the boiling water into the cleanest teapot I could find, and turned to go. "Excuse me, the men are waiting."

"But you haven't introduced yourself," Captain Douglas said in that whiny tone of his.

"Miss Figg." I gathered the sugar bowl and two teaspoons,

which were all I could find in the mess. "Now, I really must get the men their tea before it gets cold."

"Miss Figg," he repeated. "As in my favorite sweet fruit?"

"Figs are not actually fruit." I rolled my eyes. "But flowers pollinated by wasps that die in the process." I pushed past him with the tea tray, half tempted to dump it down his front.

CHAPTER 15

LUNCH WITH CAPTAIN DOUGLAS

Distracted by my encounter with the newly minted Captain Douglas, for the rest of the morning I found it difficult to concentrate on my report. With my luck, he'd been reassigned to the War Office permanently. The only way to find out was to accept his lunch invitation. As much as I despised the man, he could be helpful in getting more information on "his brilliant pal," Fredrick Fredricks. And I still had another six days before my report was due to Captain Hall. Instead of shunning him, I should try to befriend him. He was such a windbag he was bound to spill the beans if I let him rabbit on long enough. Yes, I would try my best to get along with Captain Douglas for the sake of my investigation.

Throughout the morning, I made several trips to the lavatory to check my appearance. I reapplied my lipstick, pinched my cheeks, and adjusted my hat so it covered my spiky black hair. As much as I relished reclaiming a dress, I felt quite vulnerable with so much of my body exposed. Between my self-consciousness about my hair and the men's boisterous discussion of the value of the Playfair cipher—a manual encryption technique—I couldn't concentrate on my report.

"It's absolute rubbish," Mr. Knox said. "Schoolboys could break it and—"

"Funny you should say that," Mr. Montgomery interrupted. "When the Foreign Office rejected it as too complicated, Wheatstone offered to demonstrate with a few schoolboys." He chuckled. "The Foreign Office responded, 'Schoolboys yes, but you could never teach it to attachés!'"

"You could never teach it to attachés," Mr. Grey repeated and burst out laughing.

It was good to hear the men laughing. Since the start of the war, there hadn't been much laughter in Room 40.

I glanced at my watch. Golly, it was almost noon. I slid the paper sack out from under my desk, tucked it under my arm, and headed for the lavatory. I'd intended to wait until tomorrow, when I'd have proper hair pins to attach my wig, but if I were going to lunch with Captain Douglas, I didn't want to wear this frumpy hat all afternoon.

The wig was styled in short loose curls and reminded me of Mary Pickford in Poor Little Peppina. I pulled it over my cropped mess and tugged it down onto my scalp. The transformation was startling. The color was a shade darker than my own, more auburn than flax, and the curls were unrulier than the ones I favored. But at least I didn't look like a freshly shorn sheep.

Unfortunately, I didn't look like Mary Pickford either. I touched up my make-up, re-tied the bow on my frock and secured my stockings. When I'd done all I could to improve my appearance, I returned to my desk, uncertain as to whether or not the captain would turn up.

At half past, I realized he wasn't coming, which, to my surprise, was a bit disappointing. I had been looking forward to pumping him for information about Fredricks. At one o'clock, I gave up on him completely and went into the kitchenette to fetch my ham and margarine sandwich from the icebox. I put on the kettle to make a cup of tea to wash it down. Waiting for the water to boil, I unwrapped the sandwich and took a bite. With stale bread and watery ham, it was hardly the best sandwich in London. I'd ordered it from Paul Rothe's sandwich shop to treat myself since I hadn't eaten a proper meal since yesterday's breakfast, which consisted of toast sans marmalade and tepid tea.

I devoured the sandwich standing at the counter, washing down the hard bread with sips of strong tea between each bite. I was just finishing up in the kitchenette, washing my cup and everyone else's, when Captain Douglas rounded the corner.

"I say, I've been looking for you," he said with a smile.

"You've found me."

"So I have. Lucky me."

The way he said it made me snort.

"Are we on for lunch then?" he asked.

I swallowed, blinked, and then looked at my watch. Technically, my lunch break was over. "Let me ask my boss," I said finally. "If you'll excuse me a moment, Captain Douglas." I restrained myself from giving him a lecture on punctuality.

"Clifford, please."

I left Clifford cooling his heels at a small table in the kitchenette and went to find Mr. Montgomery. I explained my plan—using Captain Clifford Douglas to find out more about the "Frenchie" before I turned in my report to the upper brass.

"Take as much time as you need." He nodded his approval and went back to his paperwork.

I returned to the kitchenette. "I'm free."

"So old Monty let you go, did he? Splendid." Captain Douglas grinned like an alley cat that had just spotted a tasty rodent. He took my elbow and led me into the hall, down the stairs, and out onto the street. If I hadn't been on a mission for information, I would have objected to such familiarity. I must say, I didn't appreciate the snide grin Mr. Knox gave me on the way out the door.

An easterly breeze mitigated the late-May warmth. As we walked up Whitehall Street, Captain Douglas pointed to an ornate building.

"Too bad I can't take you to the Constitution Club in the Old Metropole. Best lunch in London. But I'm afraid it's men only."

Too bad I'm not wearing trousers and a beard or I could sample the best lunch in London, and without an escort, if you please.

"And I'm not dressed for the Strand Palace," he said, glancing down at my attire. "Would you mind terribly taking lunch at Old Shades?" He waved in the direction of an amber stone building topped with a crown shaped like an ornate perfume bottle.

"It looks lovely," I said.

Old Shades turned out to be more public house than restaurant. Given I was on an assignment, I couldn't complain. With its dark mahogany paneling, beveled glass windows, and electric pendant lamps, it was most inviting. Between two large dining rooms sat a long wooden counter with sides in green, blue, and gold tiles, which gave it a festive feel. The floor was dotted with magnificent black-and-white mosaic tiles.

Captain Douglas took my elbow again and led me to a table in the snug, an area where women could eat and drink in private. The waiters greeted him by name. I supposed this was meant to impress me.

I looked around the place. So, this was a regular haunt of Clifford Douglas. I doubted his friend Fredricks would be caught dead in a place like this—too plebeian for his aristocratic tastes. But it suited me just fine.

"With the damned—sorry—Defense of the Realm," Captain Douglas said, "we have less than an hour before closing. It's my fault for being so late, I'm afraid. You see, I was just promoted to captain—which is jolly nice—but mostly means I have to sit through insufferably boring meetings."

"A quick lunch suits me fine, Captain Douglas," I said. "I need to be getting back to the office soon anyway."

"The mussels are quite good here," said Captain Douglas. "That's what I usually order. And do call me Clifford. Please."

"Alright, Clifford." I smiled. "Make it two orders of mussels." They couldn't be any worse than my stale sandwich.

"I say, you're a jolly good sport." Clifford grinned. The shape of his face, accentuated by a receding hairline, put me in mind of a horse, and his lips were a bit too thin. But at least he didn't have a blasted mustache like so many men nowadays. And with his pale-blue eyes and aquiline nose, he really wasn't a bad-looking sort. "Your hair is a lovely shade of auburn, if you don't mind me saying," he said, almost apologetically. "You look like an exotic film star."

I blushed. No one had ever said that before. Perhaps I should forget about growing my hair out and keep wearing the wig.

"How long have you been back from the Front?" I asked, changing the subject. I'd seen Clifford Douglas in action back at Ravenswick Abbey, flirting with Mary and Lillian Mandrake, oblivious to the fact Mary was married and Lillian was obviously smitten with Ian.

"Yes, I suppose every soldier you've met has been to the Front." He smiled wistfully and stared into space. "I was wounded in France six months ago. I was recuperating in a rather depressing convalescent home when I ran into my old friend Ernest Elliott." He glanced over at me as if he'd suddenly remembered he wasn't alone. "You've probably heard of the affair at Ravenswick? Poor Ernest. He's been wrongfully accused of murder, you see."

"I read about it in the newspaper. That poor man." As far as I knew, the poor man was guilty of cold-blooded murder.

"Yes, his poor wife, too." Clifford speared a mussel with his tiny fork.

"Must be dreadful for her." I thought of poor Mary, bearing up so well under pressure. If she'd had any designs on Dr. Vogel, they'd completely evaporated in the heat of defending her "dearest Ernest."

"I'm sure we'll be able to clear Ernest's good name. I'm helping investigate, along with my good friend the great newsman—" I could tell by the way his voice picked up steam that he was about to launch into one of his stories.

"You're a journalist too?" I asked with feigned excitement.

"Well, you know, I dabble a bit." He tilted his head in false modesty. "I've been known to help my friend from time to time."

"And who is this great reporter friend of yours?" Given I knew Clifford hadn't seen his good friend for years before their reunion at Ravenswick, I doubted they were the great pals he made them out to be.

"Oh, that is an interesting story. We met in South Africa before the war. I helped him solve the case of a big game poacher." He took a sip of his beer. "He was a suspect. Can you imagine?"

Yes, I could. I knew there was something sneaky about

the Great South African Huntsman. I wasn't surprised he was a poacher. I nodded encouragingly.

Captain Douglas waffled on nonstop throughout lunch and coffee afterward, clearly exaggerating his relationship with the "world famous hunter and great newsman."

"He taught me his method, you see," Clifford nattered on. "We don't go in for footprints and cigarette butts and all that rot. We use animal psychology to solve crime. All animals act according to their species. It's instinctual. And Fredricks is frightfully concerned with the order of the animal kingdom."

"Psychology, well that is interesting," I said. That would explain why Fredricks had those German psychology books. "You mean like that Austrian chap Sigmund Freud?" Since discovering The Interpretation of Dreams among Fredricks's possessions, I'd done some research and learned quite a bit about Mr. Freud and his outlandish theories.

"Well, yes." Captain Douglas seemed to warm to the idea. "I suppose so." He stirred sugar into his coffee.

"Do you think crime is related to sexual repression then?" I asked innocently over the rim of my cup.

"Good Lord! Sexual repression," he stammered. "Well, I never—" He dropped the teaspoon and it clattered onto the saucer.

I smiled sweetly at him from across the table. "You know, Mr. Freud attributes all neuroses, criminal and otherwise, to the Oedipal complex and one's repressed sexual feelings for one's parents." I took a sip. "He says humans are different from animals precisely because we suppress our incestuous instincts while other animals don't."

"I say!" He blushed. "What an idea." As if in protest, he loaded his coffee with another heaping spoonful of sugar.

"What do you know of Mr. Fredricks's parents? Perhaps his frightful concern with the order of things can be attributed to them?" I nonchalantly nibbled on a biscuit.

"I guess I've never asked about his family." Clifford drained his cup. "I suppose he must have had parents though."

"Unless he sprouted on a mushroom in the Australian outback or was found under a weeping wattle in South Africa." I took another bite.

"Yes, silly of me." Clifford shook his head. "Of course, he had parents. I assume they're dead. He's never mentioned them." He shrugged.

"Where is he from?"

Clifford looked confused. "Well, South Africa, of course. But he's traveled the world. He's a brilliant newsman and everyone in New York—"

"What about a wife and children?" I interrupted before he could work up a head of steam. "Does he have a family?" I drank my coffee as dispassionately as I could, given my sense of anticipation.

"Why now that you mention it, I'm not sure. I just assumed he was a bachelor." He waved his teaspoon. "Yes, he must be. The way he travels the world. He couldn't have a wife, you see." Clifford slid a biscuit off the plate. "Anyway, I can't see as any woman would put up with him always ordering everyone about and demanding things be put just so." He demonstrated by rearranging his cutlery.

"He sounds like what Mr. Freud would call an anal personality." I pressed my lips together awaiting his response.

"Good Lord!" His face turned beet red, and I thought he might choke on his biscuit.

I stifled a giggle. I was rather enjoying shocking the prudish Captain Douglas.

When he'd regained his composure, he said, "I've never met a woman quite like you, Miss Figg." He shook his head. "You're full of surprises."

Why Clifford, you don't know by halves.

After lunch, Clifford walked me back to Room 40, where we awkwardly said goodbye. I was just turning the doorknob to go inside when he asked, "Would you like to have lunch again tomorrow?" He had an apologetic look on his face, like he was sorry to impose by asking me to join him for lunch. "You do have to eat, you know," he added before I had time to accept.

"I'd be delighted." Provided you tip the wink on your great friend Fredrick Fredricks.

CHAPTER 16

MORE BRILLIANT THAN THE SUN

On the way home from the War Office, I stopped by Charing Cross Hospital to confer with Daisy Nelson about the contents of the cordial bottles. Could Daisy confirm Dr. Anderson's finding of arsenic? And was there poison in both bottles, or only one? And how much arsenic? Even a large dose of arsenic wouldn't have killed Lady Edith instantly. I still wouldn't rule out the possibility that the earl had poisoned his wife from beyond the grave using a dose of his quicksilver.

I halfway hoped the bottles contained nothing more than a delightful sloe-berry liquor, coincidentally enjoyed by the countess a few minutes before her death. For, if I discovered it contained the fatal poison, how could I ever present the evidence, and to whom? To do so would be to reveal my true identity and ruin my investigation of Fredrick Fredricks. Moreover, Captain Hall had made it painfully clear I was not to meddle in domestic criminal matters, especially those involving Scotland Yard.

When I reached the dispensary, I was met by Daisy Nelson's scrawny backside as she bent over a microscope, completely absorbed by the infinitesimal world it revealed. I hoped it was the secret world of my mysterious J's sloe-berry liquor.

My heels tapped on the hardwood floor as I approached, and Daisy spun around, her hand on her chest and her mouth agape. Her nest of mousy hair was piled atop her head with a tiny white cap perched in the middle.

"Gor! Don't sneak up on me like that." She gasped, and then her face relaxed into a smile. "Blimey, Fiona. I haven't seen you for yonks. Did the countryside calm your nerves?"

The cover story for my absence at the hospital was a nervous condition that required a restful stay in the country. "Yes, very calming," I fibbed. Wearing a disguise, spying on a deuced clever and unnecessarily handsome big game hunter, flirting with a married woman, and becoming involved in a murder trial were far from calming. Indeed, my nerves had never been so stimulated in my life.

"Did you receive the parcel I sent?" I gestured toward the microscope. "May I?"

"Tickety-boo." She moved aside. "I hope you sent Oenothera biennis. My rheumatism's been acting up something terrible."

"No, sorry, not evening primrose." I peered at the squiggly threads swimming through an obstacle course of blistering blobs. "Actually, I sent you the remnants of a homemade liquor in the hopes you could test it for plant poison."

"Stone the crows! Heracleum Mantegazzianum or Digitalis purpurea?" Daisy rubbed her calloused hands together. "Atropa Belladonna, perhaps?"

"I doubt it contains hogweed or foxglove. I'm thinking

more along the lines of Gyromitra esculenta or Amanita phalloides." I gave up trying to discern what I was looking at in the microscope and leaned against the counter.

"Poisonous mushrooms!" Daisy's gaunt face lit up.

"Exactly." The earthy smell had made me suspicious. And Dr. Elizabeth Anderson seemed to confirm the compound was organic, if not harmless. "But could be atropine and scopolamine, the toxins found in belladonna." If the countess had consumed the first bottle right before I arrived that would explain why she was feeling unwell. And then in her grief over her husband, if she drank the entirety of the second, that would have been a fatal dose.

"I never got it." Daisy shrugged. "The post is rubbish."

I thought a minute. Living at Ravenswick, I'd lost track of time. "I sent it the day of the inquest," I said more to myself than to Daisy. "That was last Friday."

"Sorry, sweetie." When she shook her head, her tiny white cap wagged at me. "So, what's this about poison?"

"Just a hunch." I paced the room surveying the various bottles and potions she had going. "I met a lady doctor, Elizabeth Anderson. She thinks it is entirely organic—"

"You met Doctor Anderson?" Her face lit up. "She's my hero—heroine. I wish I could be a doctor."

"Why can't you?"

"Cor. Go on." She blushed. "No one would believe me. But…" She lowered her voice. "As a wise woman, I might be able to conjure the poisoner without it." Her eyes sparkled.

I narrowed my brows. "What do you mean?"

"Bring me something belonging to the dodgy rascal." She pulled at her blouse and then her hair. "And I'll tell you if he —or she—used the poison."

"You want a lock of his hair?" I must have looked as confused as I felt.

Daisy scoffed. "You think it's a bunch of hocus-pocus, but

it ain't." She went back to her microscope. "If you want my help, you know where to find me."

"Alright. Thanks." I picked up a tiny green bottle and sniffed. The acrid scent sent me reeling. "So, you'll test the bottles in the parcel when it arrives?"

"Of course." She took the bottle from my hands and replaced it on the counter. "Don't touch," she said and then went back to her microscope.

"Thanks, Daisy." I started for the door.

"Toodle pip," she said without looking up.

I stopped at the threshold and turned back. "Can we keep this our little secret?"

"My lips are sealed," she said into her equipment.

"Brilliant. Thanks, Daisy." If Dr. Elizabeth Anderson was at one of the spectra of wise women, Daisy was at the other. The best of scientific medicine and the best of home-grown alchemy.

As I walked home, I cursed the British postal service. I shouldn't have let the bottles out of my sight. They could be vital evidence. At least I had the presence of mind to keep that sample, the one I gave to Elizabeth Anderson to test.

The next morning, my mind was abuzz as I went about my ablutions and prepared my toilette. I sat at my dressing table, mindlessly rearranging my boar's bristle brushes, pin trays, talcum bottles, handkerchief box, and cuticle scissors. When I got to my swans-down powder puff, I picked it up and gently stroked my cheek.

Only five days left until my report was due. I really must get something useful out of Clifford Douglas. I must say, I was doing better as Miss Figg than I had as Dr. Vogel. I still didn't understand why Captain—then Lieutenant—Douglas took such a dislike to me as Dr. Vogel, unless he truly believed I killed the countess... silly man.

So far, I'd learned Fredricks was a bit of a fashion plate—in an outdoor magazine sort of way, and a ladies' man, which was obvious to anyone who'd met him—at least to any lady who'd met him. He was Catholic, and had a wife, a daughter, and twin boys he kept hidden somewhere. I had to find out more about them. Why did he keep them secret? Even Clifford didn't seem to know about them.

Then there were his books. I suppose the German books on psychology and philosophy might be explained by his interest in the human mind. While revolutionary thinkers, Freud and Husserl were hardly the stuff of politics, let alone espionage. Perhaps I'd missed something and the books contained coded messages. Teresa of Avila claimed to have received coded messages from God, but that's another story —perhaps one worth investigating. Mr. Fredricks's Catholicism just didn't jibe with all that nonsense about lizard brains, animal instincts, and his love of killing large beasts in cold blood. Then again, the history of Catholicism wasn't exactly a cakewalk. For all of Clifford's talk of clues as rubbish and the importance of human instinct, from what I'd seen, Mr. Fredricks was as interested in old-fashioned pawprints as the next investigator-cum -hunter.

And what about the Field Guide to Poisonous Plants? Was that for his investigation, or was he planning to poison someone? Wild toadstools, anyone? Perhaps the strangest clue I'd found was the false mustache. Why would Fredricks have a false mustache? His clothes certainly looked like a costume, but not one designed to be inconspicuous. Jodhpurs? Starched white shirts. That oversized slouch hat and showy swagger stick. Come on, men only dressed like that in American films. I had to find a way to ask Clifford about that mustache.

If I were to get more information out of Clifford, I needed to look my best. I went to my wardrobe and examined my choice of dresses. Although not as beastly as last few weeks—when I was wearing trousers—it was still warm, so I concentrated on my summer wardrobe. I flipped through my dresses, but nothing seemed right. They were either too proper or not suitable for work. I settled on a pretty, plum two-piece frock with three-quarter length sleeves. The skirt fell just below my knees. The sheath was low-waisted and the outer layer had a delightful lavender border.

I'd been a man for so long, I was still struggling with the blasted corset. I wished I could just burn the damnable thing and be done with it. There was so little of me to push up or squeeze in, I didn't see the point. But who was I to buck convention? I'd seen others do it at their own peril. After lacing my corset, I slipped into the silky sheath and then sat at my dressing table and carefully rolled on my stockings. I applied a bit of face paint and stared at my reflection in my hand mirror. With my spiky black hair and deep-red rouge, I looked like one of Drury Lane's pantomime dames.

On my dressing table, the wig was draped across a hair receiver like the pelt of some animal. Too bad I couldn't pull a rat out of my hair receiver and attach it to my bristled head. Oh well, I never was a fan of pulling hair from my brushes, collecting it in my receivers, and then stuffing it into nets to use as coiffure fillers. I twirled a hatpin in its holder. I'd missed my rose china dresser set with its matching jewelry boxes, hatpin holder, and hair receivers.

I tugged the wig onto my head and maneuvered it into place. I wondered if I could give my furry friend a finger wave. I needed to do something to tame the beast. One of my turban hats would be perfect, except those were strictly for evening wear. But a pretty felt bowler might do nicely for the office. I knew just the one, my purple felt hat with the lovely lavender bow and just a touch of lace. I grabbed it off the top shelf, returned to my dressing table, held the hat in one hand and the mirror in the other, and with much effort, pinned the hat into my wig. Yes, that would do.

I pulled on matching gloves and selected an appropriate handbag, transferred my necessaries into it, and off I went. It felt so good to wear colors again. Men's clothes were more comfortable to be sure but deadly boring.

My commute to the office went like clockwork, and I arrived before the team, which gave me time to tidy the kitchenette and the men's desks and the large working table. I didn't dare move any papers though, since they each had their own system, or in the case of Mr. Dilly Knox, a royal mess. Working around the important documents, I removed old coffee cups and sandwich wrappers and straightened as best I could.

A newspaper clipping with a photograph of three shepherd children was lying among the muddle on Mr. Knox's desk. Two girls wearing heavy headscarves and thick skirts stared out at me with haunting seriousness. In between them stood a boy who wore something like a loose dark turban and held a walking stick. The smallest girl's scowl was accompanied by a defiant hand on her hip. No wonder! Poor things. They'd just been released from jail.

I removed an abandoned necktie from Mr. Knox's chair and sat down to continue reading the article. For the last year, nine-year-old Lúcia dos Santos and her two cousins had repeatedly seen apparitions of the Angel of Peace and the Virgin Mary. The Virgin appeared "more brilliant than the sun," and told them to pray using their rosaries daily to bring peace and end the war. Good Heavens! She also told them that on 13 October she would reveal her identity and perform a miracle, ending the Great War "so that all may believe." It would be a miracle if the war ended by October. If only I could have the faith of these children.

I sat back in the chair, marveling at the devotion of those so young, and wondering if this article was of interest to the War Office or if Dilly Knox was just passing the time. The article did say the children were arrested because "these events were politically disruptive." Perhaps Catholicism was more revolutionary than I had realized. I thought of Fredricks and his rosary. What was the origin of his devotion? Was he as serious and devoted as these children when he was a boy? Had he heard the voice of the Virgin?

Apparently, my focus on the photograph had tuned out the rest of the world, because I was startled when Mr. Knox's booming baritone interrupted my meditations.

"Moving in, are we?" he asked with a chuckle.

Flustered, I dropped the clipping back on his desk and popped up out of his chair. "Sorry, Mr. Knox. I didn't mean—"

"No worries, Fiona," he said with a wink. "What's mine is yours." His use of my Christian name and his impertinent wink sent me skittering off to my own desk behind the partition a few feet away. I suppose I was lucky the mischief-loving Dilly Knox had found me and not the somber Mr. Grey, or worse, the boss, Mr. Montgomery.

As the morning went on, I found myself checking my watch every half hour to see if it was lunchtime yet. I was eager to get on with my investigation. I'd typed up my notes from Ravenswick Abbey, peppering them with the tidbits I'd learned from Clifford over lunch. Still, it wasn't much. If I didn't come up with more in the next five days, I'd surely be taken off the case. I had the Great South African Huntsman in my sights now and I wasn't about to let him slip away.

I looked at my watch again. It was half past eleven, my usual lunchtime. I liked an early luncheon so I wouldn't be too full to enjoy my afternoon tea, but if yesterday was any indication, Clifford preferred a late lunch. Having had breakfast this morning, I wasn't going to eat two lunches again today. My stomach growled as I went on typing.

I continued typing and checking my watch for another hour before Captain Douglas finally poked his head around the partition.

"Are you ready for lunch?" He held up two umbrellas. "It's pouring buckets outside."

"Why don't we just go down to the canteen then?"

"Jolly good idea, if you don't mind." He leaned the brollies against the partition. "Is it alright to leave these here?"

I nodded.

The canteen was a vast room with marble pillars and wooden beams crisscrossing the high ceiling. Groups of military men, file clerks, office girls, and codebreakers sat at rows of long rectangular tables dressed with white tablecloths. Since the officers had their own dining hall next door, Clifford was the only officer of the lot.

We stood in line to get our lunch, which consisted of fish and potato pie and baked raisin pudding.

"Save the wheat, defend the fleet," I said, wishing our motto were "defend the fleet and still eat meat."

"Damn sight better than what we ate in the trenches." Clifford led me to the end of the closest table. "It was almost worth getting shot to get away from bully beef and biscuits. Dreadful stuff."

Of course, the boys in the trenches got so little to eat. I felt wretched for complaining.

"When your wound is fully healed, will you be going back?"

"To the Front? I hope the damned war is over by then." Clifford had that faraway look he got whenever we talked about the war.

I suspected in his own genteel way, he, too, suffered from shell shock.

I thought of Andrew, wounded and home six months, only to leave me for his secretary. Now, like so many women, she was alone with their baby. Not that I felt sorry for her after what she did to me. And what about what Andrew did to me? I'd taken three weeks off work to nurse him back to health after the training accident. Amazing that after the plane crash, he'd only had a broken hand. But it's deuced difficult to do anything with just one hand, especially if it was shaking constantly in terror. I thought of his beautiful hands and wanted to weep.

"Although, I must say." Clifford's voice brought me back. "I don't fancy pushing papers at a desk all day." He tucked into his lunch. "Decent fish pie."

It tasted like seaweed mixed with dirt. I swallowed the bite in my mouth and nodded politely.

"Will you continue to work with Mr. Fredricks after the war?" I asked, hoping to steer the conversation toward my prey.

"We do make a jolly good team."

"He's the brains and you're the brawn?" I raised one eyebrow. Of course I was joking. Whatever his intellect, there was no denying "Apollo" Fredricks had a physique to rival some of those I'd seen in Eugen Sandow's bodybuilding book.

"Well, I'd like to think I have some smarts of my own." He pointed his fork at his plate. "Fredricks says fish is good for the brain."

"Didn't you tell me Fredricks uses only his instincts and doesn't collect evidence or examine clues?" Of course, I'd already heard everything from Mary, but I hoped Clifford might be able to add some important details that might give me a clue as to the reporter's modus operandi.

"Well, yes. Yes, he did. I was with him of course, helping search and collect clues."

"Of course," I said with a knowing smile. "And what did you find, if you don't mind me asking?"

"Oh no, I don't mind. I rather enjoy talking about our work." He laid his fork on the table and then wiped his mouth with his napkin. "Let's see. We found the corner of a will in the fireplace grate. That was an important piece of evidence, indeed. Fredricks made a fuss over some candle grease on the floor next to a tea stain, but I don't really see the importance of those. Then there was the warm milk. Fredricks insisted on sending it out for testing even though Dr. Vogel had already had the authorities test it—"

"Dr. Vogel. I've heard of him. He's that recently arrested German spy." Who, in reality, is a very clever spy for the War Office, on a mission to trap a suspicious Boer infiltrator.

"Yes, that's right. I knew he was sinister from the moment I met him." Clifford scowled. "I never did like him. Some say I'm an excellent judge of character."

"I'm sure you are, Clifford." I repressed a giggle.

"I'm still half-convinced it was that evil man who killed the countess."

"Why would a German spy kill the countess?" Yes, indeed. Why would a spy for the Germans kill the countess? Fredricks was studying poisonous plants. Now it seemed Edith Elliott may have been poisoned with mushrooms. Perhaps the wronged lover was not to blame after all. But if the Great South African Huntsman was a German spy and did away with the countess, what in the world could be his motive? Was Edith Elliott important to the war effort? Were her good works and support for orphans and the wounded somehow more than they seemed? Were they a cover for part of the war effort? Or perhaps they were a cover for something else, something so dreadful I didn't even want to consider the possibility. Maybe that's why the War Office had been so keen to send me to Ravenswick Abbey.

Clifford thought for a moment. "You've got me there, but I knew that Vogel chap was trouble."

Ah, good captain, if you only knew. "You're so astute. I'm impressed with the evidence you found. Most people wouldn't have noticed such things as candle grease and fire-place grates."

"Oh, that's not all. I'm the one who noticed the powder on the serving tray."

"Powder?"

"Someone drugged the tea. The evidence was there on the tea tray."

HAD the pesky reporter somehow discovered Mary had put sleeping powders in the countess's tea and then snuck into the earl's bedroom as part of her plan to steal the letter from Edith's briefcase? "Who do you suspect?" I asked innocently.

"I'm not sure. Fredricks has his hypotheses, but he's not sharing them with me. It's rather frustrating. How can I help him if he doesn't confide in me?"

"Perhaps you should tell him how frustrating it is for you. If he knew how you felt, maybe he'd take you into his confidence." From what I'd seen at Ravenswick Abbey, the "famous newsman" used Clifford Douglas something terrible. In fact, Fredricks treated Clifford more like a nagging wife than a sleuthing partner. Or was Fredricks the nagging wife, and Clifford Douglas the put-upon husband? In any case, they made an odd couple indeed.

"I'm afraid he thinks I talk too much." Clifford took a sip of coffee.

I'm counting on it! "I find it all fascinating, Clifford." I smiled in as coy a fashion as I was able given my allergy to flirting.

"Do you?" He looked pleased.

"Tell me, Captain, is Mr. Fredricks a religious man?"

"Religious? Not really." He stared down at his raisin pudding. "Well, now that you mention it, he does go to church from time to time." He glanced up at me from across the table. "He was raised Catholic, you see. But I'd say he's what you'd call a lapsed Catholic."

"So his parents were Catholic?"

"Come to think of it, I remember now, he once mentioned his mother was devout. He rarely talks of her, but when he does, you'd think she was a saint."

His mother is a saint. And is her son also a saint? Or is he hiding an evil secret?

"Does Mr. Fredricks have siblings?"

"You know, I've never asked him. He might have mentioned a sister or brother, but I can't recall. You certainly are fascinated by my friend."

"He sounds like a very mysterious fellow."

"I say, would you like to meet him?" A broad smile lit up his face. "Fredricks loves attention. He's not what you'd call modest. I'm sure he'd be very pleased to meet you. We could all go out for supper. Or better yet, you could come to Paddington. We are all staying there with Mary until after Ernest's trial."

"That's very kind of you, but I couldn't impose—"

"Nonsense! You'd like Mary. She's a lovely woman. And she would absolutely adore you."

I wondered if Mary would adore me as much as she had Dr. Vogel. In any case, I didn't dare find out. If anyone would recognize me—with or without a beard—it would be Mary.

CHAPTER 17

THE BLOODBATH

*T*oday was toad-in-the hole and suet pudding, which at least meant a bit of sausage in the thick gluey pastry, and some mutton fat in the pudding. For the last two weeks, Clifford and I had lunched together, taking whatever the canteen had on offer: Each day alternated between bean soup and treacle pudding; toad-in-the-hole and suet pudding, and fish and potato pie and baked raisin pudding. The food was warm if not particularly appetizing.

Clifford didn't seem to mind. He'd happily eat just about anything. In fact, he grumbled more about Saturday night meals in Paddington when Fredricks insisted on cooking fancy French food, which didn't sit well with the captain. The way Clifford complained about Fredricks once again reminded me of an old married man complaining about his nagging wife.

I didn't learn much more about Fredricks or the murder of the countess, but it was nice to have someone to talk with, even if Clifford did most of the talking. And so far, I'd managed to put off the question of my going to supper at the Elliott house in Paddington. Furthermore, we'd compromised on the time of lunch, and I'd trained Clifford to fetch me at noon on the dot... or thereabouts.

This afternoon, instead of poking his head around the partition and asking, "Are you ready for lunch?" he stomped right up to my desk and dropped a white feather on top of my typewriter.

"The nerve," he said. "I'm going to start wearing my uniform again." He narrowed his eyes. "Horrible woman."

"I hope you don't mean me, Clifford," I said playfully as I stood up from my desk.

"Good heavens, no." He was positively fuming. "There's a band of those horrible suffragettes on Whitehall handing out white feathers. I may have been injured, but I'm no coward."

"I know," I said, patting his hand. "You have the courage of a lion." I thought of Millicent Fawcett and her conviction that women could fight along with men—from greater distance, of course.

Clifford got the strangest look on his face, like a little boy who'd just been given a sweetie. I withdrew my hand before he got any improper ideas about our relationship. My report was already finished and had been sent up to Blinker Hall, but my investigation of the Great South African Huntsman was far from over. And Clifford Douglas was my best informant. I needed to keep him close, but not too close.

Clifford and I sat at our usual table in the canteen and dutifully ate our meager lunch. Searching for the bits of sausage in my Yorkshire pudding, I asked, "Do you disapprove of the suffragettes generally or only their misplaced white feathers?"

"Why do women want to be bothered with votes and

politics and war and all that rot?" he asked, already finished with half of his toad-in-the-hole.

"Because all that rot affects their lives as much as it does a man's." I washed down the gluey pudding with my lukewarm tea. If it wasn't raining the day after tomorrow, I'd suggest we lunch at Old Shades. Tomorrow was my day off and I'd be taking lunch alone at the hospital.

"I suppose you're right," he conceded. "But women are too sensitive and fragile—"

"I don't think you'll make a good reporter thinking like that." I stopped him before he could go on with such drivel.

"Why ever not?" He looked hurt.

"You're underestimating half the population."

"Underestimating!" His lips tightened. "No, I think women are too good for all that rot. They're the fair sex—"

"Keep wearing those rose-colored glasses, and on your watch, women will get away with murder."

"What do you mean?"

"Don't you think women are just as capable of lying and cheating and stealing as men?"

"I don't know."

"They're just as capable, Clifford. They're just not as foolish."

"You think men are foolish?"

"Men started this war and all wars. If women were in charge, war wouldn't exist, and the world would be orderly and tidy." Certainly, suffragettes can also be pacifists.

"You mean if you were in charge." Clifford laughed. "I rather like the chaos of life. You never know what's going to happen."

"Give me a good filing system over the chaos of life any day."

"I really should introduce you to Fredricks. You two are birds of a feather."

"From his photograph, I'd say he's more of a peacock, and I'm just a common sparrow."

"You're far from common, Miss Figg." Clifford gazed at me from across the plank table. "I think you're a smashing girl."

I suddenly felt warm and took a drink of water. Maybe Clifford Douglas wasn't such a bad sort after all.

THE NEXT MORNING on the way to the railway station, I bought a newspaper to catch up on news of the war. We'd been at it for three years, but it seemed a lifetime.

The train was packed with women on their way to work in factories and offices, women who'd taken over men's jobs while they were away fighting. It was as if most of the young men had just disappeared one day and we were now a society of girls, women, old men and little boys. When an oversized middle-aged woman got up to get off, I took her seat. I settled in and opened my newspaper and read the front page.

Yet another peace proposal had come from the Vatican. Pope Benedict had called the Great War the "suicide of Europe," but Germany wasn't convinced the Pope was neutral, especially after he'd publicly said he wished he'd been born a Frenchman. I wondered what Mr. Fredricks would make of his Holy Father calling the war a "useless massacre."

Volunteering at the hospital, seeing so many young men's lives cut short so brutally, and witnessing the fractured lives of those who survived, made me inclined to agree with Pope Benedict. How much longer could it go on? How many more boys would be lost?

I was starting to think like a pacifist. I heard suffragist Millicent Fawcett's calm but chastising voice in my head. "It's akin to treason to talk of peace." Although I was as patriotic as the next woman, after the misery I'd seen at the hospital, I was in favor of peace, whatever it took—short of surrender, of course. The only thing worse than a steady diet of fish pie and suet pudding would be a steady diet of blutwurst and gingerbread.

I exited Charing Cross Station with a sense of foreboding. As if in response, the sky opened and rain poured down on me. Of course, I'd forgotten my brolly, so I took off running toward the hospital. Outside the entrance was a caravan of covered lorries, no doubt loaded with wounded soldiers. I dashed inside, brushing off my wet trench coat as I went. At least I'd worn a sturdy hat and lace-up leather boots.

There was a great commotion in the hall as the wounded were brought in on stretchers. I didn't need to read the newspaper to know this wasn't a good sign. Whenever we'd lost a battle, bleeding and broken soldiers poured into the hospital.

I rushed into the staff room, removed my coat and hat, replaced them with my nurse's apron and cap, washed my hands, and went to the hallway to help with the triage. A shock of sandy hair and full lips seeming to mouth my name made my pulse quicken. I ran to the soldier's side, afraid to look at his distorted countenance.

"Andrew?" I muttered, saying a silent prayer. Please God, no, not Andrew.

I inhaled sharply and looked into his face. To my relief, it wasn't Andrew. Hands trembling, I prepared to irrigate the long, deep inflamed gash that threatened to take his leg. I prepared a weak solution of sodium hypochlorite, fixed a glass container to the head of the stretcher, and proceeded with the ghastly business of packing a small rubber hose into the wound. The man cried out each time I touched the wound, but this was the only chance he had to keep his leg.

Amid the pandemonium of screaming and groaning,

wounded men called out for "mummy," doctors barked orders, and nurses darted back and forth consoling the men and assisting the doctors. There weren't enough operating rooms, so men lay on stretchers in the hallway. Some were unconscious and others writhed in agony.

It was my business to sort out the wounded as they were brought in from the ambulances and to keep them from dying before they got to the operating rooms. I had to distinguish the nearly dying from the dying. Life was leaking away, but with some it would take hours or days and with others it would be only a matter of minutes. My hands could tell all on their own one kind of cold from another. All the wounded were cold, but the chill of icy flesh was not the same as the cold that gripped their insides when life was almost extinguished. My hands could tell the difference between the natural cold of night and the stealthy cold of death. I didn't think about it, my fingers simply felt it. As if in a dream, my hands did things and knew things I didn't have time to think about.

I administered morphia to the hopeless cases and left them there to die with the names of sweethearts on their lips. Others got morphia to get them through the painful hours until their injuries could be treated. Breathless, I dashed about, cleaning wounds, applying dressings, twisting tourniquets, administering morphia, and rigging up Thomas splints, while the strongest nurses transported the soldiers hemorrhaging life from the emergency ward to the hallway outside the operating rooms. Every minute counted. Skill and reaction time determined whether a soldier would make it to the surgeons alive.

Everything happened quickly and yet as if in slow motion. As I focused on saving bits from the wreckage, the whole world disappeared. I saw only fragments of men— legs, arms, heads, a cheek, an eye, a finger. I heard only sounds, some of them phrases that sent me into action, while others sent me into a panic. The pungent smells of unwashed bodies, blood, iodine, and carbolic acid mixed with adrenaline and fear. This overload of brute sensation kept the unutterable anguish from completely destroying my spirit. It was as if time stood still and I lived an eternity in those hours of single-minded focus on saving as many men as I could.

I glanced at my watch. It was past midnight. We'd been working in the dark with only meager candlelight for hours. My eyes hurt and my hands were trembling.

When we'd done our best for the wounded and prayed for the dead, we were faced with the gruesome task of cleaning the operating theater. Along with an orderly, I began washing sheets and bedding in a big bathtub. Soon I was swimming in a sea of blood. When the lights were allowed on, we stared at one another, drenched in blood as if we'd come from a slaughterhouse. In a sense, we had.

I washed myself off as best I could and took a break for a cup of tea. As I sat in the staff room, I stared into the void, an empty shell. The warm cup and hot liquid couldn't penetrate the depths of my icy soul. What I'd seen here tonight had become so quotidian as to be a cliché, and yet it would haunt me for the rest of my life.

Still running on adrenaline, I decided to stay the night at the hospital and help out. Many poor souls were still fighting for their very lives. What were a few hours of lost sleep to me, when these men had given so much?

After another hour of attending to agony, my spirits needed lifting, so I visited the convalescent wing of the hospital where, after having been put back together again, the men were on their way to discharge. The corridor was dimly lit, and only the sound of coughing or snoring broke the silence of the night. I walked softly to keep the heels of my boots from clicking on the tile floor. The peace of knowing men were sleeping and healing and on their way home was a palliative balm on my frayed nerves.

I stopped at an open door where a light shone from the bedside table of one of the men. The room held six cots, but his was the only one occupied. How we could have used those cots in the emergency wing. I'd have to suggest moving them.

I peeked in to see if he needed anything, a cup of tea or a snack perhaps—something simple, the basic needs or the pleasures of everyday life when it wasn't thrown into the teeth of war. He beckoned me to his bedside.

When I stepped inside the room, I had the strangest sensation of déjà vu. I didn't know you were going to be here. What an odd thought to pass through my mind. I'd never met this man before in my life. I tiptoed to his bedside and introduced myself.

"I'm Miss Figg, one of the volunteer nurses."

A lock of wavy chestnut hair falling across his forehead practically dared me to reach out and sweep it out of his face. I held my hands behind my back to restrain myself.

"You're a sight for sore eyes," he said with a playful grin.

"Can I bring you something?" I asked. "Some biscuits and tea?"

He held up his bandaged right hand. "I've been trying to write a letter to my mum, but it's deuced difficult with my left hand. I wonder if you might help me write to her? She's probably worried because she hasn't heard from me."

"I'd be delighted." Finally, a task I could do with confidence and calm. I took up a blank piece of paper and pencil from the nightstand. "What should I write?"

He stared at me for a few seconds, and then asked, "What would you write to your mother?"

"My mother is dead," I said, and then regretted my abruptness.

"Oh, I am sorry." He adjusted the sheet draped over his torso, which I couldn't help but notice was lean and fit. "Do you happen to have a cigarette?"

"I'm afraid I don't smoke. Shall I try to find you one?" I set the paper and pencil back on the nightstand and made to stand up.

"No, don't leave. Just sit with me for a while." He leaned back into his pillow. "Now that I'm on the mend, it's deuced boring waiting to get out of this lockup."

I was struck by the elegance of his posture. In the light from the oil lamp on the nightstand, he looked like a nineteenth-century portrait. His soft features made me want to reach out and caress his cheek.

"Let's write to your mother, shall we?" I picked up the paper and pencil again. "Dear Mum, to start, right?"

He nodded and then brushed the provocative curl away from his face.

Together we composed a fine letter reassuring his mother he had been wounded but was safe… for now.

"I want to post this letter before I go back to South Africa," he said proudly.

"South Africa?"

"I'm working for British Intelligence. We're trying to stop another Boer uprising."

"You're a spy!"

"If I tell you, I'm afraid I'll have to kill you." When he laughed, his angelic cheeks took on devilishly handsome dimples. "I have many secrets, Miss Figg. If I divulge all of them now, what mystery will bring you back to see me tomorrow?"

"I would come back even if you were as dull as ditch water."

His smile alone was enough to inspire another trip across the hospital. And those sea-green eyes framed by dark lashes definitely warranted another look during daylight.

"Are you well acquainted with much ditch water, then?" His eyes danced mischievously, and his laughter was contagious.

I straightened my skirt and patted my wig. It wouldn't do to be giggling like a schoolgirl with a soldier I'd just met.

"Since you've been working in South Africa, have you by any chance heard of a famous big game hunter named Fredrick Fredricks? I met him recently." I shouldn't have said I'd met him since it was only Dr. Vogel who had met the Great South African Huntsman. Of course, the chance of this soldier finding out about my alter ego was slim, even if he was a spy.

"Apollo Fredricks?" he asked and narrowed his perfectly symmetrical brows. "You've met him?"

Blast it all! Why did I say I'd met him? "Well, I haven't actually met him. I've seen him. He's in town investigating a murder case. Some country gentleman who supposedly poisoned his parents."

"Blimey! Parricide among the aristocracy." He sat up in bed and ran his fingers through his thick hair.

"Yes, indeed," I said. "I understand Mr. Fredricks doesn't think this gentleman committed the crime."

"If his reputation is anything to go on, he'll find out who did."

"So you've heard of him?"

"He's a person of interest."

"What do you mean?"

"Let's just say both his hunting methods and journalistic techniques are bizarre, and he is as arrogant and commanding as Napoleon." With his good hand, he reached for a glass of water on the side table. "What's your interest in Fredricks, if you don't mind me asking?"

"If I tell you, I'm afraid I'll have to kill you," I said with a wink.

"If the bloody Germans don't do it first." He replaced the glass on the table and then held out his left hand. "I'm Archie, by the way. Archie Somersby."

When I took his hand, I felt a warm current pass between us. Perhaps it was just the contrast with the icy flesh in the emergency wing. Still, I could swear there was an electric connection. A spark of delight ignited in my chest. Suddenly, I wanted to impress this mysterious soldier.

"We have something in common," I said.

"Something besides wishing we were out of this bloody hospital?"

"That, and I work for British Intelligence, too. Room 40."

"Room 40. Impressive. Are you a codebreaker?"

"You know I can't tell you."

"Good girl. I was just testing you."

"Figures British Intelligence is interested in Fredricks." He raised his eyebrows. "Of course, all those bloody journalists are suspect. Anyone of them could be a spy." When he crossed his bare arms over his chest, the sheet slipped and I had to avert my eyes… well, I tried not to look but couldn't help myself.

His arms were smooth and tanned. I wished Archie Somersby would put on his shirt. Flustered, I said, "I'd better be getting back. There was a frightful onslaught of casualties earlier, and I'll be needed back in emergency."

"I'm being discharged the day after tomorrow. If you promise to come back before then, I promise to find out what I can about Fredricks."

He held out his hand. As I put my hand in his, I admired his long, straight fingers. We shook on it, and again I felt a warm pulse of energy that cheered me up considerably.

"Pleasure to meet you, Archie Somersby."

"The pleasure is all mine, Miss Figg."

I fairly skipped back to the triage unit.

My joy was short-lived. Another caravan of injured had arrived, even worse than the first. They'd been the targets of a new hell invented by the Germans called mustard gas.

I remembered a line from a gruesome poem about the horrors of gas: "You would not tell with such high zest, to children ardent for some desperate glory, the old Lie: Dulce et decorum est Pro patria mori," how sweet and proper it is to die for your country.

CHAPTER 18

MY WORST NIGHTMARE

I was accustomed to soldiers dying, but not to being impotent to ease their agony before they died. Even morphia was no match for the excruciating pain of skin, lungs, and eyes burned by mustard gas. The men being carried into the hospital were delirious with pain, not from gaping wounds or shrapnel, but from raw exposed nerves. Dozens of men lay on cots in the hallway, gasping for breath. Even I had to look away when a patient whose body was covered with third-degree burns also had his eyes and face marred beyond recognition. Many were so badly burned we couldn't touch them. There was nothing we could do for them but pray.

The smell of gas emanated from the men, and proximity to them caused respiratory problems for nurses too. I stood at the sink, lathering my hands over and over. Burns could easily become infected. Staring down at the white suds, my hands scalding under the hot water, I wanted to cry. But now was no time to break down. These poor brave soldiers were suffering, and many would die. Those who didn't, would suffer the effects for the rest of their lives. I wiped my hands on a clean towel, took a deep breath, and headed for the trenches.

I started my labors of assessing the men and dividing them into two groups: those who would die within the day and those who would die within the week. Of the latter group, a few lucky ones might survive—if you could call them lucky. I couldn't rely on the knowledge in my hands and fingers because I didn't dare touch most of the men. It came down to whether they could speak their names and answer my questions. Those who could answer might live through the day, those who could only cry out would not.

One young man—a boy really—had burns on his arms, scorched eyes, and was coughing. But through gritted teeth, he told me his name, "Bobby Miles," and then described how the Germans had ambushed his unit. Something about Bobby's voice reminded me of Ian Elliott, and I wondered why neither Ian nor Ernest had joined the war effort. After all, their wealth was the result of the labor of boys like Bobby.

"Try to rest. Save your strength." I called an orderly to help me rig up a croup tent around the young patient.

Weary and beaten down, but intent on easing the dying into the afterlife if we couldn't keep them alive, I went to the next cot. The man was lying on his side facing the wall. I could see why. His right shoulder was badly burned, along with his neck and the side of his head. I asked another orderly to help me turn him around so I could try to talk to him. It took four women to lift the man, cot and all, and turn the whole thing around away from the wall.

The man's eyes were closed in a tight grimace.

I knelt next to the cot to speak to him. "What is your name?"

His eyes flew open and met mine with a jolt of recognition.

No, no, no! It couldn't be.

"Andrew?" I whispered.

"Fio, is it really you?" he asked in a weak voice.

"It's me. I'm here." I fought back tears. Andrew, dear Andrew, please don't die. "Everything will be okay. I'll take care of you."

"Where am I?"

"You're in the hospital. In London."

"Shot down near Calais." He groaned. "Parachuted out just in time. Lucky to catch up with the Royal Field Artillery." He wheezed. "Bad luck to worse." He sucked in breath and then fell into a coughing fit.

"Try to rest." I quickly made up a syringe of morphia, but with him lying on his good arm, I couldn't find a place to inject it. I asked an orderly to run to the dispensary and get morphia tablets. They weren't as effective, but they were better than nothing. The orderly returned with the bottle and I tapped a double dose into my palm.

"Chew these. They will be bitter but chewing them will make them act more quickly." I knelt and slipped the tablets into his open mouth.

After several minutes that seemed like an eternity, he appeared more relaxed. Still, every time he coughed, he flinched in pain.

I asked another nurse to help me rig up a croup tent so I could administer steam to help ease his coughing. On a small burner, I boiled water in a pan and then held it close to his face so he could breathe in the steam. It was tiring on my arm, but it was the only way to soothe his burnt lungs. I should be seeing to the other men, but I didn't want to leave Andrew. The other nurses would have to cover for me.

I left him only long enough to find a doctor to help me save him. Although I knew it was hopeless, I ran from one operating theater to the next looking for a doctor to perform a miracle. Every doctor I saw was busy operating or treating another patient. I waited outside the operating room where Dr. Armstrong had just finished an amputation. Although only forty, he looked haggard and old as he exited the operating theater.

"Dr. Armstrong, can you please help me?" I heard the desperation in my voice. "It's my husband. He's been gassed."

"There's not much we can do for gas," he said.

"Please, just come. We have to try to save him."

"I'll see what I can do," he said and followed me back to the emergency ward.

I led him to Andrew's cot, where an orderly had taken over administering steam. I lifted the croup tent and Andrew stared up at us with red, glazed eyes. I had already cut away Andrew's shirt—what was left of it—and applied oil to the burns.

Dr. Armstrong took one look at Andrew and his countenance turned grave. He glanced over at me and shook his head. "Make him comfortable. That's all we can do."

The doctor's words shattered my illusions of hope. Andrew was going to die. It was only a matter of time. I vowed to stay with him however long he had left. The trauma of the night before, combined with lack of sleep and very little food, made it harder than ever to hold myself together. I felt I might break down at any minute. I had to be strong for Andrew's sake.

As I sat on a stool next to his cot holding the croup pan, it occurred to me I should get word to Nancy. No, even though she'd wrecked my marriage, I couldn't allow her to see him like this. Her last memory of Andrew should be a happy one. And, truth be told, I didn't want to share him with her. For these last precious hours, Andrew belonged to me.

"Fio." Andrew's voice interrupted my thoughts. "Tell me a story. I always loved your stories."

I smiled and pulled my stool closer to his cot. "A story. Let's see." I narrowed my brow in concentration. "Once upon a time…" It was difficult to be creative in the midst of the awful smell of mustard gas and death. "Once upon a time, there was a Great South African Huntsman named Apollo Fredricks. Apollo, who was not a modest man, thought himself the best investigative reporter in all of Europe. He dressed in fine clothes and enjoyed fine food and was generally considered a dandy of the first order." I gazed at Andrew, who seemed to be resting easier now. I could see that the sound of my voice was reassuring to him, which pleased me.

"One day," I continued, "the arrogant huntsman met his match in the fearless Miss Fiona Figg."

Andrew's laughter caused a paroxysm of coughing.

"Oh dear," I said and refilled the croup pan with water, added a drop of eucalyptus, and heated it on the little stove.

"Mrs. Andrew Cunningham," he said when the coughing subsided.

Was he delirious? Did he still think we were married?

"Former," I corrected.

"First," he replied with a grimace.

Each contortion was like a dagger through my heart. I couldn't stand to see him suffer. I checked my watch to see if I could give him another morphia tablet. Technically, we had another two hours to wait. Given the circumstances, I didn't think it would hurt to give him the tablet early. Thank God for morphia. Within half an hour after chewing another double dose, his rigid form melted into the cot. Between the steam and the drug, his cough weakened too.

Morphia. Good heavens. At that moment I realized why toxic stimulants used to poison the countess had had a delayed effect. The depressant effect of the sleeping powders Mary stirred into the countess's tea slowed the effects of the poison.

I glanced down at Andrew. I would have to file that bit of information away. I couldn't think of the countess's murder right now.

My arm began to hurt from holding the croup pan. My back smarted from leaning over beneath the croup tent. Yet more than anything, my heart ached from the intimacy of huddling so close to the love of my life. I wiped a tear from my cheek. I'd never love anyone else the way I loved Andrew. He was my first love and no one else could take his place. Dear, beautiful Andrew.

I regarded his face, now partially disfigured by gas. Oh, Andrew, don't die. Please, don't die.

"I'm sorry," Andrew whispered. "I'm so sorry, Fio." His whole body convulsed with a sob. "I treated you terribly," he said through his tears.

"Don't say that." I gently touched his hair. "You gave me the best years of my life."

"I'm so sorry," he repeated.

I slid off the stool, sat the croup pan on the floor, and stared into his bloodshot eyes. "Look at me." I took his good hand in mine. "We loved each other with all our hearts. Who could ask for more than that?" I squeezed his hand.

"I never stopped loving you," he whispered.

"I love you, my dearest Andrew." I couldn't help it. I started crying. I tried not to make a sound as the tears rolled down my cheeks. I didn't want to let go of his hand, even to wipe away my tears. I let them run.

His eyes widened and his mouth moved but no words came out.

"Georgie," he finally muttered. "Help her, Fio. Please help her," he said in hoarse desperation.

"I will." Who was Georgie? Then it dawned on me. Georgie must be his son.

"Promise me," he pleaded.

"I promise."

He held my gaze. "I love you, Fiona," he whispered and then gasped, taking his last breath.

"I love you too, dearest."

His hand went limp and his eyes glazed over. The love of my life was gone forever.

I broke down sobbing. All the pent-up emotion from the last twenty-four hours, from the last year, from our entire marriage, exploded through my wracked body. The croup tent shook as I sobbed myself dry.

"Are you okay?" an orderly asked.

I nodded.

"Did you know him?"

I nodded again.

"Come on, love, let me get you a cuppa." She took me by the elbow and led me to the break room. She put a kettle on to boil.

Unable to speak, I sat at the table and waited. Waited for what? The war to end? The grief to pass? The water to boil? Nothing mattered anymore. Nothing made sense. He'd asked me to help her take care of Georgie.

The orderly slid a cup of tea across the table. "Come on then, drink up, love. A nice cuppa will lift your spirits."

I took a sip and closed my eyes.

I don't know how long the orderly watched me from across the table. After a while, she said, "Sorry, love, but me little ones need tending. I'm going home now. Will you be alright, then?"

"I'll be alright."

She patted my hand. "Cheer up, love. You'll meet another fella. Don't seem like it now. But you's young yet."

I sat in the dark canteen sipping my tea until I'd drained the cup. As if sleepwalking, I wandered the corridors until I found myself at the entrance to Archie Somersby's room.

"You've come back," he called from his bed.

I leaned against the door frame and stared across the room.

"What's wrong?" he asked, getting out of bed.

Warm tears rolled down my cheeks.

"Oh dear," he said, taking my hand. "You look as though you've had a shock. Damned war is taking its toll." He led me into the room, and still holding my hand, sat on the edge of the bed. He patted a spot next to him.

I perched beside him, and he put his arm around my shoulders.

"There, there," he said softly. "It will be alright, you'll see."

I buried my head in his shoulder and wept.

THE FUNERAL

I awoke in Archie's arms, curled up next to him on his hospital bed. I didn't know how long I'd been asleep. Enclosed in his warmth, I didn't want to open my eyes. I longed to stay in this cozy dream and not face the harsh reality awaiting me. His body...

HIS BODY!

My eyes flew open, and I leaped out of bed. What if an orderly had seen me? I blushed all the way to my toes.

"Good afternoon," he said with a laugh. "Are you feeling a bit better?"

Flustered, I scanned the floor for my boots. Unable to put them on standing up, I moved to one of the empty cots, sat, and slipped them on. "Yes, better," I said, avoiding his gaze.

"I don't know about you, but I'm starving." When he sat up in bed, the sheet slipped, revealing his bare chest. "I could do with a full English." He got out of bed. He was wearing pajama bottoms and nothing more.

I'd never been in a bed with a man before... except Andrew. I was mortified.

"I'll settle for anything other than another hospital breakfast." Archie went to a small cupboard, opened a drawer, and removed his uniform, which was as neatly folded as a flag. "Can I take you out for a proper breakfast? I've had enough hospital food."

"What time is it?" I glanced at my watch. "Good heavens!" It was three in the afternoon. "I need to get to work."

"After what you went through last night, work can wait. A hearty breakfast is just what the doctor ordered. Then you can vanish like Cinderella."

"No, I can't. I really must be going." I headed toward the hallway without looking back.

Archie ran around me and slid to a stop in the doorway. "Are you sure you'll be alright?" He put his hand on my shoulder.

I nodded.

"Please take care of yourself." His gentle countenance almost melted my resolve. "And come back to see me tomorrow before they send me back to South Africa."

"I will."

"Promise?" He gently lifted my chin so I was gazing into his endless green eyes.

"I promise," I said, fighting the urge to kiss him. I ducked under his arm and made my escape.

I dashed across the hospital, and back to the staff room, where I gathered my clothes, handbag, and coat. I quickly changed my clothes and dropped my soiled nurse's dress and apron in the laundry basket. I dreaded looking in the mirror. I must be quite a sight. I braved the glass and immediately regretted it. Good heavens! My eyes were swollen to the size of walnuts, my complexion was wan, my wig was crooked, and I had black rings under my eyes like a raccoon where my kohl had run. I looked like a ghoul. I was embarrassed Archie had seen me at my worst. Now I'd have to visit him tomorrow… just to show him that even if I wasn't pretty, I wasn't hideous either.

I fixed my face as best I could and decided to just head home. It didn't make sense to go into work since by the time I got there it would be nearly four in the afternoon. Anyway, I wasn't up to it. I needed time to be alone with my sorrow. I thought of Nancy and little Georgie, who probably wouldn't even remember his father.

In a daze, I pushed open the heavy front door to the hospital and found myself on Charing Cross Road somehow confused about which direction to go. I'd come and gone from here so many times, yet nothing seemed familiar. My world had gone, and an impostor had taken its place.

"Miss Figg, is that you?" A tenor voice jolted me out of my stupor. "I say, what happened to you? You look terrible, as if you've just come from the trenches." Captain Clifford Douglas stood in front of me, staring me up and down.

"I feel even worse." My trench coat hung off my shoulders. Could I have shrunk in the last twenty-four hours?

"Come on. Let's get you some coffee." He took my elbow and led me to a coffee shop across the street from the hospital.

"When you didn't show up for lunch, I set out to find you," he said as he pulled me along.

"It was an awful night. First victims from a bloodbath and then mustard gas."

"Damned war!" He shook his head. "Women shouldn't have to see such horrors."

Men make the messes, and women clean them up.

The coffee shop was too loud, and the lights too bright. My head hurt and I wanted to be left alone, but I allowed

Clifford to lead me to a Derby in the back, where it was dimmer and less busy.

"Can we get two coffees?" Clifford asked the waitress. "And say, can you add some brandy." After the waitress left, he said, "Some brandy will do you good."

I leaned my elbows on the table and put my head in my hands.

"I say, cheer up, old girl."

"Andrew died last night." I looked across the table at him through my fingers.

"Oh dear. I am sorry. How did it happen?"

The waitress delivered two cups of coffee with brandy and cream. I'd never drunk brandy in coffee before. Once I got used to the taste, it was quite soothing. After my second cup, I told Clifford every detail of the nightmare hell of my last twenty-four hours. My dry eyes burned when I described the effects of the mustard gas and seeing Andrew's beautiful face burned. I had cried so much already I was out of tears.

"At least as a divorcée, he was only gone from my life. As a war widow, he's gone forever." I pulled a handkerchief out of my purse and dabbed at my swollen eyes.

Clifford reached across the table and took my hand. "Marry me, Fiona."

I was speechless.

"Marry me," he repeated.

"Are you mad?" I blinked at him.

"Why is it mad to ask you to do me the honor of becoming my wife?" He furrowed his brows.

"Because you don't want to marry me." I tightened my lips.

"I do—"

He looked so sincere and ridiculous that I laughed.

"What's so funny? I'm asking you to marry me." He got that hangdog look of his.

"And it's perfectly sweet of you. But you don't want to marry me, and I don't want to marry you."

"Oh, well," he said stiffly. "In that case—" His cheeks reddened and he withdrew his hand. "It's settled." He twisted around in his chair, trying to get the waitress's attention.

"You're a wonderful man, Clifford." I gave him a sympathetic smile. "You know, you shouldn't go around asking girls to marry you. One of them might say yes!"

"Why do you say that?" he asked haughtily. "You didn't."

"Not today, anyway." I smiled weakly. "But you've cheered me up a great deal. Thank you, dear friend."

"My word." Blushing, he returned my smile.

BY THE TIME I got home, I was so knackered I went straight to bed. Before losing consciousness, I marveled at the past twenty-four hours, during which I'd lost my husband forever, slept in a bed with a strange man, and received a marriage proposal. What bittersweet wonders would tomorrow bring?

THE NEXT MORNING, I was searching my wardrobe for a black dress for Andrew's funeral, which had already been planned for Monday. Other than my own dear mother's funeral when I was just seventeen, the countess's funeral was the first I'd attended as an adult, and there I was dressed as a man. To my surprise, my fully stocked wardrobe didn't contain a single suitable black dress, which meant I'd have to go shopping. Thankfully, when I telephoned earlier, Mr. Montgomery had given me a few days off from work.

Shopping always lifted my spirits. The depth of my

despair could be measured by the store's degree of posh. My usual, Liberty's, wouldn't do today. A trip to Knightsbridge was in order. There I could choose between Debenhams, Harvey Nicks, and Harrods, which—given the price tags—I reserved for especially bad days.

Today was an especially bad day.

An hour later, I arrived at Harrods. Harrods's art nouveau windows and giant dome gave the regal appearance of a parliament building. At Harrods, one might spot luminaries, such as cinema stars Eve Balfour and Chrissie White, or members of the royal family—who wisely changed their family name from the unwieldy Saxe-Coburg-Gotha to the less German-sounding Windsor.

Engraved over the entrance of the posh store were the words Omnia Omnibus Ubique (all things for all people, everywhere). They should have added, Praestare Possunt Provism (provided they can afford it). Harrods really did have everything. In the exotic-pets department, one could buy lemurs, and even lions, on special order. Luckily, I was only in the market for a dress and matching accessories.

Strolling through the perfume department, intoxicated by the heady scents of jasmine, bergamot, lemon, lavender, and rose, I wondered if I shouldn't splurge on a bottle. I stopped at a particularly beautiful bottle called Hammam Bouquet. The death of a husband warranted an extravagance. When I saw the price—a full month's pay—I turned on my heels and headed for ladies' wear. He was, after all, an ex-husband.

The moving staircase always unnerved me. I wished they still offered brandies after the journey like they did in the old days.

On the first floor, I took my time browsing. With time off from work, for once, I wasn't in a hurry. I liked touching the garments, even if I didn't try them on. Smooth silk, rough wool, crinkled gabardine—the textures of shopping delighted my fingertips as I flipped through dresses hanging on racks. For amusement, I held up a low-cut pale-blue lampshade tunic with a long silk skirt. Who would wear such a thing? I lingered on a gorgeous deep-purple tube sheath with a beaded bodice. How lovely! The price tag reminded me of my more practical mission. As uplifting as it was, this shopping trip wasn't just a diversion.

I gave up my research on the newest fashions and went directly to a long rack of black dresses. I chose a black crepe with full sleeves and skirt. I found a graceful crepe-trimmed Marie Stuart coif hat with a heavy veil, and black suede gloves. As a divorced woman, I wouldn't be expected to wear widow's weeds, so I didn't need more than the funeral attire.

I gulped when I added up the cost. But I wanted to look smart, especially since I was bound to see her there. I wiped the price tags from my mind and gathered up my plunder. Now all I needed was to find a small black handbag.

After searching through fancy beaded handbags, I chose a plain black clutch purse. With my wardrobe complete, it hit me that even this lovely funerary armor wouldn't protect me from the pain of seeing Andrew in a coffin or meeting his widow and little Georgie.

To take my mind off the dreadful image of Andrew on his deathbed, I decided to stop off at the hospital to visit Archie Somersby as I'd promised. I wanted to say goodbye to him before he was to be shipped back into action. Who knew if I'd ever see him again? A shiver ran down my spine. Or, if I did, would he too be gasping his last breath or lying in a coffin? It was all too beastly to bear.

Before hopping back on the train, I purchased a box of Cadbury biscuits as a going-away present for Archie.

When I exited the railway station, it was pouring rain, and like an idiot, I'd forgotten my brolly yet again. By the time I reached the hospital, my shoes were soaked through and my parcels were soggy. I put my dripping coat and packages into my locker and sloshed my way to Archie's room. Luckily, the box of biscuits was only slightly damp.

The prospect of seeing Archie's beautiful smile cheered me considerably. The closer I got to his room, the more my excitement rose. As I knocked on his door, I felt I could practically take flight from the buzzing in my chest.

"I'm back as promised," I said, as I opened the door.

The set of eyes that stared back at me were not Archie's but those of a grizzled man, no doubt prematurely aged by the war. "Nurse, I'm glad you're here," he said blushing. "I need to use the…" His voice broke off and he nodded toward a bedpan.

Blast! I'd missed Archie. He must have been discharged already. Perhaps I'd never see him again.

"Nurse," the bedridden man repeated.

"Of course, soldier," I said, depositing the box of biscuits on the side table, trading it for the required receptacle.

By Monday morning my stomach was in knots. I hadn't slept well and was dreading what lay ahead. Worried about keeping breakfast down, I only took plain tea and dry toast.

My hands shook as I drew the black veil over my face. Looking through the veil, my bedroom was blurry and dark, like looking through a sieve. Perhaps I could raise the veil until I reached the church.

The service was held at Holy Trinity Church. The chapel's façade of bright-orange bricks and beige stone stood out among the drab grays on Sloane Street. The alternating colors created a striped effect, which suggested a festive layer cake rather than a somber church.

Inside, the stained glass was magnificent. The enormous east window presented saints in individual panels featuring

Adam and Eve and a crucified Christ. The throng of mourners created a black splash against a tapestry of the rich textures and colors in the lavish church.

As I walked up the side aisle, I scanned the crowd for anyone I knew. A group of Andrew's friends wearing dark uniforms were seated to my right. Another bunch of men I recognized as coworkers from Imperial and Foreign Corporation sat together. There were many people I didn't know, and I imagined these must be Nancy's friends and family.

I took a seat at the end of a pew near the front of the chapel. When the minister appeared, the murmuring of the crowd faded into hushed silence. Wearing a long black robe and white sash, the minister began the service. He described Andrew as a hero who had given his life for his country. Next, several of Andrew's friends presented eulogies. One of his Royal Flying Corp buddies talked about his bravery and his passion for life.

I thought of our first year of marriage when Andrew was taking flying lessons and persuaded me to go with him. I was terrified, but he just laughed, his indigo eyes dancing with excitement as he loaded me in the passenger's seat. He loved adventure, and I loved him for it.

I wiped my eyes with my handkerchief and listened to funny and touching stories about Andrew from the friends who also loved him. By the end of the service, my handkerchief was sopping wet with tears of grief and regret. Andrew's disfigured face came back to haunt me.

"Help her, Fio. Please help her." Amid the horrible memories of his final night, Andrew's words came back to me. With his last request in mind, I steeled myself to pay my respects to his widow.

Nancy was standing in the front of the chapel surrounded by people extending their sympathies. I hung back and waited. When the last of the mourners left, I made my way to the front. Even veiled, her grief was overwhelming. As she cradled the baby, the boy nuzzled his sandy-haired head into her shoulder.

"Nancy," I said. "I'm so sorry for your loss. If there's anything I can do—"

When little Georgie looked up at me with his father's indigo eyes, my heart leaped into my throat. He was a miniature version of Andrew. In that moment, I resolved to do anything I could to help the boy.

CHAPTER 20

VISCOUNT ELLIOTT'S TRIAL

The next week and a half was a blur. Haunted by Andrew's gruesome death, I almost forgot all about Ravenswick Abbey, Mary and Viscount Elliott, and the Great South African Huntsman. I hid whenever Clifford came looking for me for lunch, and I buried myself in my filing system. So, I was stunned when on the following Friday, I was called on to reprise my disguise as Dr. Vogel and appear at the Old Bailey as a witness for the prosecution in the case against Viscount Elliott. And to think, my hair had finally grown out just barely enough for a finger wave. With remorse, I took my scissors and chopped off my best hope of femininity. Once again, I looked like a hedgehog.

Standing over the sink in my bathroom, I applied the pungent coal-dye to my roots and waited the requisite fifteen minutes for it to sink in before I rinsed it out. The smell of coal tar on one's head was so unpleasant, I wondered at women—and some vain men, including, no doubt, Fredricks

—who did this regularly. I rinsed my hair several times and then applied a dab of Brilliantine, which at least helped camouflage the tar smell.

Next, I set about assembling the rest of my disguise. I retrieved the dark navy suit from the back of my wardrobe and dug the beard and spirit gum out of my dresser drawer. The smell of the spirit gum burned my nostrils as I applied it to my upper lip. I pressed the beard and mustache into place, patted on the bushy eyebrows, and assessed the results in my hand mirror.

I was dreading the appearance in court even more than I had feared the inquest. For now, I'd become friends with Clifford Douglas, who was bound to be at the trial, and, as Dr. Vogel, I was friends with the wife of the accused, who was fighting for his life. How was I going to face either of my friends without them discerning my double identity? Keeping up this charade was becoming deuced difficult. I would be glad when I could be rid of Dr. Vogel forever.

Satisfied with my disguise, I grabbed my handbag and headed out the door. I was halfway down Northwick Terrace when I realized people were staring at me—not me exactly, but my handbag. Oh bother! I tucked the handbag under my arm, turned on my booted heels, and hurried back to my flat. I tossed the handbag onto the sofa and started my journey over again.

From the railway station just outside the western wall of the city, I strode up Alfred Street enjoying the freedom of a man walking alone. As I passed by St. Paul's Cathedral, I whispered a prayer for Mary… and one for little Georgie. I wished I could do more than pray, but I didn't know how else to help. Captain Hall had tied my hands when it came to the case. He forbade me from returning to Ravenswick Abbey, saying it was too risky given I'd been nearly found out. And yet, here I was, about to reprise my role as Dr.

Vogel. Hopefully for the last time. The blasted beard itched to no end.

I stopped in front of the courthouse and steeled myself for the proceedings. Only a decade old and lavishly outfitted with symbolic reminders of its virtuous purpose, the courthouse building sported a gold-leaf statue of a lady of justice perched atop a seventy-foot dome. Arms outstretched, she was holding a sword in one hand and scales in the other. Eyes wide open, she wasn't subject to the usual blindfold of justice.

As I approached the front doors, the sky opened and a rain squall drenched the three stone figures looking down from above the hall, the angels of fortitude, records, and truth. As a file clerk, I had an in with the angel of records, but as a spy, I could use help with fortitude and truth. I ducked into the doorway to get out of the rain. An inscription above the door read "Defend the children of the poor and punish the wrongdoer." The viscount was hardly a child of the poor, but was he a wrongdoer?

It took all my strength to pull open the heavy steel door. I needed to get back to my bodybuilding exercises. The interior of the Old Bailey took my breath away. With its Sicilian marble floors and allegorical paintings, it was as impressive inside as out. The oak-paneled courtroom had a spacious dock, enclosed by low partitions, and then a staircase leading directly below, presumably to the holding cells. I thought of Ernest down there and wondered how he would appear after almost a month in prison.

How difficult this must have been for Mary, not knowing whether her husband would live or die. So many wives had endured the pain of waiting, of not knowing whether their husbands would return home. And even if they did come home, nothing would ever be the same again. At least the viscount was physically whole, whatever else had been taken from him in the last few weeks—and for now at least, he was alive.

People were crowding into the courtroom, most of them jovial as if they were going to a party, an air of excitement in the room. I glanced around looking for Mary. I recognized the black felt hat she'd worn at the countess's funeral. She was sitting in the ladies' gallery, and I quickened my pace to join her. I was halfway to the ladies' gallery when I remembered that today I wasn't a lady and did an about-face.

The judge called the proceedings to order. I hurried to take a seat near the front of the room. Ernest appeared in the dock directly facing the witness box, opposite the judge. He looked a decade older than the last time I'd seen him at Ravenswick Abbey. Poor man. The jurors—who would decide his fate—sat to his right, and at a table below the judge sat the clerk, two barristers, and a woman wearing a smart skirt and matching blazer who was taking shorthand notes of the proceedings.

"Lord Ernest Gerald Elliott," the judge said with solemnity. "You are charged with the willful murder of your mother, Lady Elliott, countess of Ravenswick and your father, Lord Elliott. How do you plead?"

"Not guilty, Your Honor." Ernest looked haggard. He had dark circles under his eyes, and he needed a haircut. But his clothes were neatly pressed and he was clean-shaven.

Mr. Smith, a member of the King's Counsel, strode to the front of the room, and with much ceremony opened the case for the Crown. What he lacked in stature, he made up for in dramatic gestures.

"Gentlemen of the jury," Mr. Smith announced with

great fanfare. "I submit that Lord Ernest Elliott committed the premeditated and cold-blooded murder of his father and then his mother by means of poison." The barrister for the prosecution had an angular appearance, and when he waved his arms, it gave the impression of a knife slicing the air.

"Why would a son commit such a heinous crime as parricide?" He paused. "I will tell you why." With his craggy face, short white wig, and long black robe, he looked like an eagle ready to swoop down on his prey.

"Lord Ernest Elliott had gotten himself into such financial difficulties he killed his parents, believing he would inherit their fortune. His financial problems are the result of his gambling at the racetrack and his liaison with a neighboring widow, Mrs. Roland."

Gasps and murmurs from the crowd signaled their disapproval. I glanced up at Mary, who was staring straight ahead with a face of stone. Poor Mary. I didn't know how she soldiered on in the face of public humiliation. At least Andrew's infidelity was merely local and not national news. The thought of Andrew, and the memory of his last excruciating night on earth, made my stomach sour.

"The lady in question brought this liaison to the attention of Viscount Elliott's mother," Smith continued, "and the countess threatened to cut him out of her will. Not coincidentally, by early the next morning, she too was dead." Smith waved his hand dramatically.

Surely Mrs. Roland wouldn't have told the countess if she were having a liaison with Ernest. It just didn't make sense. Unless blackmail was her motive. Again, I glanced at Mary, who was worrying a lace handkerchief something terrible.

"The police found a full bottle of the earl's heart medicine, digitalis, in Viscount Elliott's bedroom, hidden among his undergarments in a dresser drawer." Smith's voice rose an octave as he sliced the air with his arms. "From this bottle, the lethal dose was administered by the son to the father."

If Ernest had killed his mother, he wouldn't have been so daft as to leave the poison lying about in his room. I thought of the toxic cordial bottles, most likely lost in the post thanks to my meddling and stupidity. If they contained the fatal dose, I was as much a criminal as the murderer himself. I studied the accused, whose complexion had taken on a yellowish tint that made him look positively waxy. The fact that I was hot on the trail of a notorious German spy posing as a South African huntsman-cum-journalist was my best—if not my only—defense.

"I put it to the good gentlemen of the jury, Lord Ernest Elliott murdered his father and then his mother, as she was to inherit everything and had threatened to cut him out of the will due to the liaison with Mrs. Roland." Smith's wig trembled with excitement. He glanced over at the jury before concluding, "As reasonable men, in light of the damning evidence I will present to you today, it is unthinkable for you to render a verdict other than guilty as charged." Mr. Smith sat down and mopped his forehead with a handkerchief.

The first witness for the prosecution was a detective inspector from Scotland Yard. His blondish brush mustache formed a permanent frown, which accentuated his strong chin. Aside from a gold watch chain, his attire was the usual boring three-piece suit and tie. He was no nonsense and professional as he recounted finding the poison bottle in Lord Ernest Elliott's bedroom, stuffed under some clothes in the back of a dresser drawer. Apparently, he'd received an anonymous tip.

Anonymous tip? How suspicious. Without the daily updates from Mary I had been receiving when I resided at Ravenswick Abbey, I was reliant on reports from Clifford Douglas, who obviously didn't pay as much attention to detail as Mary had. To be fair, he paid attention to details, just the wrong ones.

I was the next witness called to testify. My heart constricted in my chest as I approached the stand. I'd never spoken in front of such a large crowd, and I was mortified to be testifying for the prosecution. I didn't dare look up to the ladies' gallery where Mary was sitting. Instead, I scanned the room for Clifford and Fredrick Fredricks. I hadn't seen them in the crowd, but I knew they had to be in the room somewhere. If the great huntsman had an ace up his sleeve, now was the time to play it. If he was waiting until the eleventh hour, he certainly had a flair for the dramatic. If he waited much longer, it would be too late for Viscount Elliott.

With his manly chin and distinctive mustache, Fredricks was easy to pick out of the assembly. He and Clifford were sitting near the back of the room to my right. Once I'd located them, I avoided looking at that section of the courtroom for fear one or the other of them would find me out— Clifford because I'd seen him nearly every day for the last month, and Fredrick Fredricks because of his uncanny sense of smell.

Under the harsh lights in the courtroom, I broke out in a sweat. I patted my forehead with my handkerchief and hoped the spirit gum didn't melt in the heat. I touched my eyebrows to make sure they were still in place. The last thing I needed was my facial hair dripping down my face during my testimony.

I gave Ernest an apologetic look as I stepped into the witness box across from the dock where he stood. He remained impassive, holding onto the rail and staring straight ahead, poor man. I repeated my testimony from the inquest, telling the court how I came upon the earl in the throes of fatal poisoning, and how I tried, unsuccessfully, to revive him. I also spoke about how I recognized the symptoms of poisoning, which at the time I thought was the result of a fatal dose of mercury bichloride, but had since realized must have been digitalis, and that I was the one who insisted upon an autopsy since Dr. Derby assumed it was his heart. "A reasonable conclusion considering he had been treating him for a heart ailment," I said.

Stupefied at the brevity of the interrogation, I stepped down from the witness box, doubly relieved I hadn't said anything damning to the viscount, and even more so that my facial hair hadn't betrayed me. My testimony in no way pointed the finger at anyone. All I was asked to do was identify the symptoms of poisoning. Of course, I didn't mention the ornate cordial bottles I'd lost in the post, or the letter I'd folded into the hatband, which I was certain held the solution to the case. I'd made a real hash of it.

I took my seat in the audience and then attempted to block out the proceedings in order to recall the contents of that blasted letter. It was no use. Every time I almost pulled the words out of my subconscious the viscount's barrister Cornelius Grandville's booming voice interrupted my thoughts. He was cross-examining the frail old maid, who was gallantly defending her master.

I was glad Mary couldn't testify against her husband and wouldn't be subjected to the bombast of Cornelius Grandville or the pompous little Mr. Smith. I turned and glanced up at the ladies' gallery, where Mary sat staring out into space, a million miles away.

"It weren't him," the maid insisted.

When Grandville shook his head, his jowls in silent rage. It was hard to believe he was the barrister for the defense as he seemed intent on proving his client's guilt. I felt sorry for the poor maid. She was just trying to protect her master.

With every contradiction and twist or turn of a witness, the courtroom erupted with gasps or giggles. The judge had to use his gavel several times to call the court to order. Grandville seemed to be taking a special delight in the pandemonium, for every time the judge banged his gavel, the rotund man gave a hearty snort.

Next, Ian Elliott was called to the witness stand for the defense. He was even thinner than I remembered, and his wan complexion was paler than ever. He didn't look well. His brother's trial must have been weighing on him, either that or, like me, he had a guilty conscience. After all, with his mother out of the way, he was free to marry Lillian.

"Who would inherit Ravenswick Abbey if your brother is hanged?" The oversized barrister took a step closer to the witness box.

The crowd gasped as one.

Grandville really was too much. I wondered why Ernest had engaged such a pillock. Poor Ian. He was so mild-mannered and such a gentle lad, he didn't look like he could hurt a flea. What kind of game was Grandville playing at, sacrificing one brother for the sake of the other? Red-faced, Ernest Elliott was holding onto the rail of the dock. He looked like he might jump over it and attack his own barrister.

After humiliating poor Ian, the prosecution took over and called the prisoner himself to the witness stand. I scanned the ladies' gallery looking for Mary, but she wasn't there. I twisted around to scan the crowd behind me, and I saw her standing at the back of the courtroom near the exit. She was already dressed like a widow, in black from head to toe.

A hush fell over the audience as Ernest Elliott was moved from the dock to the witness stand.

"What was your relationship with Mrs. Roland?" The point-blank question caught everyone by surprise, not the least of whom was Ernest.

He ran a hand through his hair. "Mrs. Roland and I…" He glanced out at the audience.

I didn't dare turn around to look at Mary. Instead, I watched the jurors. It was clear from their expressions they didn't approve of Ernest's liaison with Mrs. Roland. And judging by the clucking of tongues, neither did the women in the gallery.

"Mrs. Roland's husband worked for my father," Ernest said finally. "Before he was killed in the munitions accident." He stared down at his hands. "I was merely helping her out after her husband died."

MR. SMITH CUT HIM OFF. "Is this perhaps why you found yourself in financial difficulties?"

Ernest lowered his head. "No. It's not like that—"

Obviously sensing weakness in his prey, Mr. Smith went in for the kill. "I say you murdered your own parents to continue your liaison with Mrs. Janet Roland."

Janet. Janet Roland. Good heavens. J for Janet. The sloeberry cordial came from Janet Roland. Of course! I'd been such an idiot. Why didn't I think to find out Mrs. Roland's Christian name? And then it dawned on me… E wasn't Edith but Ernest. Blimey. If the green cordial bottle was poisoned, it was intended for Ernest and not his mother. Only the red bottle was addressed to Lady Edith. More evidence that the bottle she'd polished off before my arrival, was intended not for her but for her son. Is that what killed her?

If only the little bottles hadn't been lost in the post. They had to turn up eventually. Hopefully, before Ernest Elliott was swinging from a rope. Even then, I would have to persuade Captain Hall to let me turn in the evidence to Scotland Yard. Maybe I could do it anonymously and he'd never be the wiser.

"No!" Ernest shouted and pounded his fist against the dock railing. "It's a lie! It's a lie. I didn't do it…" He broke down and buried his face in his hands.

His loss of composure did not serve him well.

"Then what of the bottle of digitalis found in your bed chamber?" Mr. Smith asked with a pointed look.

"Mutti, that is mother, asked me to fetch it since she wasn't feeling well and father was running low." Tears ran down his face.

Seeing the viscount reduced to tears put me over the edge. My head began spinning and my vision became cloudy. I absolutely had to remove myself from the sweltering courtroom before I fainted. It wouldn't do for a London doctor—a specialist in female maladies no less—to be overcome by a case of the vapors. If I collapsed on the floor and had to be revived, the jig would be up. Excusing myself as I went, I did my best not to step on well-clad toes as I made my escape from the courtroom.

Staggering outside onto Old Bailey Street, I must have looked a sight. Strangers stared as I leaned against the stone building, my hands on my knees, trying not to pass out. I closed my eyes and concentrated on my breathing. My eyes flashed open again when I overheard a group of newspapermen discussing how the forthcoming hanging of Viscount Elliott would be the biggest news of the year—a wealthy landowner swinging from a rope. I shuddered.

It was true, things were not looking good for Ernest Elliott. The noose was tightening around his neck.

I stepped away from the building and straightened myself. I stared into the street, not knowing what to do next. Should I confess to taking the letter and bottles from the countess? Should I go to Fredricks and tell him everything? Or, better yet, reveal my assignment and true identity to Scotland Yard? I still didn't understand why the War Office couldn't intervene. If we were fighting a war for justice abroad, shouldn't we be just as concerned about justice at home? Why wouldn't Captain Hall allow me to reveal myself? Was Fredrick Fredricks really so important to the war effort? Of course, I didn't want to lose my assignment. These last two months had been some of the most exciting in my life. But would I let an innocent man go to the gallows?

Mary appeared at my side. Her face was pale and her eyes were puffy. "I hate this whole proceeding, doctor," she said. "What a trap is being set for my poor Ernest."

"Perhaps tomorrow will be better," I said. Tomorrow will be worse, I thought, given the prosecution had barely begun.

Mary touched my sleeve. "Is Mr. Grandville trying to prove Ian did it?"

"I think Mr. Grandville is trying to confuse the jury so they aren't convinced beyond a doubt that Ernest did it. It's a clever strategy as far as it goes." Which was not far enough. For, despite Grandville's efforts at confusing the jurors, at the end of the day, one was left with the impression that it was indeed Lord Ernest Elliott who had given his father an overdose of digitalis in the old man's tea, and then did the same for his mother's coffee the next morning. Things were not looking good for Viscount Elliott if confusion was the best his defense had to offer.

I glimpsed Fredricks coming toward us. "I'd better be going. Stay strong, Mary." I patted her hand. "Everything will be alright."

"I hope so, doctor," she said with a melancholy smile. "That's what Mr. Fredricks says, too."

"I'm sure of it," I said, although I was far from sure of anything, particularly Mr. Fredricks. I tipped my hat and took off down the street at a brisk pace. For Mary's sake, I had to find a way to save Ernest Elliott from the gallows.

THE LETTER

Once Mary went back inside the courthouse, I ducked into the coffee shop next door. I ordered a strong cup of coffee, a margarine sandwich, and asked for a piece of paper and a pen. The waitress returned a few minutes later with all four. I took a sip and blanched. Usually a tea drinker, the coffee was brutally bitter. I added a couple teaspoons of sugar and filled the cup to the brim with cream. Ahhhh. Much better. Fountain pen in hand, I got down to business. Tuning out the din of the other patrons, I concentrated on recalling the letter. I closed my eyes and waited. Yes. Before my mind's eye, I saw the handwriting scrawled across the page. But it was blurry like I was looking through a thick glass.

My memory for documents was unlike other fleeting memories flowing by like a stream or flashing like a picture show in my mind. Books, papers, letters, documents of any kind, came back to me fully formed, as if I were looking directly at them, only sometimes they were just out of focus. I had to work to pull them closer and then miraculously they would appear before my mind as if I were seeing them anew. Dark marks on light pages became stamped onto my brain like ink from a printing press.

Distractedly eating my margarine sandwich, I let my mind wander back to the night of the earl's death. The family was waiting downstairs. I was back in his bedroom, alone, looking for clues. I spotted the briefcase, turned the key in the lock, and discovered the letter. I took the letter out and had just started to read it when Dr. Derby called out to me. I hastily folded the letter and tucked it into the hatband. I replayed the scene in my mind, pausing at the moment when I held the letter in my hands. I closed my eyes and took a few deep breaths.

Little by little, the words came into focus before my mind's eye. It was addressed to *Sehr geehrte Dame*. And of course, I remembered seeing Fredrick Fredricks name there. I repeated the words under my breath. Not that I knew what they meant. I assumed Sehr geehrte Dame was the salutation since it appeared at the top. Pen hovering over paper, I closed my eyes again and tried to recall the contents of the letter. I struggled to piece the words together. Unfortunately, I hadn't paid any more attention in my German classes than I had in my French classes.

I saw the words: Der Bombenanschlag auf Silvertown war ein Triumph. Gut gemacht. Then one line in English. Never fear. Victory will be ours. Soon we will get what we deserve.

They would get what they deserved alright. A plan was forming in my mind. A plan to retrieve the letter and trap the huntsman—hopefully in time to save Viscount Elliott from the gallows. It was truly the eleventh hour. I absolutely must recreate that blasted letter. Come on, Fiona. You can do it. I closed my eyes again, leaned my elbows on the table, and put my face into my hands. In the darkness of my palms, the smells and sounds were heightened. Coffee and cigarettes. Chatter and motorcars. I inhaled deeply and tried to tune out the world to focus on the letter.

The rest was in German. But the words were there. To me, they looked like code. But if I could just get them down on paper, then I could take them to Dilly Knox to translate. Finally, I saw the entire letter as clearly as if I were holding in my hands. I opened my eyes and scribbled the contents as fast as I could and glanced at my watch. I dropped some coins on the table and then jotted a quick note. On the way out, I paid a newspaper boy a florin to deliver it to "the tall horse-faced man in uniform queuing for a hackney carriage."

The weather had taken a turn. A cool mist hung in the air and the sky was the color of damp newsprint, as if the heavens themselves were bracing for bad news. I buttoned Dr. Vogel's jacket up to my neck and strode up Old Bailey Street, toward the Old Admiralty, weaving in and out of the crowd. When the building came into sight, I quickened my pace. I had to catch Dilly before he left the office. By the time I reached for the heavy front door, my facial hair—beard, mustache and brows—had absorbed the damp. Beads of mist covered my cheeks forming a fine film.

I took the stairs as fast as I could without falling over Dr. Vogel's oversized shoes. When I reached room 40, I was practically panting. I opened the door and all heads turned. Women looked up from their typewriters. The codebreakers —most of whom were men—stared at me. I must have looked like a drowned rat. I made a beeline for Dilly's desk. A quizzical look on his face, he asked, "Can I help you, sir?"

"It's me!" I ripped off my beard. Ouch. "Fiona."

He laughed, a big hearty belly laugh. "Aren't you dapper!" He was nearly howling now, tears in his eyes.

"Enough, already." Brows furrowed, I tightened my lips. "I need your help."

"You have a knack for costumes." He was still laughing. "Have you considered the theater."

Indeed, I had. But right now I needed him to stop auditioning for the role of village idiot and translate the blasted letter before it was too late. I pulled the transcription from my pocket. "I need you to translate this." I thrust it at him. "It's a matter of life and death."

"Oh. What is it?" He stopped laughing and took the paper. "German." He looked up at me with concern. "Where did you get it?"

"Can you translate it or not?" I stood arms akimbo.

"Of course." He adjusted his spectacles and began to translate. "The bombing of Silvertown was a triumph. Good work." His eyes went wide. "What is this?" he asked again.

"A letter I found in the possession of Lady Edith Elliott." A sinking sensation permeated my chest. I'd suspected Lady Edith was a German sympathizer. No wonder she was so distraught about the Silvertown explosion. It really had been her fault. "What else does it say?"

As Dilly continued to translate, I couldn't believe my ears. It became clear that Lady Edith was indeed using her refugee charity as a cover to smuggle in German spies and saboteurs. One of them had sabotaged the Silvertown munitions works, causing the explosion that killed dozens of people and destroyed an entire neighborhood. The author of the letter both praised her and warned her that she needed to buck up and continue the work, despite her husband. Otherwise, there would be consequences. And those consequences, the author suggested, involved Mr. Fredrick Fredricks!

After explaining everything to Dilly, who wouldn't let me leave unless I did, I tucked the letter back into my jacket pocket and headed home. If Clifford got my note, then tonight, I could put the rest of my plan in motion.

At eight o'clock on the dot, my doorbell rang. I adjusted my wig, smoothed my skirt, and answered the door. Clifford was looking rather sharp in his beige wools—Fredricks must be giving him advice on his clothes.

"Miss Figg, I got your note and came round this evening to discuss an urgent matter. Do you mind?" He pointed at my lip. "You have a bit of something just there."

I touched my upper lip and removed a tiny ball of… spirit gum. The blasted beard. "Lip balm," I said, trying to regain my composure. "Please come in." I invited him into my sitting room and offered him tea.

"Do you happen to have anything stronger? Whiskey or maybe some brandy?" he asked. "That trial has put my nerves on end."

"That's why I asked to see you."

"Were you there? I didn't see you?"

"No." In a way, it was true. Miss Figg hadn't been there. I gestured toward the sofa and Clifford sat down.

"Let me see if I still have any of Andrew's liquor in the cabinet," I said, stalling. At the mention of my husband's name, a stabbing pain struck my heart. Why did the last gruesome memory displace four years of happy ones? I'd rather remember that fateful day at his office when I found him in Nancy's arms than think of his burned body fighting for breath in the hospital.

I went into the kitchen and checked the cupboard where I'd stored Andrew's alcohol. He had a bottle of Scotch whiskey from before the war and a bottle of rough rum. I poured two glasses of Scotch, one large and one small, and returned to the sitting room.

"Do you take soda or water with your whiskey?" I asked.

"Neat is perfect," he said with a smile.

I handed the large whiskey to Clifford.

"I'm deuced worried about Ernest. The prosecution has a strong case against him. I know he didn't do it. Ernest's a topping sort and could never do a wicked thing like that." He sipped his whiskey. "I wish there were something I could do to help him."

"Perhaps there is," I said, glancing up over the lip of my glass. The smell of the strong drink was enough to bring tears to my eyes. I sipped it tentatively. At first the alcohol burned my tongue, but then the tingling gave way to pleasant flavors of smoky bergamot and a hint of citrus. Yes, to my surprise, I rather liked whiskey.

"Really?" His eyes brightened. "What?"

"Remember that fellow, Dr. Vogel, who you mentioned attended your friend's mother?"

"That blackguard!" Clifford pounded his fist on his knee.

"Be that as it may." I was somewhat annoyed at this attitude toward my good doctor. "He revealed to me the most stunning bit of information last week."

"Good Lord! You know Dr. Vogel?" He sat blinking at me.

"In a manner of speaking," I said coyly.

"How do you know that wretched fellow?" He put his glass down on the side table and gazed over at me expectantly. "Good heavens! Don't tell me he's a friend of yours."

"Not exactly."

"You don't fancy him, do you?" Flustered, he reached for his glass again.

"No, nothing like that." I sipped my whiskey.

"With that horrid black beard. I hope not." He put his glass down again, a bit too roughly. The whiskey splashed to and fro.

"I hate that beard!" There I was telling the truth. I did hate that beard. "Anyway, he's not my type."

"Who is your type?" His blue eyes shone.

The image of Archie Somersby lying shirtless in bed popped into my mind. My cheeks grew hot. "Shall we get back to saving your friend?"

"If it will help Ernest." He nodded solemnly. "You must tell me what you learned from the blighter."

"He's really not that bad, you know," I said, defending my alter ego. "If you must know, he's my doctor."

"I say. Why didn't you tell me?" He looked relieved.

"It's jolly awkward, actually." I feigned a bit of nervous laughter.

"You can tell me, I promise, I won't say a word to anyone." He looked so sincere I almost laughed. "I'm nothing if not discreet," he added. I suppressed a chuckle. Clifford Douglas was the opposite of discreet. A blabbermouth, more like.

I looked him straight in the eyes. "I see him for utero errantia during fluores menstruada." I tightened my lips.

Clifford blushed from ear to ear. "Oh dear," he whispered.

"Yes, well." I cleared my throat. "Now you see why I was reluctant to say anything to you about my association with Dr. Vogel."

"Indeed." He took a gulp of whiskey, nearly spilling his drink down his front.

I took secret delight in torturing poor Clifford. He was so easily embarrassed.

"Female maladies—"

"My word!" he interrupted, turning an even darker shade of crimson. "Good Lord, Fiona."

"Shall we get back to your friend's trial, then?" I asked to his obvious relief.

"Please." He brushed imaginary lint from the knee of his trousers.

"You must swear none of what I tell you leaves this room." I held up my hand as if swearing on a bible.

"I swear," he said, holding up his own hand. "You can trust me with your life."

"I'm sure I can, but I'm glad I don't have to." I leaned forward in my chair. "Dr. Vogel told me Mary asked him to take an incriminating letter from the countess's briefcase."

"Good Lord!"

"Exactly." I adjusted my skirt. "Now you see why you mustn't under any circumstances tell anyone about this."

"Good heavens, no." He shook his head.

"After the family left the bedroom the night the earl died, the good doctor had the letter in his possession when Dr. Derby threatened to return to the room and find him out. Thinking quickly, the clever doctor folded the letter into the hatband of the earl's gorgeous..." I stopped myself before I got carried away describing that delicious hat.

"No!"

"Yes, just so." I stood up and moved closer to the sofa.

"I knew that Vogel character was up to no good." He pounded a fist onto the edge of his chair. "Poor Mary. I don't know what she saw in him."

"I think he's rather a good egg." My lips twitched. "He didn't need to come forward with this information about the letter, you know." Was I feeling rather guilty? I suppose so. Afterall, it was my fault this beastly trial had dragged on so long. If it weren't for my assignment and my one shot at happiness, not to mention a career.

"Yes, but why didn't he mention it at the trial?" Clifford shook his head. "The bounder."

"How would it look for poor Mary, as you say, if she insti-gated a scheme to steal a letter?" I raised my eyebrows. Clif-ford may not like Dr. Vogel, but he was exceedingly fond of Mary—and every other tragic woman.

"You have a point." He took a sip of whiskey. "Poor Ernest, his wife carrying on with that horrid doctor. I can hardly believe it's true." He got a dreamy look in his eyes. "She's such a lovely creature."

"Dr. Vogel would never." Even if I really were a man, I'm quite sure I would not be the kind of bloke to commit adultery.

"How do you know what that man's capable of?" Clifford's tone was indignant.

"I know him well enough to be certain he's not the sort of man to be unfaithful or carry on liaisons with other men's wives!" My offended tone threatened to betray me.

He pouted like a scolded schoolboy.

I regained my composure. "Retrieve the letter, Clifford, and save your friend." I finished my drink and sat the glass on the side table for emphasis.

"How can this letter save Ernest?" he asked.

"The letter, you see, is not a love letter as Mary suspects. It's not about Ernest's liaison with Mrs. Roland."

"Not a love letter?" He narrowed his eyes.

"No." I leaned forward in my chair. "According to the doctor, Mary thought it implicated her husband in a liaison with some tenant's widow—" Dr. Vogel may know the widow was Mrs. Roland, but Fiona Figg wouldn't.

"Mrs. Roland," he said thoughtfully.

"Yes, that sounds right." I nodded. "You see, Mary was only using her friendship with Dr. Vogel to make her husband jealous."

"I knew Mary was a wonderful sort of woman." He lifted his glass to his lips. "I have a brilliant sense for women, you know." He smiled, pleased with himself.

"Yes, I'm sure." I tried not to laugh. "After reading about the trial, I'm convinced this letter was not about Mr. Elliott's infidelity." I went with my instinct. "Rather, it incriminates someone else entirely and he's the blackguard you should be worried about, my friend." I wished I knew who that someone else was. I had a hunch, of course, but I dare not tell Clifford. He wouldn't believe me anyway.

"Good Lord. Who then?"

"All in good time." I couldn't tell him my real suspicions or he might not go through with my plan. "Now you've got to prove it and save your friend."

"Right. I'll go straight away and fetch the letter. The hatband, you say." He arose from the sofa.

"Clifford, you can't just go retrieve the letter and reveal it to the world. What will you say? How will you explain how you knew about it? Do you want to expose Mary to vicious gossip, or worse, suspicions she had something to do with her mother-in-law's death?" I pointed at the sofa. "No, sit down please. I have a better idea."

"I suppose you're right." He dropped back into the sofa.

"Would you like another whiskey?" Best to keep him lubricated.

"Yes, I think I would." He held up his glass and I took it into the kitchen to refill.

When I returned, Clifford was pacing around my sitting room, looking pensive.

"What's troubling you?" I asked.

"WHY WOULD Dr. Vogel tell you all this?" He shook his head. "And how do we know he's telling the truth? I just don't trust the man. I mean he was arrested, after all!"

"Do you trust me?" I didn't bother explaining that Dr. Vogel wasn't actually arrested but extracted. How could I without revealing myself as an espionage agent?

"Yes, of course. What a silly question."

"Then quit pacing and sit." I pointed at the sofa again and like a puppy, he obeyed. "Now finish your whiskey like a good boy while I tell you my plan."

He took a sip and then looked up at me expectantly. "Your plan—"

"Who is the most likely person in London to solve this case?"

"You?"

I rolled my eyes. "No, not me. Who are you always telling me is the greatest investigative reporter in the world?"

"Fredricks!"

"Yes, Fredricks. But you mustn't tell him a word about our conversation, or about Dr. Vogel and Mary." I gave him a stern look. "Not one word."

"You can count on me." His eyes shone with excitement.

"Good. You wouldn't want to embarrass your poor Mary." Poor Mary would be mortified if she knew I'd told Clifford. Still, it was the only way to save her husband.

"No, indeed not." He shuddered.

"Then you must lead Fredricks to the letter." My plan was as much about retrieving the letter as it was to test Fredricks. With concentration and time, I'd made some progress on reproducing the letter from memory. I was confident, more or less, that when push came to shove, I would come through, one way or another. I hoped. And prayed. For the sake of Ernest Elliott… and my own dear life.

"And how can I do that without telling him the truth? He'll ask all kinds of questions and I'll be obliged to answer. He's not the sort of fellow who takes anything on faith."

"No, that's what I'm counting on. He will need to see for himself."

Clifford gave me a puzzled look. "What are you suggesting?"

"You've got to get Fredricks to go back to Ravenswick Abbey and make him examine the hat. It's on the earl's dressing table. You've got to make him suspect someone tampered with that hat."

"And how do I do that?"

"You say he's obsessed with the natural order of things and animal instincts?"

"Yes."

"And does he understand women's instincts?"

"Well, perhaps not as well as I do, but yes, I would say so."

I suppressed a smile.

"Dr. Vogel told me he forgot to put the hat back on the hat stand. Instead, he left it lying on the earl's dressing table. A proper gentleman wouldn't toss his hat on a table when they have a perfectly good hat stand waiting at the ready."

"Why not? I would."

"I'm beginning to wonder, dear captain, if you are really a gentleman."

He blushed.

"Its brim will become misshapen and flat." I tapped the top of my head. "Don't you know to sit your hat on its crown and not on its brim? No doubt your friend Fredricks does."

"Well, yes. I suppose he would." His lips twitched, as if he thought I was scolding him.

"In fact, I'm surprised he didn't notice the hat was not as it should be, given his obsession with propriety, as you say." I raised my eyebrows.

"Quite."

"So, if Fredricks had reason to believe someone mislaid the hat, he might suspect an interloper had entered the bedroom after the murder to tamper with important evidence."

"I say, that's genius!" he exclaimed.

I raised my glass and smiled. "Yes, isn't it just."

"How do I make Fredricks think someone tampered with the hat? He's not an easy fellow to lead down the garden path, you know." He took a sip of his drink.

"I suppose not. So, you'll have to be jolly clever."

"Yes, I suppose I will." He smiled. "You can count on me."

"Hadn't you best be going then?" I stood up.

"Yes. Yes, of course." He drained his glass. "You can count on me," he repeated, taking up his hat and overcoat.

"Hopefully, Viscount Elliott can too." I picked up the empty glasses and walked him to the front door. "His life depends upon it."

CHAPTER 22

MRS. ROLAND'S FARM

The next morning, distracted by the trial, and eager to learn whether Clifford succeeded, I missed my stop for Charing Cross Hospital. Rather than change platforms and take the train back to my stop, I decided to walk. I'd worn sensible shoes to go with my hospital uniform and —if the noxious fumes of the city streets didn't kill me—the exercise would do me good.

I'd only gone a couple of streets when I regretted my decision. It was a real pea-souper, and the smells of filth and decay hung heavy in the fog. I missed the clean country air of Ravenswick Abbey. I thought of the American Jack London's harsh commentary upon visiting London Town: "The children grow up into rotten adults, without virility or stamina, a weak-kneed, narrow-chested, listless breed." And to think, I was one of those rotten adults who'd lived here all my life. Perhaps the miasma of London had rotted the souls of traitors, who at this very moment, continued to plot against king and country to aid our enemies. I was beginning to suspect the dearly departed countess was among them.

As I turned the corner onto the Strand, I was shocked by the sight of lorries lined up in front of the hospital. You'd think I'd be used to it by now. But one never gets used to seeing young men broken in body and spirit, marked for the rest of their lives, however long they live. Perhaps there were some who could say, "Another day, another line up of lorries." But to me, every visit to Charing Cross was a brand-new tragedy as raw and haunting as the first casualties I'd witnessed, only now compounded by the horrors of Andrew's last ghastly night lying on a cot in the hallway of an overcrowded triage.

Whenever I approached those heavy entrance doors, I dreaded what awaited me on the other side.

Today, no sooner had I emerged from the locker room where I'd deposited my handbag when Daisy Nelson came straight at me, dashing up the hallway, waving her scarecrow arm above her head.

Breathless and panting, she managed to spit out the words, "Death cap."

I nodded encouragingly. "Go on."

"Your bottles finally arrived." A horse-toothed smile cracked her long face. "You were bloody right. Traces of Hygrophoropsis aurantiaca and Amanita phalloides." She shook her head. "You won't believe this." She raised her bushy eyebrows. "And Atropa Belladonna." She exhaled. "Whoever wanted her dead wasn't taking any chances."

"False chanterelles and death caps, two of the deadliest mushrooms in England." I covered my mouth with my hand. "And belladonna! Do you know what this means?"

"Whoever drank your sloe-berry had a fatal hangover." Daisy grabbed my arm. "Come on. I'll show you."

She led me down the hall and up the stairs to her laboratory behind the dispensary where the little ornate cordial bottles were standing side by side at attention on her dissection table. The red one from the briefcase, the one the countess opened and drank on the day of her death. And the emerald bottle from her nightstand, which presumably she'd drunk sometime earlier.

Daisy held up the green bottle. "This little bad boy was loaded with organic toxins."

"What would happen to someone who drank that concoction?" I pointed to the green bottle in her hand.

"Nausea, possibly convulsions, and within a day or three, death by kidney and liver failure." Daisy's hands whirled as she spoke. "And Bob's your uncle, no one's the wiser."

"A dish of mushrooms changed the destiny of Europe," I said, quoting Voltaire. Of course, he was talking about the Roman emperor Charles VI, whose death by mushroom poisoning led to the war of Austrian succession. Poisonous mushrooms followed by toxic berries for dessert. Whose fortunes had the death of the countess changed? Nearly everyone's at Ravenswick Abbey. The poisons fit with Lady Edith's symptoms. She was ill when I arrived, most likely from consuming the contents of the green bottle. And then she died after drinking the contents of the red bottle. I remembered Elizabeth Anderson's telegram. "Did you find any arsenic?"

"Funny you should mention arsenic." She picked up the other bottle, the burgundy one that Lady Edith had opened and polished off the morning she died. The one I'd found in her briefcase. "This bottle once contained a deadly brew." She smiled.

"Arsenic?"

"Yeppers."

"Are you sure?" I squinted at her. "But how? The bottle was sealed with wax when I first saw. Furthermore, would the killer use arsenic in one bottle and different organic poisons in the other?" It made no sense.

"The cork was full of the stuff." She grinned from ear to ear, obviously pleased with herself. "Can't fool a cunning woman like me."

"The cork," I repeated, my mind a whirl. So many poisons. The red bottle addressed to Lady Edith contained arsenic. The green on from the nightstand addressed just to E contained a mixture of organic poisons. I thought of the little tag I'd found along with that bottle: "To E. from J." Was E. for Edith, Ernest, or even Elliott? Which Elliott was the target of that deadly brew?

Why use two different poisons? And why spell out her name on one tag and not the other? It just didn't add up. Who had access to the bottles? Obviously, Janet Roland was the prime suspect. She made the liquor and brought it up to the big house as a gift—a poisonous gift—for Lord and Lady Elliott. Did she kill Ernest's parents in the hopes that he would inherit and then feel free to divorce Mary? Seemed a long shot to say the least. But otherwise, what was her motive?

With both parents out of the way, Ernest Elliott was next in line to inherit, which would solve the problem of his gambling debts. But I doubted he was truly in love with Janet Roland. Perhaps he was telling the truth when he said he was merely helping a poor widow. In any case, both Ernest and Ian would benefit from their mother's death. Independent of the fortune at stake, Ian Elliott benefitted in that now he was free to marry his true love, of whom his mother had most assuredly disapproved. And I don't blame her. They were related after all. And yet, if it wasn't the earl's digitalis, but poisonous mushrooms and deadly nightshade berries, combined with arsenic that killed the countess, then all bets were off. Even if a member of the family had planned to murder the countess with an overdose of heart medicine, someone else had beat them to it. The earl's death was another story. As far as I could tell, he did not consume even one drop of the poisoned cordials. And if the briefcase in his room was any indication, his wife was the last one to see him before he fell ill.

"The countess was sick when I arrived," I said more to myself than to Daisy. "Then within days, she was dead." I picked up the green bottle and examined it. Wait a second. "Mary told me Mrs. Roland delivered a basket of fresh-picked chanterelle mushrooms." Good heavens. "I've got to get back out to Ravenswick Abbey and Mrs. Roland's farm." All the organic ingredients Daisy had listed could easily be found on Mrs. Roland's farm. False chanterelles and death caps and Belladonna. Mrs. Roland had the means and the opportunity. But what was her motive?

I slid the bottle into the pocket of my apron and headed for the door.

"What's this about?" Daisy caught my arm. "I'm coming with you!"

"Impossible." I kept going and didn't look back.

Daisy rushed ahead and wedged her rangy body between me and the door. "I'm not letting you leave until you bloody well tell me where you got those bottles. Are they from this Mrs. Roland's farm?"

I stared into the brilliant eyes shining out of Daisy's leathery face and wondered whether she could be trusted. Dare I tell her the truth? More to the point, what was the truth? Had Janet Roland been the one to poison the countess? Or had she planned to poison her lover, Ernest Elliott, and instead the countess drank the fatal concoction? What was Fredrick Fredricks doing out at the farm with Mrs. Roland that evening when Mary and I were walking. I knew he was involved. Indeed, I suspected he was at the heart of the whole ordeal: the poisonings, the frame-up job, the mysterious letters. Hopefully, Clifford had succeeded in tempting the bounder back to the hatband and the letter. His reaction would tell all. Which was why I must get back to Ravenswick Abbey and pay Mrs. Roland a visit, tout de suite.

"Please let me pass." I pressed my palms.

Daisy stood with her arms wide blocking the door. "Not until you spill the beans, ducky."

What choice did I have, short of knocking her over and making a break for it? Sigh.

"No doubt you've heard about Viscount Elliott standing trial for the murder of his parents?"

"Who hasn't?"

"I found the red bottle on the floor near Lady Edith's body." I sighed. "And I found the green on in her nightstand."

"You nicked them?"

I nodded. "It's part of my job at the War Office." Not entirely true, especially since Captain Hall told me the country murders weren't any of my business. "You mustn't tell anyone." I shook my finger for emphasis.

"Don't be daft. Who would I tell?" She raised an eyebrow. "So, Miss Goody Two-Shoes Fiona Figg is actually a spy." A wry smile spread across her face. "Why, I never!"

"Not a spy exactly. More like an undercover agent." I grimaced. I never should have told her.

"You're like Nan the girl spy, from the moving pictures." She shook her head. "Cor, I never..." She looked me up and down appraisingly.

"Please let me go." I tightened my lips. "I must get back to Ravenswick Abbey and find out who poisoned this liquor. Ernest Elliott's life is at stake."

"This cunning woman is bespoke for your investigation." She tapped her breastbone. "Let me fetch my bag." She eyed me for a moment. "You won't hop it without me, will you?"

"If you're so cunning, perhaps you can tell me whodunnit and save me a trip." Many of the cunning folk around London claimed they could solve crimes through their white magic. If that were the case, why were there so many unsolved crimes? Perhaps because there weren't enough gullible people willing to pay their fees.

"I need a hair or nail clipping or tooth," Daisy said in all seriousness. "Then I can tell you if your suspects are guilty."

I rolled my eyes. "Can't you just use cards or dice or something?"

"We'd best quit faffing around." She opened the door. "If we're going to catch the murderer and save Viscount Elliott."

"Unless Viscount Elliott is the murderer." I stepped out into the hallway and wondered if I could outrun her.

"You need me." She must have read my mind. "I know a lot more about poisonous plants than you do, ducky."

Maybe Daisy was right. With her knowledge of poisonous mushrooms and berries, she could help locate their source.

"Could someone have used those mushrooms by accident?" I asked as we started to run. "Or mistaken the belladonna berries for some other fruit?"

"Only a daft apeth," she scoffed.

"You mean a daft half penny like me?"

"You didn't poison the old mutton."

I hurried to keep up with her.

"I'd like to take a butcher's at that farm." Her heels clattered as she dashed down the stairs. "Old Daisy can find your poisonous plants, lickity-split."

"Stop!" I called after her. "We need to formulate a plan. For one thing, how are we going to get out to the farm?"

Daisy paused on the landing and looked up at me. "We can take my sister's car."

"Your sister has a car?" I stammered in disbelief. "And petrol, too?"

Daisy nodded and blushed. "She's married to Viscount Falmouth."

"Your sister is Viscountess Falmouth?" You could have knocked me down with a feather!

"Close your gob. She was the prettiest parlor maid in Kent." Daisy turned on her heels. "Lucky for us, she's in town."

"Wait!" A plan was forming in my lizard brain. "We need to stop at Angel's Fancy Dress first."

Two hours later, dressed as a police constable and a land girl, we arrived at Mrs. Janet Roland's farm. Just so there was no question about who was in charge of this operation, I'd made sure I was the policewoman.

Daisy's sister, the Viscountess Falmouth, had insisted we let her driver take us in their Wolseley, which seemed ostentatious in any circumstance, but especially during the war and for members of the police force, no less. On the way, sitting comfortably on the spacious backseat, I studied the Land Army Agricultural Handbook.

Now, stepping out of the vehicle—which I had the driver park a half mile from the farm—the only thing I could remember was the warning to young women: You are doing a man's work and so you're dressed rather like a man, but remember just because you wear a smock and breeches you should take care to behave like a British girl who expects chivalry and respect from everyone she meets.

At least land girls and policewomen didn't have to wear big scratchy beards and full masculine kit. I was relieved that on this trip to Ravenswick Abbey I was dressed only rather like a man and not exactly like one.

"We have to find out if Mrs. Roland intentionally or accidentally poisoned the countess," I whispered to Daisy as we approached the farmhouse. "Keep quiet and follow my lead."

"Cor, what do you think I am? A bleeding idiot?" Daisy's jacket and breeches were held up by a thick black belt, which was the best we could do given her lanky frame. She adjusted her cap, which rode uneasily on her frizzy curls.

The farmhouse door opened. There stood the same curvaceous brunette whom Mary and I had seen riding past on that grand chestnut horse.

She arched her brows. "Can I help you?"

Her face was so open and pretty, I was tempted to trust her. Then again, the most unassuming people make the best criminals. I thought of Fredricks. Not exactly unassuming, rather the opposite. Quite charming, in fact, which was what made him so dangerous.

"I'm Miss Brown, and this is Miss Clutterbuck." The names came out of my mouth before I could think. "We're scouting for wild edibles for the Land Army. Mushrooms, berries, hedgerow, medicinal herbs, anything we might be able to use to help the war effort."

"Of course. But you're too late for early spring bloomers like the morels and forsythia. And you've just missed the wild strawberries. But the pheasant berries and crab apples should be ripe." Mrs. Roland wiped her hands on her apron. "I can show you if you like."

"If it's not too much trouble." I glanced back at Daisy, who had picked a leaf off a bush and was sniffing it. "We're especially interested in mushrooms. You know how the boys like their mushrooms on toast. And berries for jam."

Mrs. Roland nodded and then disappeared into the house. She reappeared a minute later with a basket. She'd removed her apron and had sturdy boots on under a full skirt. She was the kind of natural beauty who would be stunning no matter what she wore. No wonder Mary had been worried.

"There may still be some chanterelles in those woods." Mrs. Roland gestured toward a stand of birch.

Daisy and I trudged through the pasture, following Mrs. Roland, who, in her flowing skirt, seemed to glide above the grass like an apparition in the dusky haze.

"Over here." Mrs. Roland pointed to several patches of golden fungus.

The sun was heading toward the horizon and a purplish mist descended on the forest. I inhaled the sweet smell of flowering aster and the spicy scent of moist earth. For a moment, I closed my eyes and tried to memorize the sound of birdsong and the soft touch of the warm summer breeze.

"Oh good, there's still some left." Mrs. Roland's voice brought me back to my mission.

Daisy had stepped out ahead where several golden clumps dotted the ground in the shade of an old birch. She bent down and examined the mushrooms. She picked one and held it up in the sunlight streaming through the trees. She nodded at Mrs. Roland, opened her mouth wide, and popped the whole fungus inside.

"No!" Mrs. Roland ran to Daisy's side. "Spit it out! It's poisonous. That's false chanterelle. Spit it out now!"

Daisy opened her mouth wide again and let the mushroom drop out onto the ground. She wiped her tongue on the sleeve of her uniform. "I'm a bloomin' idiot."

"Are you okay?" I asked, rushing to where she knelt. How could she make such a mistake? I thought she was an expert on poisonous plants.

Did Daisy just wink at me? Wait! What a jolly clever girl. Daisy had just established that Mrs. Roland wouldn't have poisoned anyone by accident. If Mrs. Roland had committed the murder, she'd done so intentionally. Even at a distance, she knew a true chanterelle from a false one.

"I have it on good account you make a cordial from sloe berries." Encouraged by Daisy's demonstration, I decided to go straight to the point.

"Yes, every year I make sloe-berry liquor." Mrs. Roland smiled. "It's very popular at the big house."

Indeed. I suspected her cordial wasn't the only thing popular at the big house.

"If you don't mind me asking, when was the last time you delivered sloe-berry cordial to the big house?" I removed my gloves and tucked them into my belt.

A melancholy cloud crossed her pretty countenance. "The week before the countess's death. God rest her soul." She crossed herself. Like Fredricks, Mrs. Roland was Catholic. Merely a coincidence no doubt. "I sent up one bottle for Lady Edith and another for his lordship." She blushed.

The two cordial bottles. Both consumed by Lady Edith. One containing arsenic and the other the toxic brew of mushrooms and belladonna. "Is there any chance false chanterelles could have gotten mixed into the cordial by accident?" I asked.

Mrs. Roland's pretty face paled. "No, miss. I know my mushrooms. I dry chanterelles and grind them into a powder to add a certain sweet earthiness to the liquor. But I'm always very careful."

"What about a poisonous berry?" I tilted my head and watched her reaction. "Something like deadly nightshade, for example. Could that have got in your liquor… by accident?"

"No." She shook her head. "Absolutely not." Her cheeks flushed. Whether from anger or guilt, I didn't know.

"What's this?" Daisy held up an ugly fungus shaped like a brain. She was testing Mrs. Roland.

"Why that's a morel. It's past season. I'm surprised—"

I interrupted. "Did anyone else have access to the cordial?"

"Why are you asking me these questions about the cordial?" Mrs. Roland said softly.

"Actually, I'm with the police." I straightened my jacket.

"I didn't know women could be policemen." Her eyes darted to and fro like a rabbit running from a fox.

"Policewomen," I corrected. "With the war on, men are in short supply. I hope you don't mind answering my questions."

She nodded and bit her lip.

"We have reason to believe your cordial contained poisonous mushrooms." I took out a small notepad and pencil. I figured I'd look more official that way.

"Don't forget about the poison berries," Daisy added.

Mrs. Roland gasped. "My word. You don't think…"

"Did you?"

"No. No. I would never." She shook her head. "I couldn't. You mean the countess? No, never."

"What about Ernest Elliott?" I held her gaze. "Could you poison him?"

"Ernest? Viscount Elliott?" She wrung her hands.

"He broke it off with you, didn't he?"

"I would never." She put her hand to her chest. "I'm… fond of Viscount Elliott."

"Passion is a common motive for murder."

"Why would I put poisonous mushrooms in the cordial." Her eyes flashed. "Or poisonous berries, either one."

"How about arsenic?" I took a step closer and studied her face.

Her brows furrowed. "Arsenic?"

"Do you have arsenic around the farm?"

"No!" Her eyes flashed. "Why would I? What are you saying?"

"Do you have any more bottles of sloe-berry liquor?"

"I think I might have two left, from that same batch." Mrs. Roland gestured for us to follow her. "They're back at the house."

We followed across the field. Inside, the farmhouse was modest but very clean and cozy, and it smelled wonderful of freshly baked bread. I wondered if I could be happy in a place like this. It was so peaceful.

Mrs. Roland opened a rough wooden cupboard in the kitchen and took out two small bottles and handed them to me. They had thick red wax covering their tiny corks. The bottle I found in the countess's briefcase was sealed with the same red wax. So the poison was already in the cordial. Or, someone tampered with it. But how did they get poison into a sealed bottle?

"May I keep these?" I held up the cordials.

She nodded.

I handed the bottles to Daisy. "Let's test them back at the hospital, er, laboratory."

"Sure thing." Daisy pocketed the bottles.

"Do you always use wax to seal the bottles?"

"Yes, ma'am. Otherwise, they go off."

The one used to kill the countess had gone off, alright.

The warm yeasty smell coming from the oven was distracting. "Did anyone else have access to the cordial bottles before you sent them to the big house?" I asked, glancing around the humble kitchen looking for the source of the delicious aroma.

Mrs. Roland shook her head.

"So, you were the only person to touch those bottles?" I asked, distracted by my growling stomach. I spotted two loaves of golden-brown bread resting on a cloth. "The one you gave to the countess."

"I sent up two. One for her and one for him."

"Sent up?" I asked. "So, you didn't deliver them yourself?"

She thought a minute. "No. Mr. Fredricks hand-delivered them for me."

"The South African, er, American journalist?" I blinked. Could Fredricks have poisoned the liquor? Why would he want the countess dead?

Mrs. Roland nodded. "He came here often with the refugees. The countess had them do odd jobs. Sometimes, she would come down herself and pour tea for them. Poor souls." Her eyes drifted to the horizon.

"And the munitions explosion orphans." I watched her face. For, I knew her own husband had been the assistant foreman killed that day. "Do they visit, too?"

A pained expression marred her beauty. "I'd rather not talk about the explosion."

"Yes, a great tragedy—"

Her eyes flashed. "One that could have been prevented." She cut me off. "If only Lord Elliott had listened to Joe, my husband." The intensity of her gaze could have ignited an explosion. "I don't know how many times Joe told him." Her upper lip trembled. "Joe had a long list of safety protocols." She nearly spat. "But the old man wouldn't listen." Tears streamed down her cheeks but she didn't bother to wipe them away. "All he cared about was money." Her face softened. "Ernest tried to help me out with a loan after. But his wife got jealous, so he stopped coming by."

"What about your trips to the big house?" I touched the side of my nose. "Our sources tell us you were a frequent visitor... sometimes even going up to the family's private quarters." I raised my eyebrows and waited.

Her eyes went wide. "Who told you that?"

"Annabelle, the maid." I held my pencil over my pad, ready to make a note.

"Annabelle lost her sister in the accident." She closed her eyes.

"That doesn't answer the question as to why you were in the family's private quarters." I tilted my head, waiting.

"The old man liked me to visit…" her voice trailed off.

"By the sounds of it, you disliked the old man." I tapped the pencil on the pad. "So why would you visit him? Or care what he liked."

"If you must know." Her head jerked and she averted her eyes. "After my husband died, he gave me a break on the rent." She stared down at her feet.

Your attachment to her is unseemly and I insist you give it up at once. Lady Mary's report on what she'd overheard Lady Edith say to Ernest came back to me. She'd also told me his voice was muffled and he called his mother a traitor. I was beginning to think it wasn't Ernest, her son, who was arguing with Lady Edith, but rather Bertram, her husband.

"And when… the rent was due?" I didn't know how else to put it. Was Mrs. Roland trading favors for rent? I tried to hide my unease.

"No!" A fire ignited in her dark eyes. " I went to confront him. About the accident." She puffed and shook her head. "Some of the girls told Joe about a suspicious looking character and Joe reported it to Mr. Dunnell." If looks could kill… "But the old man waved them away. Didn't think anything of it." She threw up her hands in the air, and I jumped back. "Then the whole place blew up with Joe inside." She was sobbing now.

I reached out to pat her hand and she flinched. "I'm so sorry for your loss." I waited a beat. "You must have been livid and wanted to avenge your husband's death. Hmm?" I tilted my head to get a better look at her face.

"The old man died of a heart attack." With defiant sweeps of the backs of her hands, finally she wiped away her tears.

"That's what the inquest ruled. Natural causes. His heart." She sniffed. "So why are you coming around here questioning me?"

"Did you poison Lord Elliott?"

She shook her head. The tears started flowing again. "I don't feel well." She wiped her eyes with her elbows. "I need to go lie down."

"Just one more question and we'll leave you in peace." I slid my notepad back into my pocket. "You say Mr. Fredricks delivered the cordial for you." In my excitement, I nearly knocked off my cap. I adjusted it atop my bristly scalp lest the widow Roland notice my shorn head. "What did he say, if you don't mind me asking?"

"He promised he'd help find Jimmy." She sniffled.

"Jimmy?"

"My brother. He was shot down over Northern France. The men in his battalion, the ones still alive, think he's in a German prison camp. Mr. Fredricks pledged he'd help get him out." Mrs. Roland dug in the pocket of her tunic. "And when Jimmy comes back, Mr. Fredricks told me to be sure to give him this." She held out a folded piece of thick paper. "Says he has a special assignment for him."

I took it from her trembling hand and carefully unfolded it.

Now my hand was trembling. Written in tight cursive script was an address, an address in Paris—Paris France. The address of the Grand Hôtel, Champs Élysées.

CHAPTER 23

THE TROJAN HORSE

I spent my entire Sunday morning pacing back and forth in my flat, racking my lizard brain for what to do. I couldn't sit still long enough to eat. And even now a bite of plain toast soured my stomach. I had to do something about my discovery at Mrs. Roland's farm, but what? If only I knew for sure what I had discovered. The widow was agitated. But given the circumstances, who wouldn't be?

If the countess was indeed poisoned with the sloe-berry cordial, who added the poison? Fredrick Fredricks before he delivered the liquor? Or Mrs. Roland when she made the liquor? Fredricks was, of course, a prime suspect. The mysterious huntsman was up to no good, that much I knew. And Mrs. Roland? She hated Lord Elliott, whom she disrespectfully called the old man. She may have wanted to poison him to avenge her husband. That could be it. She made the liquor for him, to kill him, but Fredricks delivered it to the countess instead. Yes., The green cordial bottle address only to E. had to have been intended for the earl. But he never got a sip. Because his wife drank the entire bottle shortly before I arrived at Ravenswick, which was why she was ill when I met her. The green bottle contained the organic poisons from Mrs. Roland's farm. And if I was right, she intended them to kill the earl and not his wife.

The other bottle, the red one that I first discovered waxed and unopened, contained arsenic. That bottle was intended for Lady Edith and it had the tag to prove it. The tag that read To Lady Edith from J. The countess drank it, along with the arsenic it contained, the morning she died. Two cordials. Two poisons. Both consumed by the countess. Clearly, the earl died of an overdose of his own heart medicine before he could drink any of the sloe-berry liquor. Something didn't add up. Two dead aristocrats. Two cordial bottles. At least three poisons. It was bloody confusing!

Tomorrow, Daisy would be back at the hospital. Then she could test the new bottles we collected for any traces of poisonous mushrooms or berries or confirm Dr. Anderson's finding of arsenic. Hopefully, she would discover something conclusive.

My thoughts turned back to Fredricks. The South African hunter—if he truly was a hunter at all—was the last person to touch the poisonous cordials. He was the one who delivered it to the countess. He also had the means. He had access to the cordial and the false chanterelles and any other manner of poisonous plants. Why else would he have the Field Guide to Poisonous Plants in his room? If he was truly the dangerous German agent, Dionysus, he probably had access to more. Much more. Including arsenic. But why would Fredricks want to kill the countess, the woman who had shown him hospitality and taken in so many wounded war heroes, refugees, and orphans?

Exhausted from dozens of turns around my sitting room,

I headed for the kitchen to make a cup of tea. Hopefully a nice cuppa would help me concentrate. War heroes, refugees, and orphans, I repeated in my thoughts. Refugees from France, Belgium, and even Germany. As I stood at the stove waiting for the kettle to boil, a lightning bolt electrified my lizard brain. Of course, a Trojan horse! I quickly prepared my tea, drank it down, and headed to my bedroom. I loathed the idea, but it had to be done.

I retrieved my Dr. Vogel disguise from the back of my wardrobe and forced myself to don it again. Wouldn't Mary be surprised to find me on her doorstep at the Paddington house? I only hoped she'd be at home… and she'd receive me. After all, I'd hardly spoken to her since I left Ravenswick Abbey, and she'd made it abundantly clear she'd been counting on my narrow shoulders to lean on for comfort and support. Surely, I'd let her down. Poor Mary. I could only imagine what she was going through… like so many other women in our war-ravaged country, waiting to see if her husband would live or die.

It was no surprise that the houses on Harrow Road near Paddington Green were very posh. Elegant horse-drawn carriages, along with shiny motorcars, lined the street in front of a row of stately manors of white stone. How they kept the buildings so clean with all the soot in the air was a miracle. Not a miracle at all, I reminded myself, but the result of servants putting their already aching backs into it.

Number forty-four had arched columns adorned with flowers carved into the stone. Each floor of the three-story building had a balcony surrounded by wrought-iron. Lovely lilac heliotropes waved in the breeze from their window-box planters. I walked up the four marble steps to the front porch and gave the brass knocker a tap.

Annabelle, one of the parlor maids from Ravenswick

Abbey, answered the door. "Why, doctor, you've come. Thank goodness. My lady's in such a state."

She led me into the morning room and went to fetch "my lady." I took the opportunity to investigate the contents of the drawers of the writing desk. I was just shutting a drawer containing thick stationery when I heard footfalls clacking on the marble floor. Startled, I whirled around, certain guilt was written in bold letters all over my bearded face.

"My lady says to bring you upstairs." Annabelle circled around the writing desk, making sure all of the drawers were shut. "My lady's not feeling well enough to come down. If you'll follow me, doctor."

I was shocked to see Mary languishing in bed, her hair loose and uncombed, her complexion wan, and her usually bright eyes swollen and dull.

"Doctor, how good of you to come." When Mary sat up in bed, the maid plumped "my lady's" pillows.

"My dear Mary," I said, forgetting to lower my voice. I cleared my throat and started again. "Are you ill?"

"You tell me, good doctor." Her teeth chattered as she spoke.

I reached down and held the back of my hand against her forehead. "You're burning up." I may not be a real doctor, but I knew a fever this high was bad business.

"I'm worried sick about Ernest." Her lips trembled.

"That's why I'm here." I glanced at Annabelle, who was fussing around the side table, eavesdropping. On my way to fetch a chair from the dressing table, I asked the maid to go down and make us some tea. What I had to ask was not for her ears.

Once Annabelle was gone and out of earshot, and I removed my hat and sat beside the bed. I smiled down at Mary and asked in a whisper, "This may be a sensitive question, but I need to know, were any of the countess's war wounded or orphans, German?"

"Why yes, doctor." Mary's eyes brightened. "My mother-in-law took a special interest in refugees from Germany, people who wanted to escape war rather than make it."

I nodded encouragingly.

"As you know." Mary smiled weakly. "Edith's grandfather was a Saxe-Coburg. Her great-uncle was Léopold, the first king of Belgium."

The countess was German by blood. Was she also a German sympathizer?

"What does this have to do with Ernest?" Mary asked. "Aren't you here to help with the trial?"

She held out her hand. I took it in both of mine and patted it gently.

"Trust me. I am." I let go of her hand and stood up. "But now I must go."

"But, doctor," she pleaded, her eyes damp.

"Do you trust me?"

She nodded.

"Then, I must make haste if I'm to save Ernest from the…" My voice broke off. "Save your husband." I replaced my hat on my head and left the room.

I heard Mary's small voice call after me, "God bless you, Doctor Vogel."

MY MIND WAS abuzz as I stepped back out into the miasma that was the premature start of a London summer. Disoriented, I scanned the street in both directions, trying to locate the omnibus stop from whence I'd arrived.

I boarded the motorbus back to town without the foggiest notion of where to disembark. What now? I had learned that the countess was German and favored German wounded. I also knew the countess had served them tea at the farm, which could be a sign of her generosity or something much more sinister.

The countess was poisoned, perhaps at the hand of one of her beneficiaries. And now her son was fighting for his life, possibly framed for her murder. Framed by the real poisoner —whoever he or she may be—who had discovered the countess's connection to the Germans was not just in her past.

I thought of the earl's last word, derspitzel. What did it mean? If it was German, it could be Der Spitzel. But what was Spitzel? I seem to recall a Christmas cookie called a Spitzel. And Spaetzle was a German dumpling.

Swimming in questions, and moving by habit, I exited the bus on Whitehall Street. As I made my way through the crowded walkway toward the Old Admiralty, I became more convinced that my hunch was spot-on. The countess was smuggling in German spies disguised as refugees in a kind of Trojan-horse operation. Either someone had found her out— the astute Fredrick Fredricks perhaps—or she had a change of heart after the Silvertown accident. In either case, I'd wager she'd stopped working for the Germans and possibly become a double agent. It occurred to me the countess herself could have been working for the War Office.

As if conjured by my meditations, I found myself standing in front of the heavy metal doors of the Old Admiralty building. It was unlikely I'd find Mr. Montgomery or Mr. Grey working on a Sunday, but I didn't know what else to do. With the war still running full tilt, undoubtedly someone was working, evidenced by the unlocked front entrance.

In a confused sort of trance, I ascended the stairs to Room 40. I tried the doorknob, but the door was locked. I knocked and was about to give up when Mr. Knox opened the door.

"Can I help you?" he asked, looking me up and down. "If you're looking for some action, you've come to the right place." He winked.

Cheeky devil. I felt like slapping his wicked face… until I remembered the great black beard on my own. I touched the offending bushy beast.

"Mr. Knox, it's me!"

"Fiona, is that really you?" Mr. Knox let out a big belly laugh. "Well, blow me down. You are a corker!"

"Listen, I need to talk to Mr. Montgomery. Is he here?"

Mr. Knox couldn't stop laughing.

I blew out a breath. My patience was wearing thin. "Put a sock in it and tell me where I can find Mr. Montgomery."

"He isn't here," Mr. Knox gasped, still barely able to contain himself. He wiped his eyes with the back of his hands.

I glared at him. "What does Der Spitzel mean in German?"

"Did someone call you a Spitzel?" He continued laughing.

"What does it mean?" I was tempted to slap some sense into him.

"Stool pigeon." He sucked in breath.

Stool pigeon! The earl's last words were stool pigeon.

"As in spy." Amid more guffaws, he took out a handkerchief.

Spy. I turned on my heels and marched down the hall.

Stool pigeon. Spy. The earl was identifying his murderer as a stool pigeon. A stool pigeon working for the Germans or the British? Stool pigeon or spy. This put a whole new light on Edith's murder. Perhaps it wasn't personal at all. Perhaps it wasn't about the will or the inheritance or adulterous affairs. It was about the war and spies and German sympathizers. There was one person who might be able to help me find the answers. But first, I needed to talk with Captain Hall.

My heart sank as I approached the door to Captain Blinker Hall's office. I could see through the opaque window that the office was dark.

I had no choice but to try Captain Hall's flat at the other end of the building. Like others in the upper brass, he lived in a well-appointed flat on an upper floor of the far wing of Old Admiralty.

If the countess had been a German spy, either Captain Blinker Hall would already know, or he would be the one to tell. And if anyone in the blasted War Office could prevent Ernest Elliott from hanging, it would be Blinker Hall.

I hurried down the long hallway, scanning the name plates as I went. Luckily, the flats were marked, or I would never have found Captain Hall's residence. Standing before the door, I had second thoughts. After all, he'd already told me to stay out of the criminal investigation. But the poisoned cordials directly involved Fredrick Fredricks. And then there was the address on the slip of paper Fredricks had given to Mrs. Roland, which I had committed to memory. I thought it best to leave the paper with Mrs. Roland in case her brother did return and the War Office wanted to follow him.

I took a deep breath and knocked on the door. It was a Sunday, but at least it wasn't the middle of the night.

Captain Hall opened the door. He was wearing his uniform. I wondered if he slept in it too. His eyelids fluttered as he stood with his hand on the door, as if he might shut it in my face.

"Sir, I have news." My heart was racing and my stomach was doing flips. Hold yourself together, old girl! "It's about

Fredrick Fredricks, the South African big game hunter and American journalist."

"Is that you, Miss Figg, under that beard?" Captain Hall gestured for me to come in. "I knew I'd seen you before, but I couldn't place you." He smiled. "What have you learned?"

Once we were seated in his serviceable sitting room, I told him about the poisoned cordials.

He interrupted me. "You're not to interfere in domestic matters. Leave the murder case to Scotland Yard." He blinked even faster when perturbed. "The War Office can't get involved."

"But, sir…"

He scowled and shook his head.

"But, sir," I continued. "Fredrick Fredricks left an address with the assistant foreman's widow to give to her brother when he returns from the German prison."

Captain Hall quit blinking and stared at me. "What address?"

"In Paris. The Grand Hotel on the Champs Élysées."

"The French are our allies."

"The countess is a Saxe-Coburg—"

He interrupted me again. "So is our king."

"Yes, but could the countess have had German sympathies? I suspect she might have been smuggling in German spies."

"Go on." He sat on the edge of his chair.

"Well, let's say she was working for the Germans. And let's say she decided to stop… or worse, she became a double agent? Then they would want to get rid of her, right?"

"Interesting theory, Miss Figg."

I scratched at my beard. "What if the Germans sent Fredrick Fredricks to silence the countess because she knew too much about their espionage operations in England?

What if she was a double agent? And he was sent by the Germans to take her out."

Captain Hall templed his index fingers under his chin. "They told me you were smart, Miss Figg."

Now, I blinked.

"Given this was your first assignment, you were on a need-to-know basis." He relaxed his hands into his lap. "I'm afraid we couldn't tell you everything."

"Everything?"

"We've known for some time that the countess was working with the Germans and bringing in their operatives. But we needed to learn more about her involvement and try to infiltrate her operation." He stood up and started pacing the small room. "A few months ago, our informant in the household reported that the countess had a change of heart. It seems one of her associates sabotaged the Silvertown munitions plant and she couldn't live with all the blood on her hands."

"You have an informant at Ravenswick Abbey?"

"Yes, Lady Mary Elliott."

"Mary?" I gasped. "How can you allow her husband to hang for a crime he didn't commit?"

"There are larger issues at stake here. Issues of national security. I'm afraid I still can't tell you everything. You'll have to trust me."

That was exactly what I'd said to Mary. Given Captain Hall had sent me on a dangerous assignment with blinders on, I wasn't sure I could trust him.

"Leave the Elliott case to me," he said finally. "I need you to stop playing Sherlock Holmes and find out Fredrick Fredricks's next move. Can you do that?"

"Yes, sir. I'll try." I thought of all the hours I'd spent tucked up in my grandparents' barn reading Sherlock Holmes stories.

He nodded, indicating our time was up.

I was halfway out the door when he called after me, "Miss Figg."

I turned back.

"Be careful."

Now he tells me!

CHAPTER 24

*M*onday morning, I distractedly prepared my toilette, dressed for the office, drank my tea, and ate my toast. Today was the moment of truth for Ernest Elliott. Would I allow an innocent man to be sent to the gallows? To save him, would I have to come forward and reveal myself as Dr. Vogel, ruin my own investigation of the Great South African Huntsman, not to mention risk my job at the War Office? Captain Hall had forbidden me from interfering in the trial. He'd made it clear that the War Office could not get involved in domestic matters, and furthermore, my assignment was to gather intelligence on Fredrick Fredricks, not to "play Sherlock Holmes." Yet, if my hunch was right, Fredrick Fredricks was at the center of it all.

Riding the train to Whitehall, I was as jittery as a canary in a room full of cats. Clifford was the last best hope to save Viscount Elliott. Had he tricked Fredricks into finding the incriminating letter in the hatband? And if so, what had

Fredricks done when he read the letter? It was a dangerous gambit. For, if I was right, Fredricks could not under any circumstances reveal the contents of the letter to another living soul—at least not one who was also loyal to the Allies.

WHEN I ARRIVED at Room 40, the men were already gathered, heads bent over the table, presumably looking at another intercepted telegram. The excitement of the Zimmerman telegram had long worn off. The Americans had joined the Allies over a month ago, but so far that hadn't made much difference. They had yet to send a significant battalion or fleet to the Front. Mr. Grey told me the American army would grow now that they'd started conscription and made Puerto Ricans citizens so they could draft them too. Being sent off to war seemed a high price to pay for citizenship, but it's the price most men paid for citizenship these days.

"Miss Figg, come take a look at this telegram," Mr. Grey called from beyond the partition.

I filed the document I'd been holding in my hand and headed out to the planning table. Even though I was only an honorary member of the team, I was pleased when one of the men asked for my input.

"Oh for the days of splendid isolation," Mr. Knox said, "when all we had to worry about was India and the other colonies. Then that bloody archduke had to go and get himself assassinated."

It was absurd that one man's death triggered the blasted war and hundreds of thousands more deaths.

"It wasn't as simple as that Serbian nationalist shooting the archduke, and you know it," Mr. Montgomery said. "Anyway, the question now isn't how we got into the war but how we'll get out."

"First the French armies mutiny and now the Russians.

It's a bloody mess!" Mr. Knox ran his fingers through his hair.

"Has something happened in Russia?" I asked, staring down at the newspaper on the table. The headline read: "Lenin returns from exile." So it wasn't a telegram.

"We have credible information that now Lenin is back in Russia, his Bolsheviks plan a second revolution to take down the provisional government," Mr. Montgomery said. "If that happens, Russia will be out of the war and we will have lost an important ally."

"What do you think, Miss Figg?" Mr. Grey asked.

Never having understood the whole Russian situation, all I could think to say was, "Have you ever noticed the resemblance between King George and his cousin Tsar Nicholas? They look like twins!" My cheeks warmed.

"What happened to Nicholas could happen to George," Mr. Knox said. "Now that would be a rum do."

"Do you really think what happened in Russia could happen here?" I asked.

"When people are starving, anything can happen," Mr. Grey replied.

"Golly, what a mess." I sounded like a bloody schoolgirl. I couldn't imagine England without its king.

"Golly, indeed." Mr. Knox mocked me.

FOR THE REST of the morning, I absentmindedly shuffled papers around my desk until lunchtime. Sitting at the little table in the kitchenette, I took a bite out of my margarine sandwich, craving a slice of fresh tomato, or some bacon, or a nice soft cheese. Blasted war! Maybe Mr. Knox was right. Another year of war rations and we could see revolution in Britain too.

I wished Clifford would appear and whisk me off to the

canteen or Old Shades. No doubt, he was attending the last day of the trial. I glanced at my watch. Three more hours until the afternoon papers came out. Then I'd find out whether Fredricks had found the letter and saved Viscount Elliott. Or done away with poor old Clifford to save himself. If only Captain Hall would allow me to take time off work and go back to the trial. Then again, maybe he was right. Someone might recognize me and reveal Dr. Vogel as an imposture. On the other hand, a man's life was at stake, for God's sake.

I paced the length of the kitchenette, praying for a miracle. I had no appetite for more death, whether at the gallows or on the Front—nor for another bite of greasy margarine. I was rewrapping the rest of my sandwich when a familiar lanky form appeared in the doorway.

"Ready for lunch?" he asked. I was never so glad to see anyone in my life.

"Why, Clifford, you came!" So, he was still alive! "What happened at the trial? Did you get Fredricks to the hatband? What was his reaction when he read the letter?"

"Slow down." He smiled. "Wait until you hear what happened." Clearly energized by the morning's events, he was nearly bursting to tell me. "I'll take you to lunch and tell you all about it. You won't believe how terribly clever I was."

"I can't wait to hear," I said. "Let me get my hat and brolly."

"Yes, it's raining buckets."

"The canteen, then?" Who cared about the food? I was hungry for information.

"The canteen. Come on, old girl." He led me by the elbow. "Have I got a story for you!"

Over bean soup and treacle pudding, the captain recounted the events of last night and this morning. I was dying to hear how he'd enticed Fredricks to return to

Ravenswick Abbey and whether he'd discovered the damning letter and what he did when he saw it. I was also dying to tell him about the poisoned cordials, but I didn't dare. I was under strict instructions to maintain my cover for as long as possible and learn as much as I could about Fredricks, specifically his "next move." Even Clifford—especially blabbermouth, Clifford—could not find out that I was Dr. Vogel hot on the trail of a notorious German spy.

"You should have seen Fredricks." Clifford grinned. "He dashed out of the Paddington house, called for a car, and took off. Later he sent a telegram instructing me to gather everyone back at Paddington house. He does love to play to an audience." He took a swig of beer, no doubt to wash down the horrid soup.

"Go on. Then what?" I was too anxious to eat. "Did Fredricks solve the crime?" I wished the blasted man would get to the point. This was no time for one of his long-winded stories. Unless, of course, it was the story of Fredricks's real reason for coming to England.

"I was jolly clever and put the suggestion in Fredricks's head that someone had tampered with the earl's hat—"

"You said that already."

"Oh, did I? Yes, well—"

"Everyone gathered at the house, and what happened next?" I held my teacup in both hands to keep from reaching across the table and throttling him.

"Everyone gathered in the sitting room and Fredricks made quite a show of dismissing the *fausse pistes, or harengs rouges*, as he took to calling red herrings, before getting into the meat of the case." Clifford gestured with his spoon as he spoke. "Fredricks loves to show off his talent with languages. You know he speaks five languages... or is it seven?"

I scowled at him.

"Oh sorry. Right." He laid his spoon on the table. "First there was Lady Mary and the sleeping powders—"

"Mary's only crime is jealousy." I sighed. Then again, never underestimate a scorned woman.

"Yes, how did you know?" He had a look of utter surprise on his open face.

"Dr. Vogel's confession that he stole the letter on her behalf." I raised my eyebrows. "Remember?"

"Right. I'd forgotten about that." He picked up his spoon and poked at his pudding.

"Why don't we skip the fish course and go straight to the meat, as you say." I waved my spoon at him.

Clifford's face fell. I knew how he loved to milk a story for all it was worth, but awaiting the outcome of a murder trial was testing my patience. "Did Fredricks find the letter or not? Was the trial dismissed? What happened to Viscount Elliott?"

"Let me finish the story." He took another sip of beer.

"Stop nattering and get to it then!" I resisted pounding the table with my fist.

"Yes, well. Fredricks stood at the front of the room like a professor delivering a lecture and reconstructed the events leading to the countess's murder. It was really quite impressive. I wish you could have been there. You would have—"

"Clifford," I growled. At least I didn't have to watch the arrogant huntsman-cum-journalist acting like Sherlock Holmes. Although, listening to Clifford waffle on without getting to the most interesting part of the story was almost as intolerable.

"Yes, right." He gave me a sheepish smile. "As I was saying, Fredricks made a great show of rehearsing the events leading to the murder. You should—"

I furrowed my brows and tightened my lips.

"Right, sorry."

Eventually, after some prodding and scolding, Clifford related Fredricks's reconstruction of the murder: In the late afternoon, the countess had a row with Ernest over his indiscretion with Mrs. Roland. Wrong! Incensed by her son's infidelity, she made a new will leaving everything to her second son, Ian. Wrong again!

"Why would she destroy a will she'd just made, you ask?" Clifford seemed very pleased with himself.

"No, I didn't ask." I stirred my tepid bean soup. "Can't you skip to the end?"

"What fun would that be?" He smiled. "Anyway, you'll never guess how Fredricks solved the case. He was absolutely brilliant. I don't know how, but Fredricks knew about the paper. No one would think of that but Fredricks."

"You mean the letter?" I sat at attention.

"No, the writing paper."

"Oh." I closed my eyes and sighed.

"It was genius. Don't you want to hear about the paper?"

"Alright, what paper?" I let out an impatient breath and opened my eyes. "Do tell."

"The paper in the fire grate." He was beaming.

"The one that said TEST as in last will and testament?" Elbow on the table, I leaned my chin on my hand.

"Good Lord!" Clifford laughed. "Yes. Well, then…" Clifford nattered on, describing Fredricks's "genius" without so much as a hint as to whether the big game hunter was really a spy, and without telling me how he persuaded Fredricks to go back to Ravenswick Abbey. Or what they found in the letter and what Fredricks did next. Instead, he told me Fredricks had speculated that the countess went to her husband's desk to get some writing paper to write the new will, having run out herself. When she found the desk locked, she opened it using her own key. It was then that she found the love letter.

I interrupted. "A love letter? Is this my letter or a second letter?" The multiplication of letters was getting confusing. The letter I'd seen was most certainly not a love letter. From a recent chat with Dilly Knox, who'd translated it for me after I finally transcribed it from memory, I'd learned it was far from a love letter. Rather, it was a warning, a warning of a threat to the countess's life to be exact.

Geh Raus. Sie sind auf dich. Dien Leben ist in Gefar, which translated to Get out. They're on to you. Your life is in danger.

"And this is where poor Mary comes back into the picture." Clifford finished the rest of his beer. He'd retired his spoon and was now waving his napkin to punctuate the spicy bits of his story. "You see," he continued, "Mary thought the letter was from Mrs. Roland, and she was determined to retrieve it from the countess's briefcase. She knew the countess would be sound asleep because the powder I found on the serving tray was actually—"

"Sleeping powders administered by Mary herself. Yes, I know. You said that already." Now I did pound the table. "Please. Get to the bloody point. Will the viscount hang or not?"

Clifford scowled. "I really can't believe Mary would have behaved in such a deceitful manner," he continued. "I rather resented Fredricks insulting her this way. I suppose she was driven to it by jealousy, otherwise, such a wonderful woman, you know—"

I gave him a very stern look, and he stopped abruptly.

"Yes, well. Sorry."

I gave up on the watery soup and looked to my pudding.

"That's a funny story, really..." He glanced into my eyes and his voice trailed off. "Right. I'll get to the point." Again, he restarted his story. "When Fredricks learned that blackguard Dr. Vogel had been at the house for tea the night of the earl's murder, and then again the next morning with Lady Edith, he put two and two together—"

"AND GOT SEVEN." I raised an eyebrow and waited for him to go on.

"I knew it was the warm milk all along. Sometimes Fredricks is deuced disagreeable. He purposefully led me astray with the milk. I really should have put a wager on it—"

"The coroner had already established there was digitalis in the milk. But no one was willing to say it was a fatal dose." Oh, how I wished I could tell Clifford the truth and set the record straight.

"Right. Well, yes," he stuttered.

Waiting for him to finish his story, I took a tentative bite of treacle pudding. The spongy cake with warm custard was one of my favorites. Surely even the canteen couldn't ruin treacle pudding. The gluey substance stuck to the roof of my mouth quickly proved otherwise.

"Thanks to your intervention and my clever ruse, Fredricks found the letter Dr. Vogel had hidden in the hatband." He smiled. "You should have seen him! In front of everyone, he pulled the letter dramatically from his inside jacket pocket like he was some kind of magician." He waved his hand dramatically. "When he read out the letter." His eyes sparkled. "The inspector from Scotland Yard was lying in wait."

I felt the pudding sink like a rock into the pit of my stomach. "He read the letter? What did it say?" Surely, he didn't really read the letter out loud to the entire group. It would expose Lady Edith and himself as German spies.

"I told you. It was a love letter. And that's all it took for Fredricks to sus out the rest." He took a bite of pudding. "It was jolly exciting. Mary was right," he said munching. "At least in part." He took another bite and his cheeks puffed out like a chipmunk's. "What she didn't know was that Ernest had broken it off with Mrs. Roland and the woman—get this—sent poisoned milk up to the house in hopes of killing him." He shook his head and laughed. "Silly cow, didn't care who she killed, as long as she got even with Ernest."

Brows furrowed, I looked at him in disbelief. Of course, I knew better. The milk may have contained a fatal dose of digitalis, but it wasn't Mrs. Roland who put it there. "What did Ernest have to say for himself?"

"Oh, you know." Clifford continued munching. "Still denied ever having any kind of untoward liaison, denied breaking it off. His exact words were, I didn't break it off because it was never on." He punctuated each word with a dip of his spoon. He chuckled. "No self-respecting man would admit to his wife—"

I held up my hand. I didn't want to hear about unfaithful, self-respecting men. As far as I was concerned, no man who committed adultery was respectable. Period. But in this case, I was convinced Ernest was telling the truth. Even so, while he had been exonerated for murder, he was still being held liable for infidelity. I knew it. And I was hardly one to defend adulterers. "Is Ernest a free man, then?" I realized Clifford had been nattering on for half an hour and still hadn't come out and said it.

"Oh, yes." Clifford nodded. "Fredricks had persuaded Scotland Yard to bring Ernest to the Paddington house, in shackles, too." He fiddled with his spoon. "When Fredricks finished his brilliant analysis of the case, they took the rangy Mrs. Roland into custody." He drew a cross on the tablecloth. To represent Mrs. Roland, perhaps. "Good riddance to women like that. Deviants who kill instead of care." He stabbed at the cross.

I didn't bother telling him that most killers were men.

Indeed, I suspected he'd killed in the war. But that was of course legal. Poisoning the British aristocracy was not.

It took all my willpower not to burst out with Fredricks is wrong! I sat on my hands to stop myself. "Do you think attempted murder is just as criminal as actual murder?" I asked.

"Well, I suppose that depends."

"Depends on what?"

"The attempt."

"Mens rea or actus reus," I said under my breath.

"Men's what?" Clifford got a pained looked on his face, as if I'd mentioned fluores menstruada again.

"Guilty minds or guilty deeds."

"In the case of Mrs. Roland, I'd say both!" He lifted his beer bottle in the air for emphasis. "Thanks to your tip about the letter and my cleverness getting Fredricks back to find it."

Although Fredricks and I came to some of the same conclusions, we did so through very different means. And as far as motive is concerned, Fredricks claims about a love letter were nothing but harengs rouges, red herrings, designed to throw us off the track. His own track, to be precise. My report to the War Office would contain the real story and not Mr. Fredricks's fabrications. We were lucky that Fredricks didn't commit another murder to cover his tracks. Otherwise, Clifford may not be sitting here enjoying the canteen grub. And Ernest Elliott would be facing the gallows. Fredricks may not have given himself up, but he had given up an important asset for his espionage activities. The lovely Mrs. Roland, not to mention the countess—before she had a change of heart and became the most dangerous of spies, a double agent.

"Fiona, are you listening?" Clifford's question brought me

back into the moment. "Don't you want me to tell you how I got Fredricks to look in the hatband?"

"Oh yes. Right. The suspense is killing me!" I dropped my spoon and threw my hands in the air. "How did you persuade your friend Fredricks to return to Ravenswick without betraying Mary's secret? To my mind, that's the only mystery in this case."

"I was jolly good, wasn't I?"

"I don't know. What did you do? You still haven't told me!"

Clifford pulled a sheaf of paper from a satchel. "To find out, you'll have to read this." He shoved a leather-bound book across the table at me.

"What is it?" I gingerly took the book, dreading what was inside.

"Seems I have a flair for writing." He was beaming. "The Daily Times is printing my account of the whole affair, in installments."

"When did you write this?" I lifted the book. It had some heft. "You couldn't have written this whole thing last night?" I shuddered at the thought of the whole affair appearing in the pages of the Daily Times. Perhaps, I'd underestimated Clifford.

"Good heavens, no." He smiled. "I've been at it since the beginning, you see. I guess you could say I kept a diary."

"A diary?" I ran my palm across the smooth leather. "You didn't betray Dr. Vogel? Or Mary?"

"Good Lord, no." He got that familiar hangdog look on his face. "Do you take me for an idiot?"

The jury's still out.

CHAPTER 25

THE END OF THE BEGINNING

After Clifford left the canteen and I finished the last bite of my treacle pudding—which wasn't half-bad once I got used to the texture—I snatched the diary off the table and went back to Room 40. I stuffed the diary in my desk drawer and tried to forget about it. Yet, as I worked on my report, the brown book called to me. When I could resist no longer, I took a break for a cuppa and brought the diary with me to the kitchenette. I had butterflies in my stomach as I started reading. Perhaps I would finally get the dirt on Fredricks. If Clifford knew about the countess's treason, or his dear pal Fredricks's secret note left with Mrs. Roland, he hadn't let on.

I read the first few lines. Clifford Douglas said he was asked by the family to write an account of the case. Horse-feathers! I didn't believe it for a minute. I doubted any of them wanted their story in the newspaper, except, perhaps, for the pompous huntsman-cum-journalist, who would probably lap up the publicity, especially since in Clifford's account he was the hero. For a spy, the bounder adored being in the limelight.

I had to admit, Clifford was a good writer, but the diary was full of inaccuracies. I went back to my desk to fetch a red pen so I could make corrections.

Reading the diary, I learned more about Clifford Douglas than I did about the murder—or the Great South African Huntsman. First off, it was obvious from the way he described her "sleeping embers" and "fierce and feral soul bursting from a divine and elegant figure," that he fancied Mary, a married woman. And the way he carried on about his brilliant friend Fredrick Fredricks, I wondered if he didn't fancy him too. When I read about his failed proposal to Lillian Mandrake, I burst out laughing. Clifford, poor thing, proposed at the drop of a hat.

Mr. Knox came to investigate. "What's so funny?" he asked.

"Nothing, really." I put my hand over my mouth. It was just too funny. I couldn't stop laughing.

"Let me in on the joke." He came closer so he could look over my shoulder. "I could use a good laugh."

I closed the diary. "Just a friend making a fool of himself."

"Aha! A love story. My favorite."

"I bet." I'd heard the rumors about Mr. Knox's lovers, both women and men. Whereas Clifford Douglas's exploits were all in his mind, Dilly Knox was a man of action. I'd seen it in his eyes as both a woman and a man.

"Yes, well. This one's not for you." I took a sip of tea. "Anyway, it will be printed in the Daily Times. You can read it when it comes out." I made a sweeping gesture with my hand. "Now shoo."

After Mr. Knox finally left, I carried my tea and the diary back to my desk for more privacy.

I reread the part where Clifford proposed to Lillian. I couldn't help but giggle. He used the same lines on me. Clifford was nothing if not a romantic, saving damsels in distress. With this war on, if he went around proposing to every crying girl he encountered, he would spend a lot of time down on one knee.

The diary left me with the impression Fredricks had dismissed whatever Clifford said and then led him astray with red herrings before circling back around to the place where they'd begun, thereby proving Clifford right in the end, but taking full credit, all the while making the poor captain feel like a fool. With friends like that...

There was nothing in the diary to suggest Fredricks was a spy. Then again, there was nothing to prove he wasn't either. Given he was obviously smitten with the "famous hunter turned newsman," on that score, Captain Clifford Douglas was not a reliable source.

It took the great investigative journalist Fredrick Fredricks to identify the murderer, which he did by producing the damning letter I'd disclosed to Clifford. Yet, the letter he produced was most certainly not the letter I found. Of that, I was certain.

Once the photograph had been removed from the water-bath in the darkroom of my mind, it was indelible. When I'd finally been able to conjure the purloined letter before my mind's eye, and Dilly Knox translated for me, I knew it was definitely not a love letter but a warning from another German spy. Most likely Fredrick Fredricks himself. To my mind, a hunch confirmed by the fact that he'd found the German letter and lied about it being a love letter. There was only one conclusion to reach. Fredrick Fredricks was indeed a German spy. And by Captain Hall's account, a very dangerous one.

In addition to facilitating the capture of the guilty party

and saving Ernest Elliott's neck from the noose, not to mention keeping my exciting new job as an undercover agent for British Intelligence, I had the satisfaction of knowing that I was right about the case, even if I couldn't announce it to the world.

I sat Clifford's diary aside, unlocked the top drawer of my desk, and removed my own journal. Reviewing my notes, I began putting together my final report for Captain Hall. My pen flew across the page as I drafted the true account of what happened at Ravenswick Abbey.

Unbeknownst to even her husband, Lady Edith Elliott was a German sympathizer and spy who used her refugee charity as a Trojan Horse to bring in saboteurs and spies. One such person no doubt sabotaged the Silvertown munitions plant—her husband's own factory. After the explosion, seeing firsthand the consequences of her actions in the faces of those poor orphans and broken families she had a change of heart. Either she confessed to her husband or he somehow found out about her traitorous actions—perhaps he purloined her briefcase and read the German letter, which would explain why it was in his bed chamber. At that point he made a new will and cut her out in favor of Ernest. She must have promised him she would stop betraying England, and—judging by the letter—start working for our side, thus becoming a double agent. The letter was a kind of warning. For double agents were the most dangerous kind in that they knew the enemies' secrets.

Lady Edith, feeling threatened by her husband, poisoned him with his own digitalis. I surmise that if Ernest had a full bottle in his room, it was because he had purchased it at her behest. I doubt she set out to frame her own son. That was probably the work of Mrs. Roland, with the help of Annabelle, who let her into the house. Both had lost loved ones in the Silvertown explosion and, Mrs. Roland at least, desired revenge. It would have been easy enough for Lady Edith to administer the fatal dose since her husband relied on her to give him his medicine every night. The fact that Lady Edith killed her husband would also explain why I found her the next morning standing beside her neatly made, unslept-in, bed, and why she was the only person in the household who didn't rush to see what the commotion was about.

If Lady Edith killed her husband, who killed her and how? While it may have been true, although I doubted it, that Lady Edith had made a new will favoring Ian over Ernest, the burnt last will and testament I found in the fire grate was not that will. Rather, it was the new will made by her husband the evening before. The one on the form purchased by the maid and witnessed by the two gardeners. The one the earl planned to finalize with his lawyer the next day, if he had lived. If I was right, then Lady Edith burned the new will because she'd been cut out of it entirely. Now, I came to Lady Edith's death.

Although Daisy Nelson hadn't tested the cordials yet, I was sure the poison had been delivered to Lady Edith in that ornate little bottle. Dr. Anderson had confirmed the bottle I found in the briefcase contained arsenic. And yet, the countess didn't drink it until minutes before her death. So, it couldn't be what killed her. Indeed, when I first arrived at Ravenswick Abbey, Lady Edith was already unwell. She had no appetite and retired early—and not just to plan the murder of her husband. I suspected her mysterious illness arrived with Mrs. Roland's sloe-berry cordial. And it ended when she finished the bottle on the morning I found her dead on her bed.

Something in that first bottle, the one from her nightstand, had killed her. She'd already drunk an entire bottle before she drank a second bottle on the morning she died.

That bottle, the one from her briefcase, the one she drank within minutes of her death, was the second, which was consistent with the round of red wax I found on the floor near her nightstand. Lillian probably did go check on her aunt that morning before she left for the dispensary. But Lady Edith had yet to recover her briefcase from her husband's bedchamber, where she must have gone to look for it before I returned with the second cup of coffee. And I know Bertram Elliott did not drink from the cordial bottle—the red one anyway—because it was still sealed with red wax when I first saw it.

When Daisy and I visited Mrs. Roland's farm, it was obvious she was beside herself over her husband's death. She blamed Lord Elliott for the assistant foreman's death. She clearly didn't think the earl's safety protocols were up to snuff. Revenge was a powerful motive. She had the motive, the means (some poisonous substance from her farm easily added to the cordial), and the opportunity. Mary had told me that Mrs. Roland visited the house on several occasions. And once she even saw the woman upstairs near the bedrooms, which suggests that either Ernest really was having an affair with the woman—although would he be so brash as to do it in his father's house in his martial bed?—or Annabelle let her upstairs. From Bertram Elliott's lecherous comments about the woman, and Mrs. Roland's own admission of trading favors, it was clear he was the unfaithful husband. I suspected it wasn't just about the rent. I suspected that Mrs. Roland was cajoling the old man to get close enough to kill him. From my accounts, however, she failed. Instead, her poisonous brew was consumed by Lady Edith, and Mrs. Roland was guilty of killing—if unintentionally—the lady of the house rather than its master.

It was also possible that the fiendish Fredrick Fredricks added some poison of his own, say arsenic perhaps, and Lady

Edith got a double dose. For, if she'd turned and become a double agent, the Germans would be highly motivated to get rid of her. In fact, that could be why Fredricks was sent to Ravenswick Abbey. To dispose of the countess.

I fingered the leather journal, wondering why doing the right thing required concealing the truth. We were fighting a bloody war in the name of freedom, justice, and truth. And yet, we were required to keep secrets, and worse to disseminate lies in order to win the war. Lying in the name of truth. Luckily, the existential quandaries were beyond my pay grade. Indeed, after my recent conversation with Captain Hall, I'd say all but filing papers, making tea, and wearing a blasted beard were beyond my security clearance. It really would have been nice to know what I was getting into. And it would have made it considerably easier to discover the truth, had I been told it in advance. Namely, that Lady Edith Elliott was a known German sympathizer and suspected spy.

The first draft of my report finished—except for the results from Daisy's toxicology test—I went back to Clifford's fiction, which, I had to admit was entertaining if not accurate. I flipped through the pages of his diary, curious to know how he persuaded Fredricks to go back to Ravenswick Abbey and look through the earl's hats without spilling the beans about Mary and me. The telltale passage had to be somewhere near the end of the story. Running my finger down the page, I read as fast as I could. The fastidious Fredricks was bemoaning not solving the case while polishing his knee-high combat boots, an activity he claimed relaxed him. Clifford remarked on the odd activities his friend found relaxing, such as polishing combat boots and brushing slouch hats or trading out grosgrain hatbands for leather ones. A bit obvious, but hopefully effective. I read on:

"Why, I bet you hide your love letters in your hatbands."

"The volume of love letters I receive wouldn't even fit in

this boot." Fredricks held up the knee-high combat boot he was polishing.

"But where do gentlemen hide their love letters? Certainly not in combat boots."

Jolly clever, Clifford Douglas!

Fredricks laughed. "Right you are old man. Some of those gentlemen's fancy hats could hide a dozen love letters." He stopped rubbing his boot and stared over at me, eyes wide. "My God. That's it." Fredricks dropped his boot and stood up.

I was feeling rather chuffed with myself. Miss Fiona Figg would be jolly pleased with me.

Yes, Captain Douglas, she is. I continued reading:

Perhaps she'll even let me kiss her.

My dear captain, I wouldn't bet on it.

AT LEAST THIS time the supercilious newsman gave his friend the credit due him. I salute you, Clifford Douglas, very ingenious, indeed. You outfoxed the fox himself.

I had a new admiration for the captain. He was clever, and more importantly in these troubled times, he was loyal. He didn't betray me or Mary or even his nemesis, Dr. Vogel. I finally realized why he hated Dr. Vogel so much. He was jealous of Mary's attachment to the doctor. I smiled and closed the diary. Dear Clifford.

"Miss Figg," Mr. Grey interrupted my musings. "A telegram for you." He handed me a slip of paper.

"What?" Who would send me a telegram? Suddenly, the room felt cold like someone had walked on my grave. I took the paper from his hand. "Thank you, Mr. Grey."

He nodded and left me to read in peace. In these times, telegrams were dreaded, for they usually contained bad news. I racked my brain to remember what relations I had at the Front. The telegram was printed on thin paper and had been stamped several times by various officials. My hands trembled as I read it. I saw the name Archie Somersby and my pulse quickened. Why would I be notified if Archie had died or been captured? Thank goodness. The telegram was from Archie not about Archie. I finally exhaled.

I scanned it and then read it out loud to make sure I'd understood. "Fredricks's parents and siblings were killed in the Boer wars when he was a boy. More soon. Love, Archie Somersby."

I reread the telegram several times before it sank in. His entire family. Killed? Those two little boys and the baby girl in the photograph? And the dark beauty? It dawned on me. She was his mother, not his wife. I held the telegram to my chest. What a tragedy. I didn't want to think of how it happened. I'd heard horror stories from Millicent Fawcett about the British army's treatment of women and children in Africa. She knew from firsthand experience as she'd gone on a humanitarian mission to Africa. I didn't think I could ever be that brave.

A childhood tragedy could explain quite a bit about Mr. Fredrick Fredricks—his fastidious obsession with order, his religious devotion, his secrecy, his soft spot for young maids, and even his becoming a spy for the Germans. He wasn't German. He was South African. And yet, he had taken our enemy's side against us. If the British army killed his entire family in front of him, I could hardly blame him for hating us. Still, working for our enemy, and poisoning countesses, it was all beyond the pale.

It was all deuced mysterious, and I was determined to find out the truth about the secretive huntsman, who was much more than he appeared to be.

I reread the telegram again. This time, my eyes lingered

on the signature, "Love, Archie Somersby." Love. My heart skipped a beat.

"I say." A familiar voice startled me out of my daydreams.

"Curses!" My hand flew to my chest. "You scared the life out of me." I slid the telegram into my desk drawer. "Don't sneak up on me like that."

"Right. Sorry, old girl." Clifford pointed to his diary, which was still sitting on my desk. "What did you think of my writing?" His cheeks turned a lovely shade of mauve.

"Impressive." Indeed, in addition to telling a good—if inaccurate—story, Clifford's account solidified Dr. Vogel's cover by making him a real person. "I hope you don't mind, I made a few corrections. For starters, Dr. Vogel was acquitted of espionage charges."

"Oh. Right. I'll change that before it goes to print." He plucked up the diary.

"Very clever the way you tricked Fredricks into going back for the letter." I smiled.

"That was jolly clever of me, wasn't it?" He grinned.

"It was brilliant!" Too bad it wasn't the right letter.

"I say." He blushed and stammered. "I-I say, would you come to supper with me tonight? I have a surprise for you."

Oh dear. I hope he's not going to propose again. I raised one eyebrow. "What sort of surprise?"

"Well, it wouldn't be much of a surprise if I told you, now, would it?" He was beaming.

"You've got me there." I laughed.

He tucked the diary into his satchel. "Shall I pick you up at half six?" he asked hopefully.

I nodded. What could it hurt? It was only supper. Anyway, perhaps I could pump him for information about what happened to Fredricks's family.

· · ·

ON MY WAY home from work, I stopped by Charing Cross Hospital and made my way upstairs to the dispensary.

Daisy was perched on a stool at a high counter, filling an amber bottle with blue pills. She looked up and gave me a toothy grin. "Cor, you were right. The green cordial bottle was starkers. Not a trace of wax."

She went to the medicine cabinet, removed one of the new cordial bottles, and brought it back to the counter. "See?"

I joined her at the counter and watched as she pulled the wax seal off and uncorked the bottle.

"Look." She ran her finger around the lip of the bottle. "When you pull off the wax, there are still visible traces." She took a sip.

"What are you doing? That might be poisonous!"

She laughed. "It's scrummers. Want some?"

Was she nuts? I shook my head. "You tested the new bottle and it was clear of poison?"

"Don't be daft! You think I'd drink it otherwise?" She took another sip.

"If Fredricks added belladonna or poisonous toadstool to the cordial, could he have removed the wax so completely?" I stepped closer and eyed the little bottle she was holding.

"Piece of cake. Melt it off and then rub with mineral spirits." She held up the pinkish cork. "But the wax stained the cork. It absorbed traces of mineral spirits, too." She pushed it under my nose. "Smell."

A faint smell of turpentine hit my nostrils. "So, the wax could have been removed entirely and no one would be the wiser." Hmmm. "And the cork? Did he pull it out and replace it or use a syringe?"

"A syringe would have to be long enough to go through the entire cork." She held out the cork from the bottle she'd been drinking. "No holes in this one."

"I should hope not!"

She fetched a magnifying glass from a drawer and then went back to the counter where the first two corks lay. "Let's have a little look-see." One by one, she picked them up and examined them with the magnifier.

"Well?" I looked over her shoulder. "Let me see."

She handed me the glass. "See for yourself."

One of the corks had a tiny hole, barely visible. The other didn't.

"Look here." Daisy brought the cork up to my face. "See that teeny tiny hole?"

I nodded.

She smiled. "From the needle the culprit used to inject the liquor with arsenic."

My eyes went wide. "Through the wax and the cork since the bottle hadn't been opened." So, the burgundy bottle addressed to Lady Edit had been poisoned after the liquor was bottled and not before. Interesting. But the poisonous mixture of organic compounds lingering in the other bottle had most likely been brewed into the liquor before it was corked. Odd.

"Which one came from which bottle?" I asked.

"This one." Daisy held up the one with the tiny hole. "Came from the red bottle containing arsenic." She grinned. "Lemon tart, I am. I found residue of arsenic on the cork."

"Smart indeed." I squinted at her. "So, the red bottle was poisoned using a syringe. And the green bottle already had the poisonous mushrooms and belladonna in it."

"Spot on." She raised her eyebrows. "Two different poisons."

"And two different delivery methods." I paced the length of the room. "Suggesting, two different murderers." Daisy had confirmed my suspicions. Mrs. Roland had added mushrooms and belladonna to the bottle addressed with the letter

E. intended for Lord Elliott whom she blamed for the explosion that killed her husband. But Lady Edith never gave it to her husband. She kept it and drank it herself. That was the first bottle she'd consumed before I arrived, the green one I'd found in her nightstand. The second bottle she drank on the morning she died, the red one, contained the arsenic Fredricks added using a syringe. And my supposition was correct: He had been sent to Ravenswick Abbey to dispose of the countess after the Germans had discovered she'd turned and was planning to spill their secrets to our side. The warning letter mentioned Fredricks by name. And if I was right, the earl found that letter and that was how he learned the truth about his wife and her part in the sabotage at the munitions plant. Fredricks had made sure Mrs. Roland took the blame for both murders. While it was true, Lady Edith was dying already when she drank the arsenic, Fredricks was guilty of attempted murder even if someone beat him to it—someone intending to murder Lord Elliott instead of the countess. It was a deuced confusing case. But finally I'd hit upon the truth. And I resolved to bring that rotter Fredricks to justice if it was the last thing I did.

"Last sip." Daisy offered the tiny bottle to me again.

I shook my head.

"Sure you don't want any?"

"No, thanks anyway." I held up my hand. "I'd better go. I'm going out tonight."

"With your handsome Captain Douglas?" She tipped the cordial bottle and drank the last drops.

"How'd you know?"

"I'm a cunning woman, remember? Be good." She winked. "And if you can't be good, be careful."

"I'll be good and careful!" I smiled and left her to her potions.

. . .

I ARRIVED BACK at my flat with only thirty minutes to change. I bathed and applied rose water to my wrists and neck. Wrapped in a towel, I went to my wardrobe. I could do worse than Captain Clifford Douglas, I thought as I flipped through my dresses. Which one is appropriate for a June evening out with an officer? I wanted something attractive but not alluring. I didn't want to give the good captain the wrong idea… at least not yet.

I paused at a blue-gray hobble skirt that put me in mind of something I'd read about the American Secretary of the Navy's daughter, Alice, who rode in cars with boys, smoked, and kept a pet snake. Secretary Roosevelt reportedly said, "Either I can run the navy or tend to Alice, but I can't possibly do both." I chuckled. Cheers, Alice Roosevelt!

After long minutes of agonizing indecision, I chose a dark-plum two-piece with a lace bodice and straight, loose skirt that fell just above my ankles. I wore dark stockings and my favorite beaded slippers. Once I had my evening kit on, I went to my dressing table and applied my make-up—lipstick, rouge, and a touch of kohl.

Then came the wig. I tugged it into place and styled it the best I could. Clifford had complimented me on my hair. God forbid he'd see the black spikes that made me look like a wild animal. Sigh. I'd done all I could for my appearance and still was more Poor Little Peppina than pretty. But it would have to do. I glanced at my watch. Clifford, never punctual, should be arriving sometime within the next hour. Sure enough, fifteen minutes late, there he was at my door—looking jolly handsome in his evening suit.

When the car pulled up in front of Kettner's, you could have knocked me down with a feather. I hadn't eaten at Kettner's since Andrew had proposed to me over champagne and oysters five years ago. It felt like a lifetime. I thought of poor Georgie growing up without his father. The war had taken so much from so many.

"You know," Clifford said as he helped me out of the car. "They say the owner was once chef to Napoleon III. And famous authors like Oscar Wilde and that bright young thing Edgar Wallace have been spotted here."

"Is that why you chose it? Seeing as you're an aspiring author yourself?" I asked playfully.

"Well, no, actually…" he stammered. "You'll see."

"Right, the surprise." I wasn't one for surprises, but Clifford seemed so pleased. And he had kept my secret… and Dr. Vogel's too.

THE RESTAURANT WAS light and bright, with white plaster walls adorned with scalloped molding and generous mirrors framed with sculpted ribbons. The mosaic floor in the champagne bar was magnificent as light from the chandelier danced across it.

"This way, Captain Douglas," the maître d' said. "The rest of your party is already here."

The rest of the party! Clifford, the rotter, had tricked me. I turned to go but realized it was too late. Everyone was watching. I couldn't very well make a scene. I would have to bite the bullet and meet Fredricks and Mary as Miss Figg. Yet, dressed in my finest, I felt as if Miss Figg was a disguise too.

Clifford escorted me to a circular table, around which sat the party from Ravenswick Abbey, minus the deceased earl and countess, of course.

"Everyone, I'd like you to meet a friend of mine." Clifford introduced me. "Miss Fiona Figg. She also works at the War Office."

The men stood up.

I smiled. "It's a pleasure to meet you all. I've heard so much about you."

Fredricks took my hand and kissed the air above it. "Enchanté, Madame Figg."

"Miss," I corrected him. The mistake gave me an uneasy feeling. He'd done it on purpose. "Mr. Fredricks—" I wished he'd let go of my hand. Being this close to him, close enough to feel his warmth, and the scent of rosewood… and something darker, was making my head spin.

Still holding my hand, his eyes sparked as he gazed up at me and said, "You can call me Apollo." He made a great show of inhaling deeply. "Peaches." He smiled. "Fresh peaches and cream."

My cheeks burst into flames. Mortified, I swallowed hard. My heart racing, I glanced around for the nearest exit. Calm down, Fiona. Don't let the bounder get the best of you. He's toying with you like a cat with its prey. I took a deep breath and forced myself to return his smile. "Mr. Apollo."

"Miss Figg is an admirer," Clifford said. "She talks about you constantly. I thought it was high time you met."

Damn Clifford! Telling Fredricks I talked about him constantly. I had no choice but to play along. "Yes. I've read your articles about female animals who dispose of their mates." I glanced over at Mary. "Betrayal is not just a human weakness, it seems."

Mary gave me a strange look. Then a flash of recognition hit her pupils. Blast it all! Now, she'd recognized me, too.

"I'm sure they deserved it," she said with a smug smile. "Philandering husbands—no matter what the species— deserve a dose of arsenic." She touched her husband's arm. "Don't you agree, dear?"

Ernest looked down at the napkin in his lap.

"Please sit down next to me, Miss Figg," Mary said. "It seems we share a common interest in just deserts." She patted the seat next to her. So, she hadn't recognized me, except perhaps as a sister who'd also been wronged by an unfaithful husband.

I nodded and sat down.

"We're celebrating Ernest's release from that horrid business," Clifford said. "All thanks to—" He seemed to catch himself. "Ah, to my friend Fredricks."

Fredricks smiled and nodded.

"Is it true, you're one of the greatest investigative reporters in the world, Mr. Fredricks?" I asked.

He tipped an imaginary hat. "And you are the charming Miss Figg who has filled the dreams of my friend Captain Douglas."

I blushed. "I daresay his dreams can accommodate many... people."

Fredricks laughed.

"And you, Mr. Fredricks, who fills your dreams?" I was feeling rather cheeky. His muscular form and dancing eyes brought out something feral and risky.

"Aside from charming young ladies like you," he said, bowing toward me and Mary, "only wild animals and criminals."

"Perhaps you identify with them." I tilted my head, waiting for his reaction.

"Wild animals or criminals?" When he smiled the furry creature on his upper lip wiggled.

"I'm sure Mr. Fredricks hasn't committed any crimes," Mary said indignantly. "He saved my dear Ernest from the gallows. He's the dearest of men and we owe him the greatest debt."

Fredricks nodded and smiled. The arrogant chap did love flattery.

"Yes, I heard you were brilliant, Mr. Fredricks." I took a

sip of champagne. "But to inhabit the criminal mind, mustn't you have something of the criminal in your heart?"

"Ah, well," he said, taking up his glass. "Crime is my vocation, or perhaps I should say, the psychology of crime, which all comes down to animal instinct and the lizard brain."

"Your theory puts me in mind of Dr. Freud." I met his gaze. "Who says we are shaped by our childhoods. Tell us about your childhood, Mr. Fredricks."

"Fredricks was never a child," Clifford joked. "He was born full grown."

"From Zeus's head?" I asked, and then added under my breath, "The god of philandering husbands."

"Freud is a charlatan." Fredricks pounded his hearty fist on the table so hard that it caused the wine in our glasses to tremble. "We cannot blame our own evil on our parents. Each man must take responsibility for himself. Criminals must be brought to justice."

I looked him in the eyes. Freud isn't the only charlatan. "Do you take responsibility for everything you've done in your life?" I sat my glass down with a bit too much force and accidentally jettisoned the bulk of my champagne.

"I do," he said with resolve.

"Then why not tell us about your recent activities at Mrs. Roland's farm?" I asked pointedly.

"Do not confuse privacy with guilt, Miss Figg." When Fredricks stared across at me with those dark eyes, I wanted to slide under the table. I'm being too pushy, I know, but I must press on. This might be my last chance to interrogate the Great South African Huntsman.

"Stop being so serious, everybody," Lillian said, laughing. "We have an announcement to make." She tapped her fork against her glass to get everyone's attention. She whispered to Ian Elliott, who was sitting to her right.

Ian's tanned countenance turned a pretty shade of pink and he stood up. "Yes, we have an announcement."

"You're getting married," Fredricks said, pulling the rug out from under Ian's feet.

Did he have to spoil the surprise? What a prig.

"No!" Clifford looked indignant. "There you're wrong, Fredricks."

Poor Clifford. Sometimes he was so clueless.

"You said he'd snubbed you," Clifford continued, really putting his foot in it.

"That's because I'm in love with him, you silly goose." Lillian beamed up at her fiancé.

"Oh, I say." Now Clifford was blushing.

"It's true. We're engaged to be married." With a confused look on his face, Ian glanced around the table and then sat back down.

"More champagne!" Ernest said, looking around for the waiter. "Waiter, bring us more champagne." He and Mary were behaving like honeymooners, touching and giggling. Obviously, the trial had brought them closer than ever. I was glad to see Mary so happy. Although I didn't know if I could be so quick to forgive a man whom I believed to be a philandering husband. Hopefully, at the very least, he did not have the French disease.

After champagne and oysters, followed by a delicious supper of roast and potatoes, we were a jovial party, enjoying conversation while we waited for pudding. This dinner must be costing the family a fortune. Although with his parents dead, Viscount Elliott was now a very wealthy man.

"Where will you go next, Mr. Fredricks?" I asked innocently. "Now that you've recovered from your injuries and solved the murder?"

He sipped his coffee but didn't answer.

"We're off to Paris," Clifford said, his mouth full of Bakewell tart. "Grand Hôtel, to be exact."

I stifled a cough. The address on the note Fredricks left at the farm was the Grand Hôtel in Paris. "How exciting," I said, stabbing a forkful of tart and struggling to maintain my composure. "Why Paris?"

"They have an absolutely smashing restaurant," Clifford said. "Although I suppose with this beastly war, everyone and their brother is on rations." He waved a fork full of tart. "Fredricks is introducing me to his great friend, the famous dancer, Margaretha Zelle." His voice was full of excitement. "You've probably heard her stage name—"

Fredricks cut him off. "I'm sure Miss Figg isn't interested in dancing girls." From across the table, the cunning journalist was regarding me with an appraising look. "You're very familiar, Miss Figg." His eagle eyes glimmered. "The shape of your nose—"

"I have one of those faces." I forced a smile. "Everyone thinks they nose me."

The party laughed, amused by my pun.

"Perhaps you too have a nose for crime." Fredricks tilted his head and put a finger to his nose.

"I have a nose for truth." Without flinching, I returned his gaze. Then I spotted it. The tiniest bead of spirit gum attached to the end of his mustache. I knew it. Fredrick Fredricks was not who he seemed.

As we finished our pudding, I kept my eye on Fredricks. He was such a striking figure, and his mannerisms so exaggerated, he had to be acting a part. Then again, perhaps I was mistaken, and it wasn't spirit gum on his mustache. Maybe it was just aspic or a bit of Bakewell tart. Trying not to stare, I focused on the dodgy spot on his upper lip. No. I was sure it was spirit gum, and I should know.

Fredricks dabbed at his mustache with his napkin, gave a weak smile, and excused himself from the table.

Was the huntsman on to me? Or had he realized I was on to him?

CHAPTER 26

THE PANTHER HAS FLED

Fredrick Fredricks never came back to the table. Clifford was beside himself, worrying his friend had been taken ill.

"Perhaps I should return to Paddington and check," Clifford said, twisting the corner of his napkin.

"I'm sure he's fine." Ernest waved for the waiter to pour more wine.

"I really think I should check on him." Clifford was fidgeting in his chair, as nervous as an old mother hen.

"Why don't we all go?" Mary laid her hand atop her wine glass to stop her husband from pouring.

"We're celebrating!" Lillian held out her glass and Ernest obliged.

"Please don't inconvenience yourselves on my account." Clifford stood up. "But if you'll excuse me, I really think I must." He glanced at me and then at Mary. "Perhaps you can see Miss Figg home?"

Mary turned to me. "Why don't you stay the night with us?" She smiled. "We have an extra room ready if you'd like to stay the night."

"Oh no, I couldn't." The more time I spent with Mary, the more chance of her recognizing me—although now that I knew she was an informant for the War Office, I was deuced curious to talk to her. Not that my clearance level would allow it.

"At least join us for a nightcap later," Clifford said with an inviting smile. "I'm sure Mary wouldn't mind sending you back home in the car."

"Of course not." Mary took my hand. "You must join us. And Alfred can drive you home." She laid her napkin on the table. "Ernest, shall we?"

Begrudgingly, the viscount—or should I say, the count—got up from the table, settled the bill, and called for a hansom cab.

Curiosity about Fredricks won out over fear of Mary, and I joined them in the cab.

When we reached the Paddington house, we were informed by Annabelle that Mr. Fredricks had packed up and flown the coup.

"Good Lord!" Clifford paced back and forth in the foyer. "Why would he leave without telling me?"

"Maybe his newspaper called him away on another assignment?" I offered. Or maybe he knew I'd spotted the spirit gum on his upper lip and he'd fled. It dawned on me, he might even have recognized me and figured out he was being tailed. In that case, he probably knew I suspected he had had a hand in poisoning the countess. Running away was further evidence of his guilt.

I joined Clifford in pacing the foyer.

"I think we could all use a nightcap." Ernest beckoned us to follow him. "Jolly peculiar, just disappearing into the night. You'd think he was a fugitive."

"Indeed," I said, trailing the others into the drawing room.

In the middle of our speculations on what could have taken Fredricks off in such a rush, a telegram arrived with a message for Clifford.

Annabelle delivered the slip of pink paper on a silver plate. "Sir, a telegram."

Clifford looked puzzled. He slid the paper off the plate. "I say!" He glanced up at me. "It's from Fredricks."

"What does he say?" I sat bolt upright.

The others went silent in anticipation.

"The cheek of the fellow." Clifford shook his head. "Listen to this." He held up the telegram and read, "Waiting at the Grand Hôtel. Where are you? You should have been here yesterday."

If Fredrick Fredricks is already in Paris, who were we dining with tonight? And if we were dining with the huntsman, then who sent that telegram?

"What does he mean?" Mary asked. "He couldn't be in Paris already."

"Does the blasted man expect me to get there early to prepare for his grand arrival?" Clifford crumbled the telegram in his palm. "This time, he's gone too far."

"Has anyone checked his bedroom?" I asked.

"Follow me." Mary led Clifford and me up the stairs. She opened the door and gestured inside. "Do you mind if I leave you to it? I have a beastly headache."

I patted her hand. "Take some headache powders and rest." I caught myself before I fell fully into the persona of Dr. Vogel.

"Thank you, doctor," she said with a wink.

My cheeks burned. Was she on to me or was that a joke?

After Mary left us, I followed Clifford into the room.

Now was not the time to worry about being alone with a man in a boudoir, even one who'd asked me to marry him.

Fredricks's room was neatly made up and completely empty, with absolutely no sign anyone had been living there for the last month. The bed was made military style, and every ornament or vase was standing neatly aligned and at attention.

I circled the room looking for clues. There wasn't a stray hair or crumb or speck of dust anywhere. The floor was spotless and the top of the dressing table was polished to a shine. Either Ernest and Mary had excellent housekeepers, or Fredricks had left the place cleaner than when he found it. So clean, in fact, there was no trace of his existence. Fredrick Fredricks could just as well have been a phantom.

I heard a sigh of delight and glanced over at Captain Douglas, who was sipping dark liquid from a cordial glass.

"What are you drinking?" I asked, dashing over to join him at the small table in the sitting area.

"I say, it's delicious." Standing near the heavily curtained window, he held up a tiny bottle. "Fancy a taste?" He poured what was left into another cordial glass.

"Where did you get that?"

"It was sitting here." He pointed to the table. "Fredricks must have left it as a going-away gift."

"Stop!" I grabbed his hand.

"Apologies. How rude of me." He held out the glass he'd just poured. "I should have offered it to you first."

"It could be poisoned!" I took the glass by its stem and examined the viscous liquid. Was this some kind of joke? I sniffed the liquor—a sweet aroma with a hint of citrus hit my nostrils, but nothing untoward, at least nothing that my nose could detect. Mrs. Roland's sloe-berry cordial. The question was, with or without the addition of arsenic?

"Good Lord." Clifford chortled. "Fredricks may be deuced annoying sometimes, but why would he poison us?"

I had a hunch why Fredricks might want to poison me. "Trust me. Don't drink it."

He gave me a disappointed look and then dabbed at his mouth with a napkin. He'd already drank it. Or most of it. I only hoped he lived to see the morning. Silly man.

"Wait! Let me see that." I grabbed the napkin from his hands. I couldn't believe my eyes. In the corner, stamped in thick black ink, was the figure of a cat.

"I say." Clifford examined the figure. "It's a panther."

The insignia on Fredrick's pinky ring.

Clifford was using a long wooden toothpick to pick his teeth.

"Where did you get that?" I asked, pointing to the toothpick.

"What?"

"That thing in your mouth?"

"Oh, this?" He removed the toothpick and held it up. "It was in the wine glass."

"Are you daft? It's evidence."

"Evidence of what?" He gave me that hangdog look of his.

I shook my head. "Of the true identity of your friend Fredrick Fredricks."

"True identity?" Clifford wrinkled his brows. "He's a great hunter turned newsman." He shrugged. "What else is there to know?"

I bit my lip. I was bursting to tell him, but I dared not for fear of betraying my top-secret assignment. My whole body tingled with excitement. I needed to report the panther insignia to Captain Blinker Hall as soon as possible, provided the cordial Clifford just finished off didn't finish him.

I took a hanky from my handbag and gently removed the toothpick from Clifford's fingers. The thin wooden staff was about four inches long. It was dagger-sharp at one end and had a carved wooden pinecone on the other.

"Oh, my giddy aunt!" Was the arrogant huntsman so devious?

"What is it?" Clifford asked.

"A calling card." I twirled the stick inside my handkerchief. I'd recognized the staff as a thyrsus, the symbol of the Greek god of wine and chaos, Dionysus.

"I say, what does it mean?" Clifford's eyes widened.

"Didn't Fredricks tell us his friends called him Apollo?"

"I never call him Apollo," he said indignantly. He fingered the edge of my handkerchief. "The panther and the staff. What do they mean?"

"Clifford dear, we've got the wrong Greek god."

THE NEXT MORNING, I got up early, hurried my toilette, and headed to the War Office. I was eager to tell Captain Hall what I'd found.

"A wooden staff and a panther, you say?" Captain Hall's eyelashes were batting a mile a minute. "The panther is familiar, but the staff, that's new. Either that, or you're the first to notice it, Miss Figg."

I handed him the thyrsus and napkin stamped with the panther, which I still had wrapped in my handkerchief. "A symbol of Dionysus, sir."

He examined them. "So Frrr... the chap from Ravenswick Abbey is the elusive spy, Dionysus, after all."

"Just who is this Dionysus?" I stood with my hands on my hips and met his gaze, as erratic as it was. I was tired of being in the dark. Especially when my neck was on the line.

"A notorious spy." He pulled a file folder from his desk drawer and handed me a sheet of paper encased in clear cellophane. "He always leaves the panther insignia." He tapped his desk with a pencil.

I studied the panther stamp on the stationery. "Why didn't you tell me any of this before I took the assignment?"

"Classified information. Top secret." He slid the pencil behind one ear. "Anyway, we weren't sure this Frrr… chap was our man."

"So, if the spy Dionysus poisoned the countess to stop her from becoming a double agent and turning against the Germans." I thought for a minute. "Is there really a Fredrick Fredricks—the South African hunter and American journalist?" I passed the stationery back to the captain. "And who sent the telegram from Paris?" I asked under my breath.

"Either Dionysus is a clever chameleon, or we're dealing with a ring of spies."

I hadn't thought of that, but it made perfect sense. I nodded.

"So was the fellow I met at Ravenswick the real Fredrick Fredricks or the infamous spy?" I narrowed my eyes in concentration. "Was Dionysus posing as Fredricks? Or is Fredricks our spy? Or are they one and the same and he's having us on?" My head was spinning. Surely, even the brilliant Fredrick Fredricks couldn't be in two places at the same time.

"We're counting on you to find out, Miss Figg." He stood up. "We want you to continue following him and reporting back on his actions, all of them, no matter how insignificant." He removed the pencil and stabbed the air. "I want to know what he eats for breakfast, what he does before bed, his favorite color." He dropped back into his chair. "Everything there is to know. We need to know it."

"You can count on me, sir." I nodded, the buttons nearly bursting off my blouse.

"Keep up the good work, Miss Figg." His lashes were fluttering as fast as my heart. "Your assignment is to keep after this Dionysus character—or, characters. Find out how many of them there are and what they're up to."

"At least one of them is in Paris, sir." I straightened my skirt. "At the Grand Hôtel."

"Well then let's stop chin-wagging." He waved toward the door. "Get over there right away."

"To Paris?"

"Didn't you just say that's where to find our spy?"

I nodded again.

"Well, what are you waiting for?" He waved his hand as if sweeping me out the door. "Get going."

I could barely contain my grin. "With pleasure, sir."

TWO HOURS LATER—AFTER one crucial stop—I was back at my flat, packing my suitcase for Paris. Obviously, I couldn't reprise my role as Dr. Vogel. I hung my two men's suits in the back of my wardrobe. And the huntsman had seen me as Teresa the maid of the mountain. (Or had that really been Fredricks? Perhaps the man in Paris was an accomplice.) I packed the maid's outfit just in case. Then, I carefully folded my new purchase from Angel's Fancy Dress. I was jolly pleased with myself on this one. I'd found the perfect disguise for the Grand Hôtel. No one would recognize me in this getup.

Standing in front of my wardrobe, staring at the hatboxes on the top shelf, I smiled to myself. The choice of a hat was no longer just a matter of style—it was strategy. The right hat could hide my intentions, shade my suspicions, or crown my triumphs. Which hat was appropriate for top-secret espionage and outsmarting the great huntsman—not to mention his alter ego, the notorious spy?

I reached for the box containing my favorite lavender

cloche, opened it, and set the hat aside. I snapped the box shut with a decisive click and set it on the bed. Paris. The city of lights, love, and lies. Fredrick Fredricks might think himself the elusive panther. But this time, the great hunter was in my sights.

Hats off to him if he could outrun me now.

THE END

AUTHOR'S NOTE

This book, the first mystery in the Fiona Figg series, is a revised and updated version of Betrayal at Ravenswick. To align this story with the rest of the series, I included real-life characters, women who were important in history.

The Garrett sisters, Elizabeth Garrett Anderson and Millicent Garrett Fawcett were both important women in the history of Britain. Elizabeth was the first woman doctor. She opened her own dispensary in Marylebone, which eventually became a hospital. Her patients were primarily women and children. Her sister Millicent was a famous suffragist who devoted her life to fighting for the rights of women and children. She fought for the right to vote for women. And she went to Africa to campaign for better treatment for the children interned during the Boer Wars. Their father was a successful industrialist who made various sorts of steam-powered vehicles.

On 19 January, 1917, the Silvertown munitions explosion killed seventy-three people and injured over 400. The blast destroyed the munitions plant and several buildings around it. Reportedly the blast could be heard 100 miles away.

During World War I, with most men away fighting in France, women worked in the munitions factories. Because the exposure to trinitrotoluene (TNT) turned their skin and hair yellow, they were called "canary girls." Working in the munitions factories was extremely dangerous not only because the women handled explosives but also because the materials were toxic. Many women suffered the consequences of trinitrotoluene poisoning.

Fiona's nemesis, Fredrick Fredricks, is based on a real-life German spy named Fritz Duquesne, who was a spy for Germany in both World War I and World War II. Fredrick Fredricks was one of his many aliases. He was a master of disguise and his real life is as fantastical as a novel. Before the United States entered World War II, he was captured as part of the biggest FBI spy-ring bust in history. Fritz Duquesne was the ringleader.

ABOUT THE AUTHOR

Kelly Oliver is the author of four award-winning and bestselling mystery series: The Fiona Figg Mysteries, The Jessica James Mysteries, The Detection Club Mysteries, and The Pet Detective Mysteries. When she's not writing mysteries, she is a distinguished professor of philosophy emerita at Vanderbilt University. She is the author of sixteen nonfiction books, and over one hundred scholarly articles. She lives in Nashville, Tennessee with her husband and three demanding felines.

To learn more about Kelly and her books, visit her WEBSITE: https://kellyoliverbooks.com

Treasure Hunter

Geocacher

Sixteen nonfiction books

TO LEARN MORE ABOUT KELLY AND HER BOOKS, VISIT HER WEBSITE:

WWW.KELLYOLIVERBOOKS.COM